Nina Shengold

CLEARCUT

Nina Shengold won the Writers Guild Award and a
GLAAD Award nomination for *Labor of Love,* starring
Marcia Gay Harden, and the ABC Playwright Award
for *Homesteaders*. With Eric Lane, she has edited
eleven theater anthologies for Vintage Books and
Viking Penguin. She has worked in both the Olympic
and Tongass National Forests, and currently lives in
the Catskill Mountains of upstate New York with her
daughter, Maya. *Clearcut* is her first novel.

CLEARCUT

Nina Shengold

ANCHOR BOOKS

A Division of Random House, Inc.

New York

AN ANCHOR BOOKS ORIGINAL, AUGUST 2005

Grateful acknowledgment is made to the following for permission
to reprint previously published material:

Ice Nine Publishing Company, Inc.: Lyrics from *Brokedown Palace* by Robert
Hunter, copyright Ice Nine Publishing Company. Used with permission.

New Directions Publishing Corp.: Excerpt from "Logging, Part 2" by Gary
Snyder, from *Myths and Texts,* copyright © 1978 by Gary Snyder. Reprinted
by permission of New Directions Publishing Corp.

Warner Bros. Publications U.S., Inc.: "House of the Rising Sun" by Alan
Price, copyright © 1964 (Renewed) Keith Prowse Music Publishing Co.
Ltd. (UK). All rights reserved in the U.S.A. and Canada administered by
EMI Gallico Catalog Inc. (Publishing) and Warner Bros. Publications U.S.
Inc. (print); "Ramblin' Man" by Forrest Richard Betts, copyright © 1973
(Renewed) Unichappell Music Inc. (BMI) and Forrest Richard Betts
Music (BMI). All rights administered by Unichappell Music Inc.
All rights reserved. Used by permission of Warner Bros. Publications
U.S. Inc., Miami, FL 33014.

Library of Congress Cataloging-in-Publication Data
Shengold, Nina.
Clearcut : a novel / by Nina Shengold.
p.   cm.
ISBN 1-4000-7969-1 (pbk.)
1. Northwest, Pacific—Fiction.   I. Title.
PS3569.H39377C54 2004
813'.54—dc22   2004046200

Book design by Debbie Glasserman

www.anchorbooks.com

Printed in the United States of America
10 9 8 7 6 5 4 3 2 1

For my parents and Maya,
roots and branches

San Francisco 2x4s
    were the woods around Seattle;
Someone killed and someone built, a house,
    a forest, wrecked or raised
All America hung on a hook
    & burned by men, in their own praise.

—Gary Snyder, *Myths & Texts*

Mama, mama, many worlds I've come
Since I first left home.

—Grateful Dead, *Brokedown Palace*
lyrics by Robert Hunter

CLEARCUT

ONE

Earley Ritter hunched over the steering wheel, dreaming of heat. He was heading for Bogachiel campground, his jeans pocket stuffed full of dimes for the shower. He'd been shake-ratting up in Suhammish all week, and the thought of hot water was next door to sex. His skin had a serious craving for one or the other. He thought about Margie, the woman he'd met at the Cedar Bar Lounge a few Fridays ago, and wondered if she might be there tonight.

The sky threw a couple of drops on his windshield and then really let go. Rain bounced off the tarmac in sheets. Earley turned on his one working headlight, a bright, and wished he'd remembered to pick up new wiper blades. Maybe tonight, if he found a few bucks in his toolkit or under the seat. He'd stop by the Texaco as soon as he got into town, see if someone would front him. But first he would treat himself to a long shower. Of course, with this goddamn monsoon, he could just about pull over, strip and soap down in the rain. If he had any soap.

A log truck slogged past, spraying wake. Earley reached into his Drum pouch, then remembered he'd smoked the last shreds of tobacco as he picked his way down from Suhammish Creek clearcut. He rounded a curve and his lone high beam caught someone huddled up sorry and limp on the roadside. The man was wearing an olive-drab poncho, his thumb sticking out like an afterthought.

Earley braked, his heart racing. I could have killed him, he thought. Dumb fuck doesn't even have enough sense to stand out on a straight stretch of road where somebody might see him. He might have a cigarette, though, and he was closer than town. Earley twisted the wheel and pulled onto the shoulder.

The hitchhiker turned around slowly, as if he'd been out in the rain for so long he'd forgotten that someone might actually stop. He stood staring at Earley's rust-riddled hunter green pickup, then grabbed up his duffel and charged towards the truck.

Earley hoped the guy wasn't some Vietnam burnout. He rolled down the window and squinted, already regretting the impulse to let him in. The hitchhiker leaned forward, gripping the windowsill. His hands were too clean for a local, and under his soaked cuff a gold watchband glinted. He looked like a college kid, skinny and earnest, with long stringy hair and pale skin nearly blue from the cold.

"Thanks for stopping," he said.

Earley gave a curt nod, reluctant to open the door. "Where're you headed?" His voice sounded raspy and strange, and he realized he hadn't spoken aloud for a week.

"Alaska."

College, for sure. Earley's heart sank. His bones ached from working. He didn't feel up to listening to some upper-middle-class quest for adventure, not even for free cigarettes. "I'm only going a couple of miles. Hardly worth getting in."

"It's worth it to me." The hitchhiker clutched at the windowsill as if he couldn't bear to let go. He looked so desperate that Earley relented.

"All right. Chuck your gear in back, under the tarp with the tools, and come on around my side. I open that other door, it'll fall off."

The kid nodded and peeled back the tarp, setting his duffel bag down on the truckbed, next to the mud-spattered splitting maul, mallet and froe, and Husqvarna chainsaw case. Earley unfolded himself from the driver's seat. At six-five, up on spike-studded caulk boots, he towered over the hitchhiker's olive-green poncho. The kid looked startled, but all he said was, "I'm going to get your seat sopping."

That didn't even deserve a response. Earley slammed the door shut, jamming the truck back in gear. The wipers sluiced rain in an uneven wash on the windshield, over the peeling decal of a sun with a skeletal grin that some former owner had put there. Earley swerved to avoid a downed tree limb. The back of his throat ached. He looked at his passenger. "Smoke?"

"Ah, no thanks."

Earley broke into a grin, then noticed the way the kid looked at his dead gray front tooth. "You *got* a smoke?" he asked, irritated. "For me?"

"Oh. No, sorry. I don't smoke tobacco." Earley frowned, gripping the wheel at the bottom. The hitchhiker glanced at him, sizing him up. His pale eyes looked nervous. "I might have a joint, though."

"Well, now you are speaking my language for sure. Light that puppy on up."

"You bet." The hitchhiker put one foot up on the dashboard, fished in the cuff of his soaked jeans and pulled out a stray piece of tinfoil. Inside was the roach of a joint, rolled in something that looked like wet toilet paper.

Earley proffered his Drum pouch, which had half a packet of Zig-Zags inside. The hitchhiker set about rolling a fresh one, fattening it with a pinch of tobacco dust. Earley noticed his fingers were shaking.

"I'd turn on the heat but it's busted. How're you planning to get to Alaska, the state ferry up from Seattle?" The hitchhiker nodded. "'Cause you're on one hell of a detour. This road snakes around the whole fuckin' Olympic Mountains before you even *look* at the Puget Sound. And when you do get to it, you're on the wrong side."

"So why make it easy?" The hitchhiker reached for the dashboard lighter, but Earley shook his head, handing over a pea-green Bic that worked on the third or fourth try. The kid held the smoke in his nostrils and lungs as he passed Earley the joint, which was rolled as tight as a Tootsie Pop stick. An experienced stoner. The stuff wasn't bad, either. Someone had money. Earley took an appreciative toke as his passenger went on, "I'm looking for someone."

A woman, Earley guessed from his tone. He held smoke in his lungs and waited for him to continue. "She's working near some town called Forks, on a tree-planting crew. She told me to look her up on my way north."

"North from where?"

"Berkeley."

Earley let out a low whistle. "A thousand miles. Must be some kind of woman."

The hitchhiker took the joint and inhaled deeply, his eyes closed in reverie. His lashes were long and straight, like the fringe on a bedspread. "She is."

Earley nodded. He knew the refrain. The first hit had gone right to his head; he felt suddenly mellow, expansive. "Well, just as it happens I'm headed for Forks. I'm just stopping at Bogachiel for a shower. I've been up in the woods for a week and I smell like the back of a bear. If you're willing to wait—"

"Are you kidding? I'd *kill* for a shower. Get out of these clothes." The kid put his foot back up onto the dashboard and wrung out his cuff. A stream poured down onto the floor. "Oh. Sorry." His pale blue eyes darted at Earley.

"Nothing this rig hasn't seen before, nine times a day. My name's Earley."

"Reed Alton."

Now there was a preppie name. One of those which-is-the-first-name-and-which-is-the-last numbers. Rich kid en route to Alaska, trying on a blue collar to see how it felt. Earley didn't get it, but he didn't care. Everyone came from somewhere, he figured. What mattered was where they wound up, and he could attest there was plenty of flux in that. Who would have figured a red-dirt hillbilly from Georgia would find himself cutting up tree stumps in these freezing mountains, where even the rain came down sideways? He scratched the side of his beard, where the hatchet scar parted the stubble, and reached for the joint again.

"This is some mighty fine weed, Reed." Earley laughed, not so much at his rhyme as the streak of dumb luck that had gotten him high as a kite on this black, rain-slick night in the middle of nowhere, as far west as a person could get. He snapped on the radio. Eric Clapton was singing "Have You Ever Loved a Woman."

Reed moaned with pleasure. "Oh yes. *Oh* yes. Crank it."

Earley reached over and twisted the volume knob. Reed sat forward, transfixed, his head swaying back and forth as his long fingers arched, forming chords on his knees. "This is why God put six strings on electric guitars."

"If you say so."

"I do. I just did. What do you listen to, Earley?"

"Whatever there is." Earley wasn't about to go listing his tapes to some kid who played air guitar riffs on his backpacking poncho. He liked music as much as the next guy, but Reed seemed possessed. At least he's not singing along, Earley thought as he spun the wheel, veering off the main highway. I might have to hurt him.

The pickup crunched over the gravel approach road to Bogachiel State Park, its headlight a cone of white drizzle. Mist swirled through the dark tangles of club moss that hung down from cedar and fir boughs like hair. Brambles crouched in the underbrush: wild salmonberry and devil's club.

There wasn't a soul in the campground. Earley cut the engine and they got out of the truck, heading for a squat tile building with a light over its brown metal door. The air smelled of earth and wet cedar. Reed peered at a small wooden sign with a State Park insignia. "Ghost Nurse Log," he read. "What the hell is a nurse log?" He looked up at Earley, who shrugged.

"Oh, we're in the Tourist Outdoors now. Got your Teaching Trail markers, your his'n'hers potties, the whole Forest Circus nine yards. The showers are here for the campground, but you'd have to be brain-dead to camp in the West End in March. You got any dimes on you?"

Reed pulled a handful of change from his pocket and shook it. "Just one. I've got plenty of quarters."

"It only takes dimes. I might could lend you a few." Earley stuck his hand into his jeans and frowned, pulling the pocket lining inside out. It was ripped at the seam, like a cartoon demonstration of pennilessness. "Must've fallen right through."

"Check your boots," Reed suggested. "Maybe they fell in your socks."

Earley shook his head in disgust. "Ain't no dimes in my socks, man. There's dimes in the woods. Fuck a duck. I'd spit logs for a shower."

"Well, we've got *one*." Reed held out his dime.

Earley stared at his hand for a moment, then burst out laughing. "One dime? Two guys on one dime? You must be high."

"Oh god." Reed looked stricken. "That was a *drug*?"

Earley gave him a shove and Reed's deadpan dissolved into laughter. "Hey. One dime is better than nothing."

"You got that right." Earley cracked his chipped grin again, surprised by how loose he was feeling. "This'll be legend, man. We're gonna squeeze every drop from that shower."

There weren't any curtains or booths, just a chrome shower-head stuck in one wall and a large metal coin box. The tile floor sloped down to a central drain. Reed peeled off his wet sweat-socks. "I feel like I'm back in my junior high locker room."

They stood with their backs to each other, stripping their clothes off as fast as they could and tossing them onto a bench. The tiles smelled of old disinfectant.

Reed turned out to be one of those rib-skinny, bony-assed guys with a really big dong. How did that happen? Earley wondered. What freak of genetics would make a guy slender and pale as a twelve-year-old girl and then hang that rolling pin on him for laughs? It was one of those things a guy hated to notice; Earley, who'd never had any complaints in that area, didn't like feeling outgunned by a kid who came up to his chin.

But Reed didn't have any swagger. If anything, he looked self-conscious, as if he was trying to keep his eyes off Earley's work-mounded biceps and shoulders. It wasn't that often that strangers got naked together. Maybe the cold air had taken the edge off their pot high, but what had seemed funny five minutes ago now made them both ill at ease. The sensation unfolded in layers: Earley was embarrassed that he felt embarrassed. Maybe he was still a little bit stoned.

"You go under it first," he said, looking away. "It's your dime."

"You drove us here. You should go first."

It was too cold to argue. "Okay, I will." Earley turned towards the showerhead.

"We forgot towels," said Reed.

"Hell yes, we did." Earley didn't own any towels.

"And what about soap?"

"There's some of that squirty stuff by the sink. We better get lathered up first, cause a dime in this thing lasts like two or three minutes. We're gonna be sprinting."

They stood at the porcelain sink, running water and soaping themselves. The sink's hot tap was broken. With every cold slosh on his skin, Earley tried to imagine the shower's fine steam, the needling hot streams bouncing off his stiff shoulders.

Reed shivered. "It's freezing in here."

"Got your dime?"

"It fell out of my pocket." Reed pantomimed turning his pockets inside out. His cock flopped against his thighs.

"Asshole." Earley grabbed for the dime, but Reed closed his fist over it, hiding his arm behind his back. Earley lunged for it. They were both laughing. Earley twisted Reed's arm forward, prying his fingers apart with his own. Reed made a feint to the left, trying to dodge him, but Earley, stronger, forced his hand downwards. Their cold, soapy chests slid together. The skin contact startled them both. In that instant of flinching, Earley heard the amplified ping of a thin disc of metal, rolling along the sloped tiles. He dived for the floor as the dime clattered into the central drain.

"Shit!" Earley stared through the slots, down the throat of the drain. There was nothing to do. He was down on his knees on an ice-cold floor, stark naked, covered with grime, sweat and lathery slime, and their last dime was gone. He rocked back on his haunches and looked at Reed. "Welcome to life in the woods."

TWO

"So this woman you're gonna look up, she's a girlfriend or what?" They were back in Earley's truck, heading north. The rain had thinned into mist.

"You'd have to ask her that," said Reed. He stared out at the dark woods, his eyes haunted. "I guess it's or what, now."

"I surely know *that* tune. There is this girl Margie I met at the bar. We could grab a hot shower at her place, at least if her husband's still up at the logging camp."

"Why, you dirty dog." Reed grinned to show he was kidding.

Earley shrugged, rubbing the scar in his stubble. "She hit on *me*. I figure as that makes it legal." He remembered the warming surprise of Margie's hand on his bare nape that night at the Cedar, and later, the generous spill of her breasts, her doughy thighs parting for him on the waterbed. "Want me to cruise by the driveway and see if his truck's there?"

"I don't want some jerk coming after us with a chainsaw, if that's what you mean."

"That does sound a mite bit rugged. I guess it's a miss." They rolled past a bottom-lit sign that read WELCOME TO FORKS, WASHINGTON.

"Logging Capital of the World," Reed read aloud.

"Average Rainfall: Yes." Earley echoed. Reed swiveled his head to look back at the sign, where the actual rainfall was listed as 126 inches a year. "That's the local joke. *The* local joke. That was it."

Earley was feeling magnanimous. Reed had been willing to share his last dime, after all, not to mention his stash. "Wanna come with me and knock back a few at the Cedar Bar Lounge? You can call your Or What from there."

"She doesn't have a phone. She told me she'd leave me a note on the bulletin board at the laundromat, but it's got to be closed by now."

"Says you." Earley pulled a wide U-turn, brakes screeching. "Twenty-four hours, man. This is *downtown*. You can soak your highwaters in Cheer at four in the a.m. if you get the urge." He pulled onto a side street and drove to the Suds Hut. Sure enough, it was brightly lit, surrounded by pickups and old station wagons. They parked and went in.

A couple of crewcut small boys drag-raced laundry carts

over broken linoleum tiles while their mother, in bathrobe and curlers, folded a huge pile of men's flannel shirts. Two women sat side by side, watching clothes swirl around in the buff and orange dryers as if it were prime-time TV. The radio droned about gas lines and President Ford playing golf at Camp David. Reed snorted. "I still can't hear 'President Ford' without getting a rash. I miss hating Nixon."

"Same difference," said Earley.

"Right. Coke or Pepsi. They both make you sick."

Earley nodded, preoccupied. The fluorescent lights and machine noise made his head throb; he wished he was back on the road. He led Reed to the bulletin board, which was layered with note cards and handwritten want ads. They scanned offers for truck chains, bait, sheds built to order, a size 18 bridal gown LIKE NEW, BEST OFFER.

"This it?" Earley pointed to a stained looseleaf page folded into sixteenths. A single red tack was jabbed through the initials R.A.

Reed nodded, pulling it off the board. Earley heard his breath catch as he fumbled to open the paper. It sounded like somebody had a bad case of the wishfuls. Reed scanned the note quickly, then showed it to Earley. The writing was jagged and urgent, like something that came off a life-support needle.

REED! It is virtually IMPOSSIBLE for you to get to me. Treeplanters' camp is up about 10 miles of unmarked dirt roads. IF you can find a ride (4WD only!!), the turnoff is 7/10 mi past the road to La Push. Right turn onto logging road, go 3-4 mi till it forks (after wrecked car with Fuck You in spray paint.) Bear left, then right, cross creekbed and keep going another 5 miles or so till road almost disappears, follow ruts along ridge till you get to our tents. See you soon!—Z.

Reed sighed. "It's impossible. See you soon. That sounds like Zan, all right."

Earley laid a big hand on Reed's shoulder. The grime-crusted duct tape that bound up a gash on his knuckle was twisting loose. "How 'bout that beer?" he said.

The Cedar Bar Lounge was so full it took time to get inside the door. The Friday night crowd was lined up three deep at the knife-scratched bar, jostling for schooners of Oly or double shots, shouting to make themselves heard above Tammy Wynette on the jukebox. Earley spotted a few guys he knew, but none who looked likely to front him a loan. If Margie was here, she might slip him a couple of bucks. Or a bourbon.

"What are you drinking?" Reed yelled in his ear.

"Whatever the tide brings in."

"Beer?"

"That'll do me. I'm gonna go find us a seat." Margie might be in the back room, watching the guys shoot pool. It was worth a look, anyhow. He didn't want to sponge too many beers off of Reed, and he needed to rustle up someplace to sleep.

Earley threaded his way through the crowd. There were loggers in hickory shirts and faded suspenders, a handful of wives and a few unidentified hippies. The sound of them talking and laughing at once seemed insanely amplified. The Suhammish Creek clearcut where Earley was working was roadless, dead still. Whenever he paused in his splitting or sawing, he could hear birdsong from miles away, the low whoosh of the distant Hoh River. Sometimes he found himself humming and wondered what moron was making that din.

Earley stepped through the stripped cedar columns that framed the back room. A woman was circling the pool table. Under her red flannel shirt she was wearing a man's scoop-necked undershirt, and when she bent over her cue, he could see her breasts swell through the fabric's thin ribs, the dark slice of heaven between them. A low-hanging lamp spilled a blaze of light over the kelly-green felt as she lined up her shots, knocking ball after ball into the pockets. Her hair was dark, coarse as a horse's mane. She shoved it behind one ear and leaned down towards the cue ball. A small crowd had gathered to watch her play. Some of the loggers were whistling and placing bets. Earley didn't care whether she won or lost, as long as she kept leaning over the table.

Reed appeared at Earley's shoulder, holding a pitcher and

two glasses, beady with water. The woman was eyeing a tight-angled bank shot. She slid her cue back and forth through her hooked finger and drew it back.

"Zan?" The cue ball went wide. She had missed her shot.

"Jesus Christ, Reeder, you *found* me!" Her cue clattered onto the floor as she flung herself onto Reed's neck, splashing beer foam all over him. "I don't believe this. Our first night in town in a *month*, I'm not kidding, and you roll in. Talk about karma!"

"How about the game?" asked the man she'd been playing with, frowning possessively.

"Fuck it, you won," said Zan, slinging her arm around Reed. "Is one of those glasses for me?"

Reed's eyes darted towards Earley.

"You bet it is," Earley said. "I'll go get me another."

"This is my new buddy, Earley," said Reed. Zan's eyes traveled up Earley's height and came to rest on his. Earley felt nakeder than he had been in the shower with Reed. Her dark eyes were appraising and frank; a slight curve of her lip let him know that she liked what she saw. Earley knew that he wasn't a good-looking guy, with his twice-broken nose and gray tooth adding insult to injury, but he was tall and broad as a tree trunk, and most of the time, he'd found, women accepted the details. Maybe the turn-on was how much he worshiped them. Earley had made love to women of all shapes and sizes, half his age, twice his age, and he could honestly say he had never been inside a pussy he hadn't enjoyed.

"Zan?" he said stupidly.

"Alexandra, but who has the time? Good to meet you."

"I'll go get a glass," said Earley. He was hitting the conversational highlights, all right, really rolling them out. All his life he'd reacted to chemical lust with a thickened tongue. He could practically feel his IQ dropping as he stared at Zan's bristling eyebrows, the way her lips glistened. This woman was *fierce*. She could eat you for breakfast, or thought she could, anyway.

Reed had a chewed-up-and-spat kind of look on his face, like he'd already been through the mill and was hoping for more. It was Earley's job, right now, to get the hell out of their way. He should head for the bar like a good boy and get himself sidetracked, let Reed have his shot. But his feet wouldn't move. The spikes of his caulk boots were anchored, set into the floor, as if he were standing atop a downed trunk that was slick with rain, treacherous.

"So you're a shake-rat?" Zan picked up her near-empty beer glass, staring at Earley. They'd moved to a booth in the back corner. Zan and Reed squeezed together on one bench and Earley hunched onto the other. Zan's treeplanter friends stood across the room, laughing and goofing around at the pool tables.

"Stumpfucker, yeah."

"Hard work." She set down her glass and Reed filled it.

"It's work," Earley said. "Not so different from tree-planting, except for the chainsaw. Your basic bend over and kill yourself."

"What's a shake-rat?" asked Reed.

"I cut up cedar salvage for roof shakes," said Earley, squirming a bit under Zan's intense gaze. He'd felt out of place and self-conscious when she and Reed traded news without filling him in, as if they were speaking a dense private code. Now that she'd shifted the spotlight to him, he wished they would talk about Berkeley again. I'm out of practice with people, he thought, thinking again of the hush that surrounded him when he stopped working and gazed down the mountain, when he lit an oil lamp and reheated something for dinner, eating it right from the skillet.

"You work by yourself?"

"Had a partner cut out on me, couple weeks back." Earley picked up his beer and took a long slug. Dean had quit back in December; he wondered why he'd felt the urge to downplay the amount of time he'd been living alone. It would take him a couple more drinks to feel back in the world.

"Do you think I could do it?" asked Reed. "Do you need any special—"

Zan interrupted him. "Look at his hands." She pointed at Earley's black nails and split knuckles.

"I'm not playing anyway."

"Then you're a jerk," said Zan, dropping her arm from Reed's shoulders and grabbing her beer mug. "Reed is a fucking amazing musician," she told Earley. "But he'd rather piss it away."

"Zan, if I *was* amazing, or even half good—"

"You *are*," said Zan angrily, slamming her beer on the table. She looked at her treeplanter friends. "It's our crew leader's birthday today, that guy with the beard and bandanna. He just turned thirty. All day he's been walking around in a daze with his tree-bags strapped onto his ass, saying over and over, 'I'm thirty years old, and I'm climbing up hills in the rain poking holes in the ground.' You want to be him?"

Earley was twenty-nine. He could relate. All three of his sisters had families already, and even his kid brother owned a few acres he'd bought with his disability checks from the navy. Earley's net worth was a beat-up old schoolbus, a truck with one door and a six-year-old chainsaw—a Husqy, he told himself, top of the line, but still.

"Yeah," Reed was saying, "maybe I do. Maybe I'd like to be planting a forest, or giving some family a new roof, or *something*. Something that isn't just me being me."

"You're a jerk, Reed." Zan picked up his hand, pressed her lips to his fingertips, then moved downwards to nuzzle his palm. Reed cradled her cheek, and her eyes closed. "I missed you," she murmured. Earley watched as Reed kissed her hair, breathing the scent of her, drinking it in with his lips. They'd forgotten that Earley was there. This was his exit for sure. He was horny enough without watching them kiss.

Earley unfolded himself from the bench, but Zan's other hand caught his sleeve. "You don't have to go," she said.

Earley looked down at the two of them, trying to shoot Reed a glance that meant, I'm clearing out, bud, don't worry. "Taking a leak," he said. "Too full of beer."

Zan's gaze didn't leave him. "Come back," she said.

Earley looked at himself in the mirror above the cracked sink. This wasn't a thing a guy did; there were rules of behavior here. Margie was different. She'd married an asshole who slept around plenty, would probably screw a damn gas tank if you left the cap off. Earley was poaching, he knew, but he figured her husband deserved it. Reed was a buddy.

Or was he? Earley had met the guy, what, maybe two or three hours ago. They'd smoked some weed, had a couple of laughs, that was all. They were strangers. Reed had told Earley himself that he and Zan weren't really together, least not any-more. And damn it, the way she *looked* at him.

Earley was hedging, he knew it. The right thing to do was to walk out the door of the men's room and just keep on going. He turned off the water tap, wiping his hands on his shirttail. A Quileute Indian built like a hot water heater walked through the door, tilting his chin up in greeting. That's how men were with each other. They gave ground, they maintained their dignity. Leave now, Earley said to himself. If you don't, there'll be trouble.

He walked out of the men's room, his head held high, swinging the door back so forcefully that it slammed into the women's room door as Zan came out, smiling. "Don't know your own strength," she said, eyeing Earley's broad shoulders. He followed her back to the booth, watching the way her ass moved in her jeans, how the men she passed swiveled and how she ignored them. It was like watching the wake of a ship.

Zan slid back in next to Reed. "Did you find my map in the laundromat?"

Reed nodded. "I would have walked if I had to."

"Good thing Earley rescued you." There was that smile again, mocking, inviting. "Treeplanting camp is a hell of a hike."

"How'd you wind up there?"

Zan shrugged. "I was heading for Vancouver Island. Met a guy from Australia who'd just joined the crew." Reed's face went taut. Her lips curved as she answered the question before he could ask it. "He quit the first week. Couldn't hack it. It's backbreaking, boring, hard work."

Earley wondered what kind of a moron would pass up a chance at Zan because planting a couple of trees was too hard. "But you stayed on?"

"I liked it."

"Why?" Earley asked her.

Zan turned to look at him. Her eyes were unreadable, dark as molasses. "It's making me strong," she said. "Why do you work in the woods?"

"I'm good at it," Earley said. He leaned backwards and folded his forearms across his chest.

Reed drained his beer. Earley noticed the group of tree-planters was starting to layer on jackets and raingear. A girl with a hip-length honey-blonde braid slouched over to Zan. "The crummy's about to take off. Are you coming?"

"Give me a minute." The blonde girl nodded, looking at Earley's arms. She flashed him a tentative smile, then rejoined the bandanna-wrapped crew chief, the one who'd turned thirty. Zan turned towards Reed, draping a hand on his shoulder. "So where are you guys gonna stay tonight?"

Reed and Earley looked at each other. "Got me," said Earley.

"We haven't, ah, gotten that far," said Reed. "How about you?"

Zan traced her hand up the side of his neck. "I've got a leaky tent up in the woods. With a roommate."

"I've got a bus in the woods," said Earley.

"I've got a dorm room in Berkeley," said Reed.

Earley shook his head, grinning. "Well, this is a sorry-ass state of affairs. I could drive y'all twenty miles back to my bus, but it's none too deluxe up there."

"Got to be better than treeplanters' camp."

Reed looked at Zan, then at Earley. "Is there a motel in town?"

"Sort of. Guy I know works the front desk. If he's not feeling surly he might find us some kind of rack. He's stood me to plenty of Friday nights."

Zan's lips crinkled into a smile, "Yeah, I bet." Earley wasn't imagining it. She was flirting with him, with her fingers entwined in Reed's hair. He tried to envision the sleeping arrangement. Whatever it was, he was on for the ride. He tossed the keys to his truck onto the tabletop, next to the empty beer pitcher.

Zan twisted around towards the crew chief. "Yo, birthday boy, I'm going to stay with my friends tonight." She waved at him, blithely ignoring his frown. Then she turned back, drained her beer glass and looked from Earley to Reed. "Ready?"

They stood at the same moment. Reed tossed a handful of change on the tabletop next to the pitcher. Earley couldn't imagine why someone would leave a tip when nobody had served him. He spotted a couple of dimes in the mix. You son of a bitch, he thought, staring down at the coins. You better have just picked those up at the bar. He looked over at Reed, who was pulling Zan tight to his hipbones, his hands roaming over the seat of her jeans.

"You bet," said Reed. "Ready for anything."

THREE

Scoter Gillies was practically prone in his swivel chair, watching a snow-crackled mini TV. He heard the door open but didn't look up. Earley leaned over the counter and pinged seven times on the customer service bell. Scoter twisted his head around. "Earley, you fuck."

Earley raised his chin towards the TV. "That the one about killer piranhas?"

"I'm not gonna lend you a cent till you bring back my drill."

"It's up at the bus. But I got some collateral." He laid one of Reed's tightly rolled joints on the guest register. Scoter's eyebrows went up. "It's serious weed. California Hawaiian."

Earley set down a second joint next to the first one, then glanced at the key rack. There were still a few numbered fobs hanging down from their hooks. "Could you spare me a couple of honeymoon suites for the evening?"

"A couple? How many wives have you got out there?"

"Second room's for my friend from the grassfields of Maui. He's here with a lady." Scoter swung his desk chair around, grabbing one room key. He threw it at Earley. "Tell your friend and his lady I take cash or charge."

Earley slammed the aluminum door and went to the idling pickup. The VACANCY sign spilled a wet slick of red through the parking lot's puddles. He opened the door and held up his room key. "Best I could do. You guys take it. I'll sleep in the truck."

"That's not fair. He's your friend."

"It's your weed. And there's two of you."

Zan said, "I think we'll all fit." Reed stared at her. She shrugged. "I've slept in an army cot under a pup tent the last couple months. It's got two double beds, right?"

"The hell with the beds," Earley said. "It's the shower I'm dreaming of."

The hot water splashed in the fake marble sink, clouding the mirror with steam. Earley was shaving his neck. He had worked up a lather with Cameo soap, and was carefully mowing a half inch of fuzz from the base of his throat. He bent his knees lower to look in a mirror positioned for somebody half a foot shorter. His Adam's apple stuck out like a growth, ris-

ing and falling with every gulp. He could hear Zan and Reed
through the door. They'd turned on the TV for some semblance
of privacy; Earley heard an ominous soundtrack and wondered if it was the same killer fish movie Scoter was watching. Reed let out a moan as Zan's voice rose and fell in a
flirtatious lilt.

Earley pictured her peeling that undershirt over her breasts,
how they'd rise with her arms, nipples jutting like fingers. He
heard the bed creak. Were they already at it? Did Zan have her
legs wrapped around his bare back, was she riding on top? He
imagined the wetness inside her, the gasp with each thrust,
how she'd draw a man deeper and deeper. What must that feel
like, he wondered, to pull someone inside your body, surround
him? He was getting a boner. Forget the damn beard, he could
clean it up later. He stripped off his longjohns and pulled back
the blue shower curtain. Inside the tub was a plumber's kit.
Both of the faucets were off.

"Shit!" Earley kicked the tub so hard his toes hurt. He
grabbed at the curtain and ripped it off, shredding its grom-
mets. He pounded the wall.

". . . You okay in there?" Reed's voice sounded strained. Earley pictured him stuck in mid-hump, straddling Zan as he
turned towards the bathroom wall, wondering what kind of
gonzo had picked him up hitching.

"Gonna kill that sumbitch. Gonna murder his scrawny white
ass," Earley sputtered. He scooped up his blue jeans and jerked

them on angrily, stepping back into his unlaced caulks. Hell with socks. Hell with his wool shirt. He grabbed his stained T-shirt in one hand and pushed through the bathroom door.

Zan and Reed sat side by side on the edge of the bed. They weren't even undressed yet. College kids. He would have had her flat out by now. Reed must be one of those talkers. Earley clomped through the bedroom in loose caulks and dangling suspenders. "Be back sooner or later," he mumbled, aware of Zan's eyes on his torso, the damp froth of Cameo sliding from throat to bare chest. "I got a shower to take."

Scoter stuck his hand into a big bag of Fritos. "You get what you pay for." He stared at the screen, where the Amazon River was roiling. "These fish are *intense*. Check the jaw on that thing."

"You got three other rooms. Half an hour," Earley begged.

"No can do, man. It's bar night. God only knows what's about to roll in here. I gave you the room I knew wouldn't be renting."

"Ten minutes. I'll get you some more of that Maui."

"I'm already fucked up. That stuff's killer."

"What'd I tell you? Ten minutes. I'll wipe down the tub, change the towels . . ."

"Look, Earley, I need this piece of shit job, okay? Put your damn shirt on. If my boss comes in here and sees you like that, he'll ream us both hollow." Scoter swiveled his chair towards the screen, where a blonde in a wet shirt was screaming. Earley stared at his back. He decided it wasn't worth saying fuck you; he might need a free bed again someday. He pulled on his shirt and went out in the rain.

"Lost your key again?" Margie Walkonis swung open the door of her double-wide trailer. She had on a loose purple T-shirt and sweatpants. No bra, Earley noticed at once. Her loose breasts rolled down to her waistband. "Earley Ritter!" she sputtered, one hand flying up to her untidy hair.

"I know, I'm a sight for sore eyes." Earley grinned. "Make 'em sore if they wasn't already. Did I wake you up?"

"God no. I thought you were Harlan."

"Harlan's in town?" Earley tried to sound casual.

"'Sposed to be. Not that he bothered to stop by or nothing. He's probably knocking back shots at the Cedar."

"I just came from there. I was hoping I'd see you."

"You were?" Margie smiled. Earley could see she'd been pretty before all the weight, the darkening under her eyes, the stripe of gray splitting her rust-colored hair. Probably a cheerleader, big tits, big teeth, willing. He tried picturing her twenty years ago, doing a split, but got stuck on her powder blue sweatpants and belly roll. "Can I get you a beer?"

"Listen, Margie, if Harlan's in town—"

"If he's not at the Cedar he's probably passed out at the

Shamrock. He won't make it home till closing time, if he shows his face then. I'm not on the top of his playlist these days." Margie wasn't complaining, just stating the facts. She reminded Earley of women he'd known back home, who'd gotten unlucky in high school and wound up with men their adult selves would never have chosen. His sister Judene. Not to mention his mom. "Besides, you can hear his damn diesel a mile away. Where'd you park?"

"Down the street. I remembered." Earley had left his truck in the grown-over lot at the end of the cul-de-sac, outside the development no one had ever developed.

"Good boy," Margie said, pressing closer against him. Her tits were like couch cushions, welcoming, warm. He could smell something winy and sweet on her breath. "I'm so glad you're here. I was climbing the walls. Amber Ann's at the hockey game with that Mexican boy, and whenever he drives, I can't help it . . ."

Earley took hold of her arm. "I could go for that beer," he said. "You?" Margie nodded and led him back into her kitchen. Earley dipped his head under the Plexiglas chandelier, wondering whether his boot spikes would tear up the shag rug. He didn't feel right about taking them off until he was invited.

"How about a shot of Harlan's Wild Turkey?"

"That sounds mighty excellent, thank you," he said, overdoing his accent to make her smile. She was a good lady, Margie, seen more than her share of hard times. She'd cried in his arms that first night on the waterbed, and he'd found out later that it was her thirty-sixth birthday. She'd already buried two children: a daughter who'd died in her crib, and a nine-year-old son who'd been clipped by a van on his way to a Little League game. Now her oldest was running around with an eighteen-year-old with two DWIs, and her husband was screwing some truck driver's wife. Earley figured as Margie deserved any comfort she found in this lifetime. Even if it was just him.

Margie poured him a generous bolt in a grape jelly jar, then swung the fridge open and refilled a glass of peach-colored wine cooler. She wore open-toed terrycloth scuffs, and Earley noticed her toenails were striped with a peeling magenta glaze. He pictured her sitting alone on her bedspread, cotton balls stuffed in between every toe, the radio on and a glass of that wine cooler, trying to make herself feel better. The bathroom he'd shared with his sisters back home had been littered with curling devices, mascara wands, small crusty bottles of makeup. Earley thought about all the time women spent doing things that men didn't care about, really. It made him sad. He walked up behind Margie and slipped his arms around her. "Could we take a shower together?"

"Ooh, kinky," said Margie, turning around to face into his hug. She was too short to kiss him without his help; even when he slouched against the counter, her lips grazed his collarbone. She pulled Earley's hand underneath her shirt, placing his palm on her nipple.

"It's a humanitarian project," said Earley. "I stink to the sky."

"You know what I'd like some day?" Margie unsnapped

his jeans. "One of those hot-tubby things with the bubbles. Jacuzzis."

Earley could feel his dick stiffening. Margie's hand slid around the shaft.

"Mm," she said.

Earley put down his Wild Turkey. The shower could wait. So could everything else. They stripped, groping each other. Earley pushed open the door to the bedroom. "I've got to go put in my thing," Margie said. He nodded, deflating.

Margie disappeared into the bathroom. Earley went in and lay down on the waterbed, feeling its slosh and embrace. His mind drifted to the motel room; he wondered if Reed was still chatting, or if Zan was jumping his bones. She didn't look like the patient type. Earley thought of her circling the pool table, bending to shoot. It went right to his groin, and he groaned out loud, feeling disloyal to Margie and eager to get inside her. He knew Margie felt the same way about him: horny, grateful, just tender enough not to feel like a shithead.

Earley rolled back onto one of the pillows. He wondered if Harlan would pick up his musk like a hunting hound, sniffing the forest green comforter cover for traces of woodsmoke, tobacco and week-old sweat.

Margie stood in the doorway. She'd slipped on a shiny night-gown that featured her cleavage, and Earley noticed that she'd brushed her hair. "You look good," he said.

"You're full of shit," Margie answered, and then added shyly,

"But thanks." She came to the edge of the bed and held out one hand. Earley reached over and pulled her down, feeling the lurch of the waterbed. They got right down to it. He liked the way Margie kissed back, warm and hungry, how she ran the backs of her fingernails over his spine and massaged his bare butt as he arched himself over her body. The waterbed added an undersea roll to his thrusts. He felt like a sea lion mating.

Earley had started to sleep with girls when he was thirteen years old; it was one of the few things he knew he did well. Fucking, drinking and splitting wood. Not a long list. I could do this forever, he thought, but Margie was already churning her way towards a climax and he obliged, pumping faster and filling her, bringing her with him, her breath getting deeper, more guttural.

"Was that a car?"

"Shit," she gasped. "Bring me home. Do it." And Earley dove in deep and stayed there, lifting up onto his arms as Margie shuddered beneath him. "God," she moaned. "That was incredible. Go out the kitchen door."

Earley jumped up and yanked on his underwear, then scooped up the rest of his clothes, nearly dropping his jeans as he grabbed his caulk boots. He wondered how Margie was going to explain her glazed sheen of sweat and heaving breath. He figured that was her problem. His was getting the sliding door open and hiding somewhere in the darkness before Harlan boomed through the living room, waving a shotgun.

Earley scrambled out onto the back deck, bare feet slipping on the wet wood. He could see headlights bounce onto the wall as a pickup pulled into the driveway. He dodged around the far side of the trailer, crouching next to a tank of propane. He looked up with a start as a light snapped on over his head, behind a small, louvered window. That would be Margie, rushing into the bathroom to throw on her bathrobe and squirt some cologne. Earley bent down to pull on his jeans. From the opposite side of the trailer he heard a car door swinging open, an engine on idle, a woman's flirtatious laugh. Had Harlan brought somebody home?

"'Cause I *said* so." A breathy voice, singsong. "Come *on*." A male voice said something too low to make out, and the girl answered, "Yeah, well, tell that to my mom."

It was Amber Ann, coming home early and worried about what her mother would think, while Margie was probably inside with a big wad of kleenex, trying to blot up the rest of his come. Earley swore to himself he'd stop messing with other men's women. He'd just slept with somebody's *mother*, and here he was squatting behind a propane tank, trying to sort out his tangled suspenders, like the punchline of some dirty joke. What had happened to his self-respect? He thought of Zan's crew chief, stomping around in the rain on his birthday, then shivered and pulled up his jeans. What did he have to show for his twenty-nine years on the planet? Hell, he couldn't even get clean.

Earley had wild thoughts of pounding on some stranger's door, striding into the bathroom shower and taking his due, the way Scoter Gillies' old man once came home skunked from a hunting trip and carried his rifle right into the frozen food aisle of the FoodMart, where he'd plugged a Butterball turkey, slung it over his shoulder and left before anyone got it together to stop him.

Where else could he go? It was Friday night; none of the guys would be home yet unless they were getting a piece of some action. Maybe Chester Marczupiak, from the Texaco station, but he'd been so down since his wife left that Earley couldn't face the idea of listening to him, not even for soap and hot water. He supposed he could pick up a new roll of dimes and drive back to Bogachiel, but he knew he was too beat to make the round trip. He thought briefly of doing it anyway, just leaving Reed and Zan in the motel and not coming back; it wasn't like he owed them anything, really. Then he remembered that he'd brought his chainsaw inside the motel room for safekeeping. No way was he going to abandon his Husqy. That saw was his livelihood, his prize possession. And he'd left his wool shirt and best socks on the bathmat.

All right, then. Earley had to go back for his stuff, so it wasn't just about wanting to see Zan again. Though he certainly did want to see her. Reed too, he thought, feeling guilty; he liked the guy. Earley didn't know why they'd washed up on his shore, like a tangle of kelp, but he already felt they belonged with each other.

There wasn't much light in the motel room when Earley let himself through the door. He could make out Zan's hair on the pillow, the twist of Reed's torso beneath the white sheet. He hoped they'd pretend they were sleeping, at least till he got to the bathroom. He closed the door quietly, twisting the brass knob, and bent down to take off his caulks. Trying to walk softly in those was like trying to tiptoe in horseshoes. The smell of his feet hit him full in the face. Damn the faucets. He'd just have to improvise.

The ceiling light in the bathroom was bluish white, with a fluttering filament. Earley lifted the plumber's kit out of the tub—goddamn Scoter—and stripped off his clothes. He could sponge-bath it, anyway. There was a plastic ice bucket on top of the toilet, along with two glasses. Earley set it on the edge of the sink, within reach of the tub. He turned on the hot water tap in the sink and twisted a towel underneath it until it steamed. He stepped into the bathtub and rubbed himself with the hot towel. It felt so good he moaned. He worked up a lather of Cameo soap, then filled up the ice bucket, pouring it over his shoulders. The hot water ran down his back, trickling over his buttocks. He did it again and again, scrubbing his arms and legs with the steaming towel, then lathering, rinsing, holding the bucket up high to pour over his head like a waterfall.

By the time he reached over to turn off the tap, the mirror

was fogged and the air in the bathroom felt tropical. Earley stepped out and rubbed himself down with a dry towel. This is more like it, he thought. It had been a long day, starting out with a rot-riddled oldgrowth stump the size of a Pontiac. He was ready for bed.

Earley clutched the towel around his hips, switching off the fluorescent light as he emerged from the bathroom, surrounded by steam. He moved stealthily past the foot of Zan and Reed's queen-size, then paused. The aisle between the two beds wasn't more than a foot across. Earley would have to take off his towel to get into bed, and his ass would wind up half a foot from—which one was on his side? Zan.

She'd rolled over. Her arm was thrown back on the pillow, her face twisted sideways. The sheet had slipped down so that most of one breast was exposed.

Earley's breath caught. He could feel himself getting a boner again. Better get under the covers before things got embarrassing. He edged in between the two beds and pulled back his bedcovers, sliding in, towel and all. The bed was too short for his legs, but the clean sheets were cool. He shifted his weight on the pillow, then reached under the covers to peel off his towel, feeling the rub of damp terrycloth over his groin. Zan was inches away, she was naked beneath that thin sheet. He stuck out his hand, dropping his damp towel onto the rug.

"Night, Earley," Zan whispered. Her hand reached across so their fingers touched, hanging in midair between the two beds.

FOUR

Zan's description of how to get out to the treeplanters' camp had been accurate, though without her there, wedged into the front seat between him and Reed, animatedly pointing out landmarks, Earley doubted that he would have spotted the final turn. The skeletal road was grown over with brush, and the more recent ruts on each side could have passed for an elk trail.

Earley heard stiff canes of devil's club scraping the truck's undercarriage as they bounced along over rocks. His front tooth hurt. Reed had taken them out for a Pancake House breakfast, surreptitiously paying the bill with his Visa, and Earley had drenched his two stacks with a strawberry syrup that worked its way under his gums. He could feel the side order of sausage churning around in his belly. Where was this place, anyway? They were almost as deep in the woods as his bus, and the thought of picking his way back through this thicket of criss-crossing dirt roads, driving twenty more miles down the highway and clambering back up his own maze of log roads was daunting. Kiss this day good-bye for a wage-earner.

"Just up this ridge," Zan was saying, and Earley saw something that looked like a tipi loom out of the mist.

"What the hell?"

"Oh, that's Young Nick's wickiup. He pitched it up there for the view, and it's blown down three times. Just around this next bend."

The treeplanters' camp was laid out in a cross, on the intersection of the washed-out road they were on and another, still worse, road that led to the creek. There were several tan canvas tents, a two-tone VW van, a vintage Ford truck with a yellow and red gypsy wagon built onto the back, and a lavender step-van lettered TAKE BACK THE NIGHT parked along the crossed roads, raying out from a slightly collapsed, bright blue dome in the center. The place looked abandoned, except for a mangy dog padding along the ridge next to the wickiup and a thin plume of smoke from the stovepipe that jutted up from the blue dome's sagging roof.

"They must be out planting already," Zan said.

"Well, it *is* almost noon," said Reed. He was the only one wearing a watch. It looked old and expensive, a gift from some uncle or grandfather who'd have his name on a college dorm.

"I bet Just Nick will be pissed at me. Wonder who's camp-tending?"

"Where should I park?" Earley asked.

"Wherever you think you won't sink in the mud," Zan said. "Oh, it's Cassie."

The flap of the blue dome had opened. A girl's face peered out, drawn by the sound of the truck's engine. It was the same girl they'd seen last night at the Cedar, the one with the honey-blonde braid. Zan waved, pulled Reed out of the pickup and strode towards the dome tent, leaving the passenger door dangling off its lone hinge.

"Where is everybody?"

"They got started early for once," the girl answered. "Just Nick was in one of his shake-it-up moods." She watched Earley approach.

"Are they gonna come back here for lunch?"

"I sure hope so. I cooked up a ton of food. I heard your truck coming and figured it must be the crummy." The girl flashed a shy smile at Earley, flipping her braid over one of her shoulders. "I'm Cassie. Hey."

"Earley and Reed," Zan said, without indicating which one was which. Earley nodded and Reed echoed, "Hey."

Cassie was wearing an inside-out sweatshirt and overalls, and hadn't bothered to pull on her raingear when she stepped outside. "Come into the yurt," she said, folding her arms with a shiver. "I'm getting wet." If that's an issue, thought Earley, you picked the wrong job, sister.

Reed followed Zan into the dome tent. Cassie held the flap open for Earley, who needed to bend nearly double to get through the doorway. Even when he was inside, his head grazed the roof. It was surprisingly cozy, with a Coleman lantern hung over a long plank table and stools made from stumps on a matted straw floor. Pots and pans and stray twists of dried herbs dangled down from the dome struts alongside a sizable woodstove. The air was close, smelling of garlic and cedar smoke.

"You guys want some soup?" Cassie touched her hair again, looking at Earley. She lifted the top off a pot, revealing some brown, indefinable bean mass.

"Ah, no thanks," said Earley. "I'm full of bad pancakes. It might send me over the edge."

"I'd love some," said Reed. Cassie smiled and reached into a crate for a bowl. She had very straight teeth. In a different circumstance Earley might have thought she was attractive, but Cassie quite literally paled beside Zan. Her fair hair looked wan, her skin sallow. There was a gentle, drifting fluidity in her movements that might have been graceful, but struck Earley instead as unfocussed and woolly. It made him impatient to watch how slowly her wooden spoon circled around in the bean pot; he felt like grabbing it out of her hands and giving that mess a good stir.

"I'm gonna go out for a smoke," he said, bending to fit through the doorflap. He felt better as soon as he got back outside, filling his lungs with cool air that tingled with mist. He took out his Drum pouch and made his way down to the creek. It was fast-moving and nearly opaque, clotted silver with silt. A crisscrossing thicket of alder trunks lined the far bank. Beyond the bare twigs of the alder hell, he could make out the dish of a mountainside, partially clearcut, its peak disappearing in veils of low clouds. That bald patch was probably where they were planting. Earley squinted up at it, wondering if someone had already cleared out the cedar. If not, he could put in a claim, move his bus a bit closer to civilization. To Zan.

He hunkered down on a flat rock, scooping out some tobacco and rolling a smoke. He didn't know how to proceed. Zan and Reed had been talking at breakfast about whether Reed might find work with the treeplanting crew. Should Earley hang around, waiting with him to find out? Did he owe Reed a ride back to town if the answer was no? It was too far to walk, not to mention good odds on him losing his way. But why should that be Earley's problem?

He took out his lighter and struck it, remembering the joint they'd shared in his pickup cab, laughing like fools. Getting naked together, the dime falling into the drain. The touch of Zan's fingers last night in the dark, like a promise.

Maybe Reed would get hired and wind up with that pale chick who couldn't cook beans. Maybe Zan would get sick of his oversized dong and gold watch and decide what she needed to make life complete was a penniless shake-rat with rotting front teeth. Maybe Earley should get in his truck and move on. He was wasting his time.

He spotted a shadow above the gray water. An osprey. The bird swooped low, winging upstream as it searched for fish. Without warning it plummeted, sinking its talons deep into the sides of a trout. The silver fish writhed in its grasp as the osprey flew off, disappearing into the mist. That was how quickly a life could be over.

Earley tossed his cigarette butt in the creek and watched it tumble downstream. He'd stay a bit longer. At least till he'd worked out some way to see Zan again.

He got back to the kitchen yurt just as the treeplanters' crummy rolled into the campsite. It was an old flatbed truck with a plywood cabin built onto the back. There were metal racks on either side of the back door for mud-spattered hoedads and treebags, and when the door opened, he could see benches along both side walls where the treeplanters sat like spent paratroopers preparing to jump.

Cassie came out with a steaming washbasin and a quart of Dr. Bronner's Peppermint Soap, which she laid on a rock just outside of the yurt as the planters humped out of their truck. They were muddy and sullen, a sad-looking outfit, thought Earley. Not one of them seemed to take note of a six-foot-five stranger standing next to their kitchen tent. Then the crew chief stepped out of the driver's seat. He looked right at Earley, pegging him as the same guy he'd seen in the Cedar—the one

Zan had stayed with last night—and his jaw clicked into a frown. Just like that, they were enemies.

Earley and Reed stayed for lunch, at Zan's invitation. The black-bearded crew chief kept eyeing them, trying to figure out which one he ought to resent. The other planters all called him Just Nick, apparently to distinguish him from Young Nick, the wickiup owner, who wore hawk feathers tied to his Dutch Boy-blond braids, without pissing him off with Old Nick.

The Nicks weren't the only treeplanters who'd renamed themselves. Earley caught wind of a Robbo, a Graywolf, a Japanese girl named Susu and a ham-faced girl with a crewcut who called herself Mum. He found himself edging towards people with names like Dave, Bob and Eric. True, he had sort of a weird name himself, but he'd come by it honestly: his mother had christened him for Jubal Early, a Confederate general whose gravesite was in her hometown, though she'd mis-remembered the spelling and added an extra "e." But nobody's mom named him Graywolf.

Reed looked in his element, perched on a ten-gallon drum of tahini and scarfing down seconds of Cassie's inedible beans. He was doing his damnedest to get himself hired, asking all sorts of questions about the treeplanters' coop, how they bid for jobs from the government and logging companies, what kind of tools they used, how many trees they were planting per acre. In Ear-ley's opinion, Reed's eagerness exposed him as a virgin to woods work. There was a clear hierarchy, with tree-toppers and sawyers on top of the heap, cat skinners, buckers and choker dogs a notch below. Shake-rats were sneered at as scavengers, living off loggers' dropped bones, but at least they used chainsaws.

Treeplanters weren't even part of the food chain, although, as they liked to point out, no one else in the woods would have jobs if they ran out of trees. Which could happen: the old-growth near Forks had been logged out from every place skidders could reach, and no one had thought to replace them till recently, when the Forest Service and private owners like Royalton Timber had started to contract out reforestation. The tree plugs the co-ops were planting would take thirty years to mature. Treeplanting was grunt work, undertaken exclusively, it seemed, by people who had a perverse sort of downward mobility, suburbanites seeking out hardship in hopes it would make them feel real. Scratch a treeplanter and you'd find a master's in Eastern philosophy, a family fortune in stocks or tobacco. Reed and his watch ought to fit right in.

Earley had asked him at breakfast how he and Zan had first met. "Reed played in the coffeehouse where I was waitressing," Zan answered, taking Reed's hand.

"I'd been buying my lunch there for months and she never looked at me twice," added Reed. Zan smiled and shrugged.

"A skinny white guy with a pile of poli-sci textbooks in Berkeley. One of a thousand. But I took you home the first night I heard you play. That counts."

"Oh, it counted, all right," said Reed, kissing her fingers one by one. Earley sliced his fork through both his fried egg yolks and smeared his pancakes through the glop. Zan and Reed seemed reluctant to volunteer any more about their shared past, so they traded birthplaces instead of more recent events.

"Waycross, Georgia," said Earley.

"Marblehead, Mass," said Reed, adding, "Near Boston," when Earley looked blank.

"Guam," said Zan.

Earley hadn't expected that. "Your dad's in the service?" he asked her.

"They're *both* in the service." Zan stuck her butter knife into the jelly as if she were trying to kill something with it. She licked the knife clean. Reed looked disconcerted.

So Zan was an army brat. Earley figured that made her a novelty item: a hippie treeplanter with working-class roots. He wondered how long she'd been up in the woods. Not very long, he bet. She was too restless to settle for this kind of life. Even the way she sat was impatient, like an engine that idles too high when it's parked. Earley couldn't imagine her staying in any one place, or with any one man. He wondered why she had ditched Reed back in Berkeley and then pulled him back like a magnet. And he wondered if he would be next.

Zan crossed the yurt to refill her tin cup with green tea. Earley could feel the molecules shift in the tent as she lifted the speckleware pot from the woodstove and circled the hay bales, refilling men's cups. Cassie nursed her juice, sullen. The other two women, the slim Japanese girl and crop-haired Mum, sat close together, thighs touching like lovers. The Nicks were arguing over the wisdom of hiring Reed. "We're barely making our nut as is," said Just Nick. "If we took on another hourly wage—"

"But if we had another guy working, we'd cover more ground." Young Nick reached into his bowl and scooped out some tempeh to feed to his dog.

"Ever planted before?" Just Nick turned to Reed, his gaze challenging.

"Marigolds, corn, sensemilla. A few windowboxes." Reed seemed to know he was being obnoxious; he just didn't like the guy's tone.

Just Nick frowned. "We don't need more rookies. Too late in the season to break you in. We're finishing up our last contract."

"I work like hell," said Reed. "I'm an obsessed man. Ask Zan."

Just Nick shook his head. "Can't afford you."

"Okay," said Reed, stung. "It's your party."

Earley looked at Zan. She'd been silent throughout, and showed no disappointment. Was he imagining things, or did she seem a little relieved that Reed wouldn't be sharing her tent? Earley could not put his finger on what they had going.

Zan wasn't in love with Reed, that much was clear, but she wasn't just playing him either. There was something that glowed in her eyes when she mentioned his music, a lingering cling in her touch when she reached for his face. They were tied to each other in some indefinable way, an invisible rope Reed might yet use to hang himself.

Zan walked them back out to the truck after lunch. The rest of the planters were pulling their raingear back on and clambering into the crummy. Earley busied himself rearranging the tarp in the back of his pickup as Zan moved towards Reed. "You could stay for a couple of days, at least."

Reed shook his head. "I don't get the feeling I'm wanted."

"Oh, fuck Just Nick—he's been trying to get in my pants for a month. You can stay here with me."

"And do what all day long while you're planting?"

Zan opened her mouth to say something, then nodded. She didn't look happy. "So what'll you do?"

"Head on up to Alaska, I guess. Find a job there."

"You don't have to do this, you know."

"But I want to." Reed's pale blue eyes went opaque. Zan stepped in closer. She lifted Reed's hands in hers, kissing his fingers. Then she set his hands onto her hips and pressed her body against his, her lips open wide for his kiss. Reed's eyes closed, as if he were trying to memorize every sensation. They kissed for so long that Earley looked down at the toes of his boots, feeling like an intruder. Zan pulled away first, and Reed let out an audible sigh.

"Take care of yourself, Reed." He nodded and Zan turned towards Earley, searching his face with a gaze so intense the heat rose in his ears. Was she wondering how she might see him again? She stepped towards him and gave him a hug, rising up onto her toes so her lips grazed his throat.

"Catch you later," she said. Then she turned from them both and walked into the crummy without looking back.

Neither one of them spoke for a long stretch of road. The landmarks seemed clearer on the way down, brought to life by the echo of Zan's vivid comments. There was the split fir with the ZZ Top beard, the boulder that looked like a crouching baboon, the moss-covered stump with the fungus ears. Earley stopped at the junction of two muddy roads. "Don't remember this one. Left or right?"

Reed looked around. "I don't know. Left?"

"Got to be one or the other," said Earley. He turned to the left. "Why Alaska?"

"Why not?" said Reed.

Earley shrugged. "If you say so." It was raining again. He switched on the wipers, cursing the warped blade that smeared the left side of the windshield.

Reed looked over at him. His wide eyes looked as pale as a malamute's. "I just got sick of myself and the stuff I was doing." His voice had a choked, hollow sound; he was trying to say something true, but not finding the words. "I've never stepped off the track: high school, summer camp, college. I needed some air."

That sounded like way less than half of the story, but Earley accepted it. Maybe Reed didn't actually know what had made him roll up all his things in a duffel and stick out his thumb. People rarely knew why they did anything. Earley had no clue, for instance, why he'd stuck with Reed since he picked him up yesterday—or why he was, even now, struggling to find the right way of framing the question he had on his mind.

Reed was still talking. "Maybe I'll sign up to be a fire look-out, like all those Beat poets. Jack Kerouac, Gary Snyder, Phil Whalen—they all did time in the Cascades. Kerouac couldn't hack it—he kept bopping down to the bars—but Snyder wrote book after book about life in the woods."

"Would you want to try working together?"

Reed turned his head. "Cutting cedar?"

"You mentioned it yesterday. It's not a great gig, but—"

"Yes. Absolutely. *Yes.*" Reed burst into a broad, sudden grin. Earley hoped that he hadn't just blown it. He did need a part-ner, but breaking in someone this green would be hard on them both. Not to mention the issue of having a person *around* all the time, in his space, in his way. He'd gotten used to his own way of living. Whenever he went into town to refuel and get drunk, he felt jangled for days till he found his way back to the slow, patient rhythms of living in nature.

"Don't jump up and down till you see what the work's like. Not to mention my bus. It's no suite at the Ritz. Got a hell of a view, though." Earley had angled his parking space so that the view from his window was two oldgrowth firs, framing the snowcap of Mount Olympus.

"Sounds perfect."

"The last guy I worked with, we split sixty-forty. That okay by you?"

Reed nodded quickly. "But I've never worked with a chain-saw."

"Don't have to. I'll saw and you'll split. It goes faster like that."

"I'm stoked," said Reed. "Thank you."

"I don't know as you ought to be thanking me," Earley said. "You're gonna be aching in places you didn't know you have. And I don't mean to sound like Just Prick, but it's not gonna work if you can't keep the pace."

"I ran track in high school. I've done a few marathons. I'm pretty good at just keeping on going."

"You'll need it," said Earley, imagining Reed in his bus's tight space. He felt hemmed in already. Well, why not? he thought. Even if Reed couldn't hack the work, Earley would have some company for a few days or weeks, not to mention a good source of weed. And he'd get to see Zan again. That wasn't the only reason he'd asked Reed to stay, Earley told himself, but if someone had asked him at gunpoint, he'd have to admit it was high on the list.

Earley rounded a curve and stepped on the brake. The dirt road they'd been driving on came to a dead end ahead, at the foot of a cliff. They looked at each other and started to laugh. "Guess that left was a right, huh?" Reed deadpanned.

"Last time I listen to *you*, city boy." Earley slung his right arm over Reed's seat and backed up as fast as he could. "We're in my mountains now."

FIVE

Earley's bus had been parked in the grown-over turnout of an abandoned access road for ten months, and he figured that he hadn't actually looked at his spread, really *seen* it, for nine of them. There were a few dozen beer bottles lying around, for example, that he'd never noticed. Three rusted-out fuel cans, a spare tire, the dented tin cap for his pickup. A few cords of firewood that he'd never gotten around to stacking. That old-fashioned Coke machine he'd grabbed out of a landfill in case it might work as a fridge. Some spare links of stovepipe. It looked like a front yard from the lower-rent section of Way-cross, except for the midnight-blue schoolbus with stars on its roof and the glaciated volcanic cone looming up over the clouds. The fir trees that framed his small clearing were heavy with rain, needles glistening. Earley turned off the pickup.

"Well, this is it. My brokedown palace."

Reed didn't say anything right away. He stepped out of the truck and looked up at the mountain, spellbound. Earley noticed the stillness around them, a silence so absolute that he could hear droplets of rain shifting down through the trees and the sound of a woodpecker drilling on some distant ridge. This was his home. He was grateful that Reed hadn't cheapened it with an immediate comment. If he had that kind of awe around woods he'd do fine, even if he was a scrawny college kid with no back to speak of. The strength you could build, but that silent acceptance that lets two men work side by side all day long in the rain was something you had or you didn't.

Earley's last partner, Dean, hadn't had it at all. They'd been in each other's face since the day Dean arrived with his tape deck and toaster oven, sapping the generator to play Lynyrd Skynyrd and heat up his Pop-Tarts. The bus was a constant hum of activity, appliances whirring above thumping drum-beats, the drone of the generator's engine, Dean's loud braying voice as he "shot the shit," his favorite phrase. He'd been able to match Earley's pace as a splitter, his one saving grace, but he'd kept track of every last nickel and whined about how little profit they made, and how he could pull twice as much at the sawmill, and how much the rain sucked, until it had all blown sky-high in a fight about who'd gotten crumbs in the butter.

Dean had stormed to his bedroom and put on "Free Bird" for the four hundredth time; Earley had stomped a caulk boot through his eight-track. They'd punched each other a couple of times, Dean's lip had split, he'd packed up his stuff in a fury and skidded out of the clearing, hurling the word "loser" out his rear window. A couple of days later, Earley had taken the toaster oven down to the river and shot it. Let someone find it and wonder, he thought as it tumbled downstream.

Reed was still gazing up at Mount Olympus. Earley pulled back the truck tarp and shouldered his duffel bag. "Come on inside," he said.

The bus was about as well-kept as the yard. The macramé dream catcher that hung from the rearview glinted with spider webs. Earley wondered when all those gray socks and dead leaves had piled up on the floor, but Reed didn't seem to care. His eyes scanned the place in approval, noting the raingear that hung from pegs over the driver's seat, the sideways kitchen with its cast-iron boat stove and counter hewn out of a cedar slab, tin basin and wash pitcher, jars of dried grains, the dinette seats made out of the bus's old benches. The twin rows of windows enlarged the space, striping its walls with sunlight and shadows of firs. Earley noticed with envy that Reed could stand any-where under the arched roof without the reflexive hunch he'd developed whenever he strayed from the center aisle.

He ushered Reed into the bus's midsection and set down his duffel bag, watching Reed's face as he cased the joint. It was a living room of sorts, with a thick striped mattress tucked half out of sight behind an old couch and a beanbag chair. "That'll be your rack," said Earley. A brightly striped Mexican blanket stretched up to the ceiling, so the "bedroom" behind it resembled a circus tent. "I sleep in the back."

Reed looked to the rear of the bus, where a door said EMER-GENCY EXIT. Earley's extra-large futon was heaped with big pillows and bordered by Indian bedspreads strung from the ceiling with clothesline. The copper and cinnamon paisleys gave it a seraglio look, accented by a *Playboy* centerfold taped to a milk crate of books and tapes. There was a hurricane lamp on a wire spool alongside the bed, with a clamshell ashtray, some incense, a jar of hawk feathers. The rest of the room was a jumble of clothes, boots and beer bottles, landsliding down from plank shelves to the rug.

"Do you play?" Reed asked, pointing at something. Earley had to look twice before he realized Reed didn't mean the pouty brunette weighing her tits in both hands, but the scuffed guitar in the corner.

"Not me. It belongs to this girl I was seeing a couple of months ago, her teenage son. He brought it out here one night, played some 'Kum Ba Yah' shit till we fell asleep."

Reed picked up the guitar, idly tuning the strings. Then he sat on the edge of the futon and started to play, notes cascading in ripples and runs as his fingers flew over the fretboard. He stopped just as suddenly, frowning at something he'd done. He set down the guitar and looked over at Earley. "It's not my main instrument."

"Shit, man, what is?"

"Mandolin. Dobro. I fiddle a bit." Reed stood up, wiping his hands on his jeans. "Doesn't matter."

Earley knew when a subject was closed. "You cook at all, Reed?"

"I can open a can."

Earley shrugged. "I've got plenty of cans."

"I was kidding," Reed said. "I can cook."

"Good, it's all yours. Wanna fix dinner?"

Reed looked a bit startled. "I guess. Sure." He set off for the kitchen.

"No rush," Earley said. "I'm still toting six pounds of beans in my guts from that treeplanter stew. Go hang up your stuff or whatever. It's too late to work today."

"Show me," said Reed.

"Show you what?"

"What we're going to be doing."

Earley wasn't sure what to make of Reed's eagerness. From his standpoint, the kid was just begging to be abused. "Yeah, okay," he said. "Gotta start a fire in here anyway. Might as well burn up some cedar." And find out if you've got the stones for the job, he thought. Your Visa card isn't worth shit in the clearcut.

He grabbed hold of the joystick that opened the bus's pneumatic door. Reed followed him back out and paused on the steps. "Where's the toilet?" he asked.

"You're looking at it," said Earley. "I dug a pit back by those two hemlocks right there. Paper's in a tin can."

Reed nodded and walked off. His stride had a vertical lilt, as if every step he took might be the one that would lift him up into the sky. Earley took out his Drum pouch and rolled a smoke, squinting. He still wasn't sure why he'd asked Reed to join him. He could have made plans to see Zan on his own, with Reed halfway to Fairbanks and out of the running. He wondered if they'd bring her up here for weekends, if she'd fall for his bus in the woods like her buddy had.

Earley noticed his mind steering clear of the word "boyfriend" and reminded himself she was sleeping with Reed. He thought of their two bodies sprawled beneath moonlit sheets, and that moment when Zan had reached out for his hand, twining her fingers through his in the darkened motel room, their bodies so close he could feel her breathing. If Reed was enough for her, she wouldn't have left him to travel up north by herself, and she sure as hell wouldn't be hitting on Earley.

"So what do I do?" said Reed.

Earley turned, startled to see him so close. He dropped his cigarette into the mud, ground it under his heel and led Reed to the chopping block.

Earley jerked his axe out of the stump with one hand and set a big cedar round down in its place. "We're cutting up salvage. Some of it's logs that got left on the ground back when cedar was trash wood, some of it's stumps. When a logger falls trees all day long, he's gonna work at a comfortable height for himself. That leaves a few feet of saleable stump for the shake-rats, but we're always working below the waist. Hope your back's not too bad."

"It's fine."

"*Now* it's fine," Earley said. "Tell me about it next week." His own back had hurt him for years now, a dull ache so constant he'd almost forgotten how he'd feel without it. "I buck up the logs into rounds, and you knock off the bark, cull out the rot-wood and knots and split them into bolts. The cedar mill bevels them down into roof shakes. You ever split wood?"

"Boy Scouts, summer camp."

Earley gave Reed a splitting wedge. "Place it."

Reed hefted the five-pound wedge like a shotput and jammed its sharp edge in the cedar. Earley nodded, feeling a slight edge of irritation that Reed had done it correctly. "Right. Go with the grain, never cross it." He picked up a sledgehammer and brought it down square on the wedge with an effortless one-handed swing, as if he were tapping a nail into plywood. A thick chunk of cedar fell down to the ground.

"That's probably simplest to start. Once you get the feel, you might switch to a mallet and froe"—Earley swung a wedge-ended froe down with one hand and the sledgehammer down with the other, snapping another chunk clean off the cedar—"or a splitting maul. Whatever you think you can keep up all day." He handed the sledgehammer to Reed and stepped back to watch.

Reed swung it surprisingly clean, unfazed by the eight-pound weight. It took him a few swings to pound the wedge through, but he brought the sledge up in a smooth, fluid arc and his aim was not bad. Eagle Scout, Earley thought to himself, Merit Badge for Camping. But let's see you do it all day in the wind and sleet.

Earley watched Reed's long fingers slide down the battered ash handle. "Be right back," he said. Reed kept on working. The metal blows rang through the clearing and echoed off a distant rockface.

Reed had split the whole round and was on to the next by the time Earley found what he was looking for. "Here," he said, tossing a pair of Dean's grimy suede work gloves onto the chopping block. Reed paused, his face flushed from exertion. "I don't need those," he said.

"Yes you do," Earley said. "Your hands'll get blistered right down to the bone, and then we both lose money." Reed looked at him, wiping a damp strand of hair from his forehead. He put on the gloves and went back to work. Earley watched his thin shoulders rise as he lifted the hammer and crashed it back down. You'll do fine, he thought, wondering why he felt so grudging about it. You'll work out just fine.

SIX

Earley got up first, chunked wood in the stove and made coffee. Reed had left the coffee tin on the wrong shelf, and the basin was still full of dishes from last night's supper. He frowned and thought, no more free ride. He went in to wake Reed. They ate quickly and got in the truck.

It was barely dawn and the rain needled down in a fine, sleety mist. The high peaks were veiled. Earley squinted, but couldn't make out any sort of horizon. The silhouettes of fir trees loomed out of swirling clouds. Earley drove with his coffee mug in one hand, shifting gears on the bone-jarring ruts of the access road without ever setting it down. Reed was wearing an old pair of Earley's rain overalls, with the cuffs rolled up a few times around new-looking hiking boots. He'd put on a red chamois cloth shirt that looked so pristine that Earley couldn't help wondering if Reed's mother had sent it for Christmas. He had Dean's suede gloves in his lap.

Neither one of them spoke. This is it, Earley thought. This is where we find out what you're made of. He slurped on his coffee. He used plenty of sugar and never stirred; by the time he got down to the dregs, it tasted like warm coffee ice cream. He'd sited his bus several miles from the clearcut on purpose: along with the view of Olympus, the twice-a-day drive cleared his head.

They rounded a curve and Earley braked suddenly, swerving. Reed grabbed at the dashboard. "Shit," he said, breathing hard. There was a downed hemlock across the road, just in front of their bumper. The trunk was at least two feet thick.

"Must've been wicked windy last night," Earley said. "That's still green." He left the truck idling and went to the back for his Husqy. The saw purred to life on the first tug. Earley carried it close to his hip like a bass guitar, as relaxed as if it were part of his body. He lopped off a few branches, revving the saw as he moved alongside the trunk. He nosed the tip upwards and sliced out an undercut, then angled down from above and burned into it, easing the saw free before the tree split. He walked down a few feet and repeated the motions. A section of trunk fell free.

Earley sliced off three more lengths and turned off his saw. "Firewood," he said. "We can pick it up on our way home."

Reed got out of the truck cab and rolled the logs off to the side of the road while Earley put his Husqy back under the tarp. He did that without being asked, Earley thought. That's a good sign. They drove right between the cut ends of the blowdown, heading for Suhammish Creek Unit A-46.

It was colder up here, longjohn weather. The mud of the road had a hard, frozen look, and the rims of the puddles crackled with ice. Earley remembered the rawness of his first northern winter, how he'd felt like he'd never get warm. A person could get used to anything, given a chance; now he'd probably wilt if he went back to Georgia. He tipped back his coffee mug, slurping the sweet, sandy dregs. He could feel his front tooth throb. The truck burrowed upwards and finally broke through the treeline, into the midsection landing where Earley parked.

"Jesus Christ," said Reed, staring. Earley looked out the windshield and realized: he'd never been in a clearcut before. The land was bald, scarred as a battlefield. Limbs lay twisted on top of each other, their needles dead brown, and giant stumps loomed through the mist like so many tombstones. The ground was a wash of mud, crisscrossed with skidder tracks. A few limbless spar trees still stood where the yarders had been. Reed's eyes traveled up and down the bare acres of mountainside; nothing green anywhere. "Jesus," he said again.

Earley had nothing to add to that. "Let's get to work," he said.

.   . .   .

Earley's saw kicked up a backwash of warm cedar sawdust, as fragrant as cinnamon. It was a scent that infused his skin through every pore, but he never got sick of the fresh dusting that started each work day. He eased his saw into the side of a log about four feet across, burning a kerf to the heartwood.

Reed worked like a virgin. At first Earley slowed down his pace so he wouldn't lose heart, and once or twice he quit bucking logs and helped Reed split bolts, but he soon got impatient with how far behind Reed was dragging. This guy's costing me money, not helping, he thought. He's not going to cut it. But Reed never complained or looked at his watch. He seemed startled, though grateful, when Earley told him it was time for a lunch break.

They put down their tools and set off for the truck. They'd been working high up, and the grade seemed even steeper on the way down, a sheer scoop of earth. Reed lost his footing a lot as they clambered through downed limbs and slash. His new hikers were slathered with mud. Earley slowed down.

"If you take to the job, we'll buy you some caulks next time we're in town."

"I have taken to it," said Reed. "Mud, sleet and backache. What's not to love?"

Earley didn't like his sarcastic tone. He'd be hard put to say why he loved being a shake-rat so much, but love it he did.

Independence, he guessed. Getting to work in the weather all day, with no roof and no walls, just the wilderness rising around him. He could call his own shots, without some boss getting into his face, like every other lame job he'd had. Earley had scabbed on a road crew, unloaded semis, baled hay, picked chilies, pumped gas, hauled garbage and worked in a lumber mill. Somebody had to do all of those things; he was damn glad that it wasn't him. They climbed down past the last cords of shake bolts he'd cut with Dean.

"What happens next?" asked Reed, eyeing the tall stack of cedar.

"We bring 'em on down to the mill, in the pickup if we can get close enough. If it's too far off-road, like we're working today, we sling the bolts into a bundle and copter it out. I've already cleared out the bottom landing where most of the money logs were. We're down to the dregs on this unit, not more than a couple weeks left."

Reed looked back up the mountain, its acres of stumps jutting up from the mud. Earley shrugged. "There's a point where it's not worth the time it takes getting there. Factor in all the slogging up and downhill, we'd make more flipping fries at McDicks."

Reed nodded. "So then what?"

"We start on the next hillside over. Or move the bus some-place else and stake out a new claim. I spotted some clearcuts up by the planters' camp that probably haven't been picked over yet. We could cruise over and check it out."

Reed looked at him. Earley rolled his shoulders to loosen his neck muscles, wondering if he'd tipped his hand about wanting to see more of Zan. He should just keep his mouth shut, he reckoned; he'd never been able to hide much of anything. "Zan doesn't know," Reed said quietly. Earley met his blue eyes with a surge of guilt. "That I'm working with you. When we said good-bye, I was on my way up to Alaska."

Earley realized this must be true. He kept his voice carefully neutral. "No phones in the woods. We could drive up and see her next weekend."

Reed looked at him for a moment too long. "I'd like that" was all he said.

We, Earley thought; dead giveaway. I should have said, "I could drive *you* up." He wondered why he felt so guilty; he hadn't done anything yet. And he didn't owe Reed a damn thing, he reminded himself. Zan could make her own choices. He doubted, in fact, that she'd ever done anything else.

Earley had packed their lunch, something else that Reed could start doing tomorrow. They sat in the cab of the truck, drinking sweet coffee from one thermos and ladling pork and beans out of the other. There were peanut butter and banana sandwiches on thick slabs of bread, a couple of apples, some chips. Reed could eat pretty well for a little guy. "How are your hands?" Earley asked.

Reed held them up. There was a wedge of grime under his nails, and the skin was so blackened from glove sweat he looked like he'd been fingerprinted. The joint between pointer and thumb was chafed, but the skin wasn't broken. "Not bad," he said.

"Cool," Earley said, biting into his apple.

The afternoon lagged. The sun that had lightened one patch of the sky disappeared under heavy gray clouds, and the wind stung their skins with invisible rain. Reed didn't complain, but Earley could see he was lifting the mallet with effort. *I wore you right down, city boy,* he thought, gloating a little. *And I'm only working at half speed. Wait till we really start humping.*

"Let's hit the road," he said. "Woods'll still be here tomorrow." Reed nodded, exhausted and grateful. They headed for home.

A mat of low clouds had rolled over the clearing, the color of dirty sheep. They shook off their raingear and clumped up the steps to the bus. Earley sat on the driver's seat, unlacing his caulks in the half-dark while Reed hung his rain overalls on a peg. "This is when we need that shower," he said, rubbing his stiff, blackened fingers. Earley struck a match to the hurricane lamp, stoked up the woodstove and put on the cast-iron kettle. He reached into the cooler and got them both beers.

"Day One," he said. "Cheers."

"Amen," said Reed, clunking his bottle on Earley's. The head foamed over and spilled on the floor.

"Not to worry," said Earley, sprawling out on the dinette bench, his grubby wool socks in the air. "It's just part of the ambience here at the casa."

"You want me to spritz a bit more?" asked Reed.

"Nah," said Earley. "I don't want to fuck with the gestalt."

"The gestalt?" Reed's eyebrows went up.

"Don't they have that at Berkeley?"

"Oh, Berkeley's got everything. Fruits, flakes and nuts." Reed sat down on the dinette bench and swigged his beer. "It just didn't sound like you. Let me guess. The same girl with the 'Kum Ba Yah' kid?"

"Her sister."

"You're kidding."

"I am." Earley's grin split his face as he tipped back his beer.

"Thank God. I was starting to think you'd screwed every woman in Washington State."

"I'm still missing a few," Earley said. "Life is long."

Reed tipped back his bottle and chugged it dry, setting it down with a satisfied clunk. "I feel like a Miller commercial," he said, overdoing his "Aahhhh."

"They never drink," Earley said. "Ever notice? The guys in those ads, they're always like shoulder to shoulder at bars, watching the Super Bowl, or flipping burgers outside on the grill, and they're laughing and pouring and clinking their glasses, but they never get the damn beer in their mouth."

"They ought to film shake-rats," said Reed.

"Oh, now *that* would sell big. The American Dream. Bust your ass in the rain for a nonliving wage." Earley raised his beer, toasting their mud-spattered raingear.

"You don't even have a TV, do you?"

"Why? Have they started to make something I'd want to watch?"

"Not in the least," said Reed. "Most people turn it on anyway, just for the brainwash. You don't miss having phones and TVs and that shit?"

"I miss plumbing," said Earley. "The rest can drop dead." He loped to the stove, where the cast-iron kettle was spouting a fine jet of steam. He poured the hot water into a wash basin, fished out a dishrag and cake of Chandrika soap, which he offered to Reed. "Here you go, buddy. Gestalt yourself."

They slid into an easy routine. As the week wore on, Earley noticed that Reed had stopped wearing his watch. He woke soon after dawn, stoked the woodstove, made coffee, even went down to the creek and hauled water, something Dean had never done once without bitching. He was quiet at work, decent company evenings; he knew when to keep to himself. It was working out better than Earley had hoped. They weren't making their quota—not even close—but Reed was still struggling with blisters and finding his rhythm. He'd pick up speed.

Even the weather had gotten a little bit better. The air was still moist, but less icy. The alder buds down by the creek were maroon; any day now, they'd pop. Pussy willows would start forming catkins. Earley couldn't remember which day spring began. It was probably soon, or might even have happened already. He could have asked Reed, but it seemed like too stupid a question. What was more on his mind was the countdown of days till they drove back to the treeplanters' camp. Earley was careful to keep it from Reed, but he couldn't stop thinking of Zan. He carried her with him wherever he went, on the slopes, in the truck. She was there in his thoughts every night when he blew out the candle for bed, as constant as last year's Miss June.

Reed was telling the truth when he said he could cook. He could throw things together and come up with huevos rancheros or vegetable curries and stir-fries. One night he made tempura fritters from leftover chicken and yams. Earley wondered who'd taught him, if there'd been some spicy immigrant cooking in his family's kitchen, or if it was just something he'd picked up in Berkeley. Whatever. It beat cans of beans.

After dinner they'd hang out and listen to music, or play a Chinese game called Go that Reed had in his duffel. It was a flat wooden board with black and white marbles; the goal was to wall off free space. Earley had never been much good at games, but he didn't mind this one too much, especially when Reed lit a joint while he pondered his move. The tape deck was playing the Stones' *Sticky Fingers*. Earley noticed that Reed kept rubbing his shoulder and neck.

"Got a cramp?"

Reed nodded. "It kind of seized up on the slope. I figured if I just kept going, it'd work itself out." He moved a white marble and put his hand back on his neck.

"Want some Tiger Balm?"

"What?"

Earley got to his feet. "It's Chinese Ben-Gay." He padded into his room and came back with a small red tin. "I don't hold stock with most of this herbal crap—some of these hippies around here would cut off their leg and try to heal it with some goddamn tincture. My mom had an aunt like that, always chasing us down with the cod liver oil and boneset tea. Sometimes you just need a natural-born drug."

Reed took a deep drag on the end of his joint and passed it to him. Earley smiled and filled up his lungs while Reed pried off the cap of the Tiger Balm, sniffing it.

"What do I do with this?"

"Rub it in. Here." Earley scooped his forefinger into the waxy green substance and rubbed it along Reed's neck, working it in with his fingertips. "Give it a minute. You'll start to feel heat."

Reed nodded and closed his eyes. The tendons that ran down his neck were tight cords. Earley heard a sharp intake of breath, felt Reed tense as he worked the Tiger Balm into the muscle knot. "You've taken a beating this week. Am I on it?"

Reed hesitated. "A bit farther down."

Earley slid his hand down through the neck of Reed's T-shirt. "Now don't take this personally."

"No worries," said Reed. "I'll pretend you're Zan."

Earley groaned inwardly. I wish *you* were Zan, he thought. I'd massage you for real. His fingers were starting to heat up. "Can you feel that?"

"Whoa," said Reed. "What the hell's *in* this shit?"

"Got me," said Earley, "but it works." The burning sensation was spreading along his hands. "You don't want to play with yourself for a while after doing this. I took a piss once and nearly passed out." He was feeling a throb in his temples now, sympathetic heat. He wondered if it was the fumes or the joint.

He thought about Zan as he worked the balm into Reed's shoulder. He imagined her doing the same thing to him, pressing her fingertips into his skin, kneading, stroking, her hands sliding under his shirt, moving downwards.

Reed let out a sigh. Earley's fingers stopped moving.

"Feel better?"

Reed nodded, opening his eyes. "Want me to do you?"

Earley looked at him. "I don't hurt," he said, putting the lid on the tin.

Reed picked up the roach and inhaled once more, sucking the smoke deep into his lungs. He stubbed out the blackened twist in the shell Earley used as an ashtray and studied the Go board. "Your move," he said.

Earley pushed a black marble. He wanted to talk about Zan. It was like having an itch, poison oak or wild sumac or something. He knew it was better to leave it alone, but he couldn't help himself. He asked Reed again how they'd met, what the restaurant was like, whether Zan wore a uniform ("Not on your life" was the answer), what kind of music Reed had been playing the night that she took him home. He asked things that he wasn't interested in, just to keep the ball rolling and hear her name spoken aloud. Reed was eager to talk; he'd been storing this up, Earley sensed, since the moment he dropped out of college to follow Zan to the Olympics.

"Why did she leave California?"

Reed hesitated and looked at the floor. "She had her reasons," he mumbled, the lines of his face dissolving in layers of misery. Zan could do that to a guy, Earley reckoned. She'd probably cut quite a swath on her journey north.

Zan. He liked saying her name to himself, the way the sounds buzzed on his tongue. Her last name was Koutros. Greek on both sides, she had told him. Zan Koutros. Zan. Alexandra, but who has the time?

I do, he wanted to scream at her, I have the time. It was more than just lust. It was something he'd seen in Zan's eyes, behind all the swagger and flash, some deep bruise of longing, some untended wound Earley told himself he could help heal. He could care for her, soothe her. He wanted to wash her feet. Hadn't Jesus done that in the Bible? Or no, it was Mary Magdalene who had washed his feet, and she'd dried them off with her hair. How did *that* work? Earley wondered, and thought to himself, I am really stoned. Dangerous.

Don't say too much, he thought, letting his eyes close. Don't mention her lips, her wild, throaty laugh, how she chews on the side of her thumbnail, and for God's sake don't mention her breasts. He thought of Zan lying under that twisted motel sheet, the curve of her hips like a landform.

Mick Jagger was singing "Wild Horses." The heat of the Tiger Balm surged through Earley's fingertips, right where Zan had touched him that night. He could feel his blood circling his body, his heart filling and emptying, pumping warm gallons of life. He imagined Zan's heart beating with his, skin pressed against skin, how their bodies would move with each other, the way she would taste. His mouth felt as dry as a desert. He took a deep breath.

"Are you falling asleep?" Reed's voice seemed to come from a long way away. Oh, yeah, Earley thought, there was some-body else in the room. He opened his eyes, feeling dizzy. Reed was right next to him, hand on his shoulder.

"I'm wasted," Earley drawled, lolling back in his chair and rubbing a hand on his belly. "Better hit the sack."

Reed swallowed hard. "Yeah."

Earley rose, wavering. "Night," he said, touching Reed's arm.

SEVEN

Friday finally came. Earley was too impatient to cut wood for long. He and Reed knocked off after lunch and loaded the truck with shake bolts, climbing back and forth up the scree, lugging wood like a pair of pack oxen—a huge waste of time, Earley thought, when he'd have to shell out for a copter to fly out the rest in a couple of weeks, but he needed some cash. If they all wound up at the Cedar, he wanted to buy Zan a drink. If they wound up at his place, he wanted to fix her a quality dinner. Their pantry was down to the bone. Reed had switched last night's menu from arroz con pollo to arroz con arroz, and they'd run out of bread this morning and had to make sandwiches out of cold pancakes. Reed needed a pair of acceptable boots; those prep school hikers of his were slowing them

down. And like it or lump it, the laundry had to be done. Neither one of them smelled like a man that a woman would want
to undress.

Scoter Gillies' old man weighed them out at the cedar mill. He
paid Earley in cash, only grumbling a little when Earley asked
him to trade in a ten-spot for dimes. Vern Gillies slammed
open the register and gave Earley a change roll, his eyes dripping scorn for anybody who needed to shower his sad ass in
some public campground. Earley stuck the roll into his jeans
pocket and turned to go.

"You're working up in Suhammish, that right? The B unit?"

Earley shook his head. "A-46."

Vern lobbed a wet gob of chewing tobacco into a Coke bottle next to the cashbox. "I heard there's a couple of timber
cruisers from Royalton sniffing around your way. Could be a
big operation."

Earley frowned. The last thing he wanted was somebody's
logging show in his backyard. "They've already shaved every
hill they could get to."

"Don't be too sure," said Vern, popping a fresh pinch of
snoose underneath his lip. "Those boys are hardcore. They'd
shave Mount Olympus right up to the glaciers if they could get
past Uncle Sam. Whole lot of oldgrowth up there in Suhammish."

"You got that right," said Earley. "I like it that way." He looked out through the screen door, frowning. Reed had wandered away from his pickup and into the sorting yard next to the mill. Earley went out to round him up.

A hard-hatted crew was offloading an eighteen-wheel log truck. Earley nodded to two guys he knew and loped over to Reed, who was watching the crane as it swung the severed logs onto a stacker. The towering piles stretched all the way back to the chain-link fence, where a couple of piggyback log trucks sat waiting, and out to the sheds where the shrill whine of bandsaws shredded the air. "So many trees," said Reed. He looked stricken. "I had no idea."

Where did you think all your newspapers came from? thought Earley. He squinted at the incinerator and said, "It's a boneyard, all right." He hoped Reed wasn't going to go off on some East Coast liberal tear about spotted owls. *I'm* an endangered species, he thought. Red dirt shake-rat.

"Let's go scrape off a few layers." Earley twisted the dime roll in two halves and gave one to Reed. "This oughta last you a couple of showers." He'd remembered the soap, plus some towels he'd lifted from Scoter's motel. A deluxe operation, thought Earley, relieved that they each had some change.

After they showered at Bogachiel, Earley got dressed in his laundromat outfit: gray sweats and a Grateful Dead T-shirt some girlfriend had given him. He caught a glimpse of himself with a rainbow of teddy bears trucking across his chest, felt like a fool and put it back on inside out. He could see Reed in the mirror, pulling on clothes that Earley had never seen before, an open-necked shirt made of Indian cotton and loose drawstring pants. This must have been his musician suit, Earley figured, but why the guy packed it to go to Alaska was anyone's guess. Maybe he figured he'd pick up some bucks on the coffeehouse circuit in Nome. If that was what Zan went for, Earley was sunk. He scratched his chest. Maybe he'd change after they did their laundry.

"Ready?" he asked and Reed nodded, adjusting his pants.

They sauntered back out to the truck. Reed fiddled around with the radio dial as Earley backed up. He paused at a news station, listening to a report about Watergate pardons. "Fucking baboons," he said. "How can they let these guys *off?* It's like they can't even be bothered to cover their tracks anymore. 'Of course we can lie, cheat and steal; we're the government.'"

"Uncle Sham," Earley said. "Put on some music."

"What makes you think I can find any?" Reed twisted the dial from country to the Bee Gees. "These guys sound like castrated hamsters. Who *listens* to this?"

He tried a new station, groaning out loud at Olivia Newton-John. "Somebody shoot this chick. Put her out of our misery."

The way Reed talked about music reminded Earley of how guys he'd grown up with had talked about sports: loud and impassioned and sure they were right. Reed changed stations again, cursing his way through the Top Ten and a preacher or two till he landed on "This Wheel's on Fire" by The Band.

"Now these motherfuckers can play their instruments. Listen to this." Reed's fingers drummed over his knees as Garth Hudson soloed on organ. "Have you ever *seen* this dude? His head is the size of a barrel. You get him hunched over the keyboard and he looks like Ludwig van Beethoven."

"Isn't Beethoven deaf?"

"Beethoven's dead. He's dead *and* deaf. Most dead people are deaf."

"God, I hope so," said Earley.

Reed cracked up. He seemed looser these days, Earley noticed. The Band had put him in a good mood. His hands seemed to play some invisible instrument as he looked out the window, the wind whipping through his hair. The next song began, and Reed pinned it in two notes. "Van Morrison—now you've gotta give this cat big points for balls. He's four-foot-six, looks like a weasel, he's from fuckin' *Ireland* and he thinks he's a Negro. This must be a college station."

"How can you tell?"

"Songs are more than a week old. Any minute now, some chick with a wispy voice and no mike technique is gonna come on and say, 'Hey. That was, um, Van? Yeah.'"

"You had one, didn't you?" Reed looked at him, puzzled. "College radio show."

"God, no. Who'd listen to me?"

"I would," said Earley, mock-solemn. "I'd be your Number One Fan."

"Fuck you!"

"You and Olivia Neutron Bomb." Earley pulled into the laundromat parking lot, cutting Van Morrison off in mid-yelp.

They dumped all their stuff into two machines, one for the mud-crusted blue jeans and one for everything else, and took off for the grocery store. At the register Earley picked up a fresh pouch of tobacco and Reed bought three newspapers.

Both loads were done by the time they got back. Reed's red chamois cloth shirt had stained their longjohns and socks an uneven cherry pink. "Sorry," he muttered.

Earley looked at his underwear, trying to hide his annoyance. He shrugged. "Little tie-dye. Who cares?" They filled up two dryers with quarters and took off again, this time for Keneally's.

Fergus Keneally's wife Gladys was working the register. She took them both in at a glance and decided they didn't rate greeting. Earley led Reed back to the boot section, past counters of hickory shirts, brown Carhartt overalls, highwater jeans and a couple stray items that looked as if they'd been sitting there waiting for purchase since World War II.

"Those are what I wear," said Earley, pointing to a pair of

black work boots with lug soles and spikes. "But these lowboys are cheaper." Reed picked up one of the high-cut caulk boots and winced at the price.

"They don't sell these used, do they?"

"You don't wanna look at 'em used," Earley said, "much less smell them. I'll front you your forty percent if you need." He was nearing the end of his wad, but this wasn't a luxury item. The spikes gave a footing on sheer slopes and wet bark that could save a guy's life. He'd seen more than one logger wind up at the Cedar Bar minus an arm or leg from falling on top of his chainsaw. Reed wasn't using a saw, but he'd taken some serious tumbles. Earley didn't want to be packing him out on a stretcher.

Gladys came over, her plump arms folded. "You boys buying something?"

"He wants to try these," Earley said.

"Size twelve and a half," said Reed. Gladys looked him up and down.

"What the hell do you call them trousers?"

"Um . . . pants?" said Reed. Earley stifled a laugh as Gladys stalked back to the stockroom, her mouth a thin line. "What's her problem?" Reed asked him.

Earley shrugged. "We're shake-rats," he said.

A couple of old-timers slouched through the door. Earley knew one of them, Gus Ritchie. He'd worked for him once, as a greenhorn just up from Georgia. Gus had taken one look at

Earley's back and hired him on doing gruntwork, rolling logs with a peavey pole, loading up trucks. He'd started out all gruff and fatherly, promising Earley he'd work his way up, setting chokers and learning to top, but it never panned out. A couple months later, Earley found out that Gus had been gouging his paycheck and popped the guy one, nearly breaking his jaw. Gus hadn't sacked him right off, but he'd made Earley's life such hell that Earley had walked off the job a week later, hitch-hiking home from a clearcut some twenty miles north, up by Clallam Bay.

Gus looked Earley's way and gave him a curt nod. The old geezer with him just stared. He wore his suspenders clipped onto his belt, as if neither could manage the job, and was working a big wad of snoose in one cheek. Earley wondered if he would come right out and spit on the floor.

Gladys emerged from the stockroom, shoved a carton at Reed and went to the counter, beaming at Gus and the chewer. "What can I do for you fellas?"

"Fergus here?"

"Last time Fergus worked on a Friday night, Ike was in office. Try the Shamrock." Gus nodded. The snoose chewer spit. They went back out the door.

Reed was lacing up one of the caulks. Earley turned to him. "How's it feel? Can you wiggle your toes?"

"Uh-huh. These things are heavy as hell."

"'Sposed to be. Keeping you upright is what they're about."

"Not a bad plan," said Reed. He laced up the second boot, then stood. The thick soles, boot heels and spikes brought him a little bit closer to Earley's height. He took a few paces, flexing his knees. "I feel like a rocker," he said. "Like Lou Reed."

"Not in those *trousers*," said Earley.

"And fuck you too."

"Keep that mouth in the woods," Gladys snapped. "This is a Christian store."

Earley walked through the laundromat door and found himself staring at Margie and Amber Walkonis. Margie flashed him a welcoming smile, but Earley wasn't sure how to proceed with her daughter right there. The memory of crouching behind that propane tank was all too vivid; it wasn't a feeling he welcomed. He hoped that his ears weren't flaming. He gave Margie a stiff nod and walked right past her. Reed glanced up at his face, read between the lines, and headed across the room.

Earley busied himself with the dryer, taking out clothes and stuffing them into a brown lawn and leaf bag. The glass door made a mirror of sorts; he could see Margie, stung by his slight, sorting out her underwire bras from Harlan's boxers. Well, what did she want him to do, bend her backwards and suck on her tongue right in front of her daughter? He saw Amber Ann smirk at his cherry pink longjohns and thought, *I could give you a few things to smirk about, sister.*

Reed's voice caught his ear. Earley turned, wondering who he was talking to, and spotted him shuffling in place, speaking into a pay phone. ". . . I don't *have* a phone number. It's way out in the woods, there isn't a. . . . What?" Reed held the receiver away from his ear and turned towards Earley. "Do we have a mailing address?"

"Um . . . G.P.O., Forks, Wash."

Reed nodded and relayed the news. "No, I'm not . . . No. Look, I like what I'm doing, I'm happy. You don't have to understand it." He hung up and stared at the floor, exhaled hard and walked back towards Earley. "Well, *that* went well."

Earley could feel Margie listening, wondering who this guy was. "Your parents?"

"My mom. She can pass it along to my dad and his wife at their next fight." Reed kicked at the base of a Wascomat triple-loader. Earley was glad that Reed didn't have on his new caulks; he might have done damage. He opened up their second dryer and stuck in his hand. He was itching to get up to treeplanters' camp.

"Dry enough for me." Earley scooped out the damp blue jeans and piled them on top of the rest of the clothes, then realized he'd have to walk right past Margie again. He slung the sack over his shoulder and made for the exit, muttering, "See you," as he passed her washing machine. As he pushed through the door, he heard Amber say, "Mom?" and Margie's too-loud "He's a friend of your dad's."

"I bet," smirked Reed, catching up in the parking lot. "Real bosom buddy."

"Shut the fuck up," Earley growled, tossing their clothes in the back of the truck like a feed sack. He didn't see what was funny about hurting girls' feelings and having to slink around like a low dog.

Reed seemed taken aback by his tone. He said, "Sorry, man."

Earley slammed into the driver's seat. He stomped on the gas and backed up too fast. If you think my sex life is such a big joke, he thought, see how you like it when I hit on Zan.

EIGHT

They'd forgotten the map. Reed and Earley agreed on the first several turns, but when they got up to the creekwash, Reed started insisting that Earley had made a mistake. "I remember that stump," he said. "We were supposed to bear right."

"Not the same stump."

"Yes it was. I remember the way it stuck up on the top."

"Every stump that's been cut with a chainsaw sticks up on the top."

"Not like that one. It looked like a skyline."

Earley stepped hard on the brake. "Do you have a *clue* how many goddamn stumps I've seen?"

Reed looked surprised at his vehemence. He lifted his hands. "Okay, fine. I'm just saying—"

"I heard you," growled Earley.

They drove for the next several minutes in silence. Reed stared out the window, as if he had never seen clouds and wet trees before. He's pouting, thought Earley. Spoiled brat. He dug into his Drum pouch, fished out a paper and rolled a cigarette one-handed. Reed reached over to steady the wheel as Earley twisted the ends tight and lit it up, setting his hands back onto the wheel without saying a word.

Earley was loath to admit it, but he didn't recognize this stretch of road. They seemed to be heading away from the creek, not along it, and gaining too much elevation. Reed glanced over at him once or twice, but said nothing. He seemed to be waiting for Earley to say he'd messed up. Earley sucked on his cigarette end and peered into the gathering dusk. He was damned if he'd give Reed the pleasure of proving him wrong. Maybe the road they were on would lead to the treeplanters' camp from a different direction. The ruts he was driving on looked pretty fresh. They rounded the next several curves and came out at the top of a clearcut, even broader and steeper than Suhammish A-46 and crevassed with mudslides and snarls of dead branches. It looked like the side of the moon.

"Damn," said Reed, staring down at it. "That was a forest."

Earley squinted. He'd noticed a thin wisp of smoke rising beyond the next ridge. "Somebody down there," he said, jerking his chin towards a dark, moving dot on the side of the mountain.

Reed followed his gaze. "Oh yeah," he said. "Two of them."

"Planters," said Earley. He eased the truck back into gear and continued along the road, towards the smoke. The dots looked a bit clearer now, and there were more of them, fanned out over the slope, some slogging upward, some heading back down in an uneven zigzag. One of those dots must be Zan, he thought, rounding the bend.

The treeplanters' crummy was parked in the landing ahead of them. Earley parked right behind it and cut the ignition. The door to the crummy's small cabin swung open and the guy with the blond braids stepped out, raising his right hand in greeting. He didn't have feathers today, but the last inch or two of his plaits was wrapped in red leather cords. Probably started their natural life out as shoelaces, Earley thought. "Hey," he said. "Nick, right?"

Young Nick nodded. "You're Zan's old man," he said, looking from Earley to Reed. "She's on her way up. Want some tea?"

"Sounds good," said Reed. Earley followed him up the three steps, bending under the low wooden doorframe. The cabin was hot and close, with a tiny boatstove stoked up in one corner. Four or five planters sprawled out on the plank benches lining the walls. They looked muddy and wasted. The crewcut girl had her arm around Susu.

Young Nick lifted the kettle and poured steaming water through a homemade basket strainer. "I gathered the herbs on this land," he said. "Nettles and raspberry leaf. They have serious medicine for us." His voice was so solemn that Earley could barely resist saying, "Ugh!" What made white guys decide to pretend they were Indians? The Makah brothers who'd worked on his sawmill crew, Leroy and Vance, would've drunk their own piss before they made tea out of nettles. Earley picked up a tube full of honey and squirted a lot of it into his teacup. It still tasted nasty.

"I'm going back out," he said. "Hot in here."

He ducked back through the door, taking his tea with him and slopping it into a puddle outside. He looked down at the figures crisscrossing the darkening hillside. He could make out the bunched silhouettes of their treebags and the stop-and-start rhythm of planting: swing hoedad, pull back, set the root plug, stomp shut. He spotted a red-bandannaed head moving faster than anyone else, traversing the bowl of the slope like a skier. Must be the other Nick, Nick who'd turned thirty, the one they called Just Nick. Beside him, and moving more slowly, pausing at every tree site, was someone he pegged as that camptender chick who'd stirred the bean soup for so long that he'd wanted to strangle her. Impatiently he scanned the rest of the clearcut for Zan.

There she was. Off to the left, attacking the slope in a sharp, unpredictable zigzag, backtracking to fill in the gaps. Earley watched every movement she made: the fierce way she swung up her hoedad and slammed it down into the mud, rocking back on it, freeing the blade. He watched her twist backwards to grab a tree plug from one of the twin canvas bags crisscrossed onto her hips, watched her fan its roots before setting it in the ground. She moved like a mountain goat, facing into the hillside and changing position with quick, darting strides, moving up and back downwards, but mostly up, coming his way.

The door of the crummy swung open and Reed stepped out, banging the door against the rear-mounted tool rack. The mud-covered hoedads clattered like swords. Way down on the hillside, Zan heard the sound and turned.

"Reeder!" She dropped her hoedad and charged up the hill. Her treebags flapped behind her like low-slung wings as she let out a whoop and propelled herself into Reed's arms, flushed and panting from running uphill. He staggered backwards but held her. Her legs wrapped around his back as she covered his whole head with kisses. Reed tipped his chin up and caught one full on the mouth. Lucky bastard, thought Earley. His tongue felt thick.

"What are you *doing* here?" Zan said. "I thought you were halfway to Juneau!"

"I'm working with Earley."

Zan turned and saw him. She slid down Reed's body and smiled. There was mud streaked across her left cheek and her hair stuck out under her watch cap in two thick, unraveling braids. She's gorgeous, thought Earley. God help me.

"Good to see you again, Earley."

"Yeah," Earley managed. Life of the party, he thought, that'll really impress her.

Zan threw her arm over Reed's shoulder and nuzzled the side of his neck. She was wearing a vivid orange sweater beneath her green raingear, and the tips of the last several sapling plugs poked from her treebags like little green tails. Reed reached over and pulled one out. It was barely more than a foot long, a bristle of needles that looked like a bottle brush topping a test tube-shaped root cluster.

"What kind of tree?" he asked.

"Doug. Douglas fir."

Reed looked down at the great swath of mud. "So in thirty more years . . ."

"They'll be bound for the pulp mill." Reed looked stricken. Zan shrugged. "We're just sowing a crop." She was right, Earley thought, though it startled him to hear her say it so bluntly.

"We don't know that," Young Nick intoned through the open door of the crummy. "We don't know what people's consciousness will be thirty years from now."

Zan's eyebrows went up. "Yeah, I'm sure they'll care less about money by then." She spotted Just Nick striding towards them, hefting her hoedad along with his own. "Oops. Busted!"

Just Nick walked past them, the twin blades curved over his shoulder like scythes. "Remember my friends Reed and Earley?" asked Zan. Just Nick's eyes swept from one to the other. Reed was clutching the miniature sapling and Earley still held

Young Nick's Earth First mug. Just Nick nodded in silence and went to the crummy, swinging the two hoedads into the rack on the back.

"Cassie, Robbo and Zach are still in the hole," he said to the other treeplanters, peeling off his wet bandanna and wiping his face with it. Earley noticed his long hair was sparse at the crown. "When they come up, we'll roll."

"Dinner," moaned one of the planters, a gangly guy with matted brown hair and a slight walleye. "I'm fuckin' dying here."

"Ditto," his buddy said.

Zan turned to Reed. "You'll stay for the weekend." It wasn't a question.

Reed looked over at Earley. "I'd like that," he said. Earley stared stupidly back at him. This wasn't at all what he'd had in mind, but when he really pictured it, what he'd had in mind didn't make much more sense. Zan's hands had been all over Reed since the moment she saw him, and sharing his bus with a couple in heat had its definite downside.

Zan looked at him too. "Can you stay for dinner?" she asked. "Graywolf's camptending. He's a great cook."

"I've already got plans," Earley lied, looking Zan in the eye so she'd know he was lying, that he was just being a gentleman, stepping aside. And maybe, if she was a good enough reader, she'd even pick up how he felt about that, how he felt about her.

Zan held onto his gaze for a few beats too long. Her eyes were so dark they looked black in the twilight. "Some other time." She reached over and took Earley's hand, one fingertip tracing his palm. She still had her other arm slung around Reed. "I can drive him back Sunday," she said. "You have fun tonight."

Earley had had way too many, but not enough to think that the world didn't suck. The crowd at the Cedar was louder than ever, and everyone seemed to be there with a date. He tried to get Big Jim's attention by raising his shotglass, but he was pouring out two sudsy pitchers of Oly for some high school team and their giggling blonde girlfriends. Probably all under-age; Big Jim could lose his whole outfit. The hell with it.

Earley slammed down the shotglass. He slid off his barstool and tested his balance. Still vertical. He figured a trip to the men's room would set him straight, drain off a bit of the Maker's Mark. As he lurched past the pool room, he saw a familiar wide back in a rose-colored sweatshirt, angrily jamming a pin-ball machine. Had she really been here all this time? How the hell had he missed her?

Earley hoisted up his sagging sweatpants with one hand and walked over to where she was standing. "Margie."

She jammed on a flipper. "You shithead."

"Your daughter was with you."

"You could have said hi."

Earley leaned forward and kissed her neck, sliding his hands down her sides.

"What the hell are you doing? There's people here!"

"See?" Earley said. He backed off her and leaned on the end of the pinball machine, looking back at her face. Margie looked pretty fearsome, but he could still tell she was putting on an act. "You're not really mad at me."

"Wanna place bets?"

"That's not what I want and you know it." He hated the sound of his voice, but he saw she was softening. "Come on, Margie, cut me a break. I was just thinking of Amber Ann. Didn't want to get you into trouble."

Margie pushed hard on both buttons at once, but her ball rolled between flippers and sank out of sight. "Look what you made me do."

She sounded so angry he might have believed her, except for the way that her hand reached up, smoothing her hair. She still wants to look nice for me, Earley thought. All is not lost. He leaned on the pinball machine.

"I'm a low piece of snakeskin," he said. "Always was."

Margie pulled back the trigger and slammed a new ball up the chute. "Who was your friend in the wiggy pants?"

"No one. Forget him." He reached for her hand, but she elbowed him off.

"Hey, I'm playing." Her ball slid up onto a platform and set off a volley of bells.

"I'll be in my truck, right outside," Earley said. "When you finish your game . . ."

"Dream on," Margie told him.

Earley brushed past her, bending his lips towards the top of her head. "I want you," he said, and walked out of the bar.

It hadn't worked. Earley had been in his truck for at least fifteen minutes. He'd finished the beer he brought with him and now he sat, mesmerized by the pulse of the red neon "E" as it flicked on and off at the tail end of "Lounge." This wasn't his night. In a lifetime of nights that weren't his, this was up on the charts. He didn't know which he felt worse about, playing the sleazeball with Margie or failing to hook her. Or thinking of Zan and Reed fucking their brains out in some goddamn tent.

Earley sighed. Might as well sulk in the comforts of home. He reached into his pocket for car keys and dropped them. Of course. When you'd already lost your last shred of dignity, why not add to the picture by having to scrabble around on the wet rubber floor for your goddamn. . . . Wait. He craned up towards the window, where a dark shape was blocking the red neon light.

It was Margie. Earley reached across quickly to steady the hinge as she opened the passenger door and got in.

"You don't deserve this."

"I know I don't." Earley leaned down and buried his face in her hair. Her shampoo had a strawberry scent, like something you'd find on an auto air freshener. He was so grateful he thought he would weep.

"You think I'm some fish on a string," Margie said. "You can just reel me in when you get the urge and toss me back over the side when you don't. Big man with a pole."

"I don't think that at all," Earley said. "I think we've both got other lives, with a whole lot of crap coming down from all sides, and when we can manage a few hours together, it makes us both happier. That's what I think. Am I wrong?"

Margie looked at him, frowning. "Damn you, Earley," she said. "It's a good thing I like your sad ass. Let's get out of here. All's I need now is some damn friend of Harlan's to see me in your truck."

Earley picked up Margie's hand, squeezed it and started the pickup. They drove through the outskirts of town. Margie gazed out the window without saying much, and Earley got the feeling that he was still on probation. He pulled a flat pouch of Drum from his pocket and veered the truck into the parking lot of a gas station convenience store. "Right back," he said, slamming the door before Margie could join him.

The pickings were slim. Pennzoil, canned string beans and Special K were not going to help him get back into Margie's good graces. Earley went up to the counter and spotted some half-priced selections left over from Valentine's Day. "Bingo," he muttered, and reached in his pocket. There were two dollar bills in his wallet and seven loose shower dimes. He dug out his emergency fund—the fiver he always kept wadded up under his Buck knife—and loped out of the store with a small box of Russell Stover cremes and a single silk rose in a plastic tube.

"Here," he said, handing Margie the chocolates and rose. She stared at them.

"Shit," she said.

"It was all they had," Earley said hastily. Margie shook her head.

"Harlan would never . . ." she said, and looked up at him, biting her lip. Her eyes shone in the fluorescent spill of the parking lot lights.

"I wish . . ." she whispered, then shook her head. "Thanks, Earley."

Scoter swiveled around in his desk chair. The TV was playing a dog food commercial. "Two weeks in a row, Ritter? Pushing your luck."

"What luck?" said Earley, and slipped him a twenty. His last.

"That about pays for last time," said Scoter. "You got any more of that weed?"

"I'll give you a raincheck," said Earley. The TV ad changed to a blonde in a bathing suit, filling her palm full of shaving cream. "Take it all off," she intoned in a thick Swedish accent.

"I wish," Scoter said. He threw Earley a room key. "Two hours. You go falling asleep on me, I'm coming in after your girlfriend. Whoever she is."

Margie's nipples were big as fried eggs. Earley could not get enough of them. They'd made love the second they got through the door, barely stopping to tear off their clothes, and now he was leaning against the headboard with Margie curled into him, resting her back on his chest while he played with her tits.

"That feels nice," Margie murmured.

"I'll say," he said, slipping his palms underneath them and lifting them up, like Miss June in the pinup he kept by his bed.

"You should've seen me before I had kids. I had beautiful boobs."

"You still do," Earley told her.

"If you only meant half the stuff that you say," Margie said.

"I do mean it." He did, too. He loved to watch Margie unhook her stiff bras, the way she spilled out like a jackpot. He loved licking her nipples until they got hard, the way that she moaned underneath him, the touch of her fingernails over his back.

She rolled over and looked at him. "What are you doing with me, Earley?"

"What do you mean?" he said. He wasn't ready for this, not tonight.

"Look at yourself, for Christ's sake." Margie ran her hand over his chest muscles, tracing the taper of hair that bisected his belly and led down towards his groin. "You're a big healthy animal. How come you don't have a girl of your own?"

Earley wished she would leave it alone. This was not going

anywhere good. He tried keeping it light. "I've got half of two nickels. A secondhand bus and a '58 pickup. I'm no one's Prince Charming."

"I don't want Prince Charming. I want someone who tells me he still likes my body, and fucks like he means it." She was looking him right in the eye.

"Well, you got me," said Earley, shifting his weight on the pillow.

"Don't give me this crap. If I wasn't married to Harlan, you'd head for the hills."

Earley could have come up with some line, he supposed, but he figured he owed Margie better. "I already live in the hills," he said, stroking her cheek.

"I know," Margie said, "God, do I know," and she closed her eyes.

Earley looked down at his sweatpants and shirt, tangled on the blue carpet with Margie's bra. He wished he could slip on his clothes and go back to the bar.

"I'm sorry," said Margie. "I'm dumping on you. Got a lot on my mind. It's my little girl's birthday tomorrow."

"Amber Ann?"

Margie shook her head. "The one that I lost. She'd be eighteen years old. The same age I was when I had her. Half my life ago. I can't hardly believe it."

Earley touched her hair. "What was her name?"

"Angelica Dawn," Margie said. "Three weeks old." Earley

didn't know what to say. There was nothing that didn't feel hollow, inadequate. He wrapped his big arms around Margie and she closed her eyes again, letting him rock her.

"I don't think Harlan even remembers the date," she said. "He never talks about her at all. Not even when Pete got hit."

"Harlan's an asshole," said Earley.

"I know," she said. "But he wasn't back then. He slid into assholedom bit by bit."

"Just like we all do," said Earley, feeling sheepish that he'd called her husband an asshole.

Margie looked at him. "What if he leaves me for good this time? Would that make a difference?"

Earley hadn't expected that. He could feel Margie's eyes on him. "He'll be back," he said.

"I don't know that I want him back," Margie said, resting her lips on his collarbone. "I could get used to this."

"I'm not your kids' father," said Earley.

"No. You're not." Margie threaded her fingers through his. "Did you ever want kids, Earley?" He was taken aback, not so much by her asking the question as the fact that she'd put it in past tense, as if he had already missed his chance. Well, she had her first kid at eighteen, Earley thought, and Amber the year after that. By the time she was my age, her littlest was riding his bike to Little League.

"I never did think so, but maybe. Yeah. I think I might."

"They break your heart," Margie said. "Break it in pieces,

and grow you a bigger one." Earley thought of his mother, wedged into a trailer with four screaming kids and a husband who got drunk and beat on her. Somehow she'd loved them all anyway. Maybe the trick was just *having* the family, sowing your seed in whatever sad patch of ground you had to work with. He looked down at Margie's left hand, where her flesh had trapped her in a zircon engagement and wedding set two or three sizes too small. I don't know how to do this, he thought. Never have, never will.

"I'm making you sad," Margie said.

"No you're not." He had to kiss her now. It was what Margie expected. Earley leaned forward and opened his mouth around hers, feeling the grateful thrust of her tongue and the quick surge of heat that reminded him why men and women had bodies. He slid his palms over her breasts, but a part of his brain was already weighing his options and wondering how to head back to his bus without hurting her feelings. Why couldn't anything ever be easy? Margie's arms roamed over his back, and she rolled over, taking him with her.

NINE

Earley woke up squinting. Something was off, and it took him a moment to figure out what it was: the sun was out. Sunlight poured in through the bus's twin rows of windows. It steamed off the soaked branches outside, turned the snow-covered crest of Olympus a bright golden pink. It might have been gorgeous, but all Earley knew was that his eyes ached, his head hurt, and he needed to piss. He stumbled up from his bed and went out the emergency exit, releasing a stream in the dirt.

The sun wasn't fair. The view of Olympus was stunning, one of those hand-of-God vistas that was supposed to lift up your spirits and fill you with awe, instead of reminding you what a hungover, stale piece of shit you were. Earley sighed and went inside to brew some strong coffee. The stove was dead cold; he'd come home too wasted last night to refresh it. The kindling hopper was empty—Reed's job, he thought, kicking it so hard it rattled.

He picked up his olive-drab thermos and opened it. Nothing. He lifted the lid of the coffee pot in the wash basin. There were some dregs, a bit grainy with grounds, but at least it would give him a jumpstart. He drained the pot into a nearly clean mug and poured in some sugar. The milk in the cooler was sour. There was more in the truck—he'd forgotten to unload the groceries last night, Earley realized—but it had probably gone sour too in this goddamn sun. He dumped in a few lumps of powdered milk, stirred it and choked it down, gritting his teeth. This is no way to live, he thought, and the second his mind formed the words, he knew they would stick in his head all day long like a tack, like a mantra.

He got through the chores. Split the kindling. Relit the stove. Made a new pot of coffee, some oatmeal and toast. He unloaded the groceries from the truck, sniffing and tossing the milk, a pound of ground chuck that was starting to rot and a whole fryer chicken he thought might be dicey. He got out his poacher's spade and dug a grave for the meat so coyotes and bears wouldn't come around. He put away laundry and hung his damp jeans from a tree. Then he went to the truck for his Husqy. He sat down on a stump round, took off the saw chain and cleaned it methodically, picking out black clots of fuel and sawdust and sharpening each tooth with a file. The sunshine was warm on his back. He heard the high liquid song of some bird that he realized he hadn't heard once all winter, and spotted a Steller's jay watching him work from the crest of a tree.

Earley tugged the chain back onto the bar of his Husqy and realized that he was sweating, with twin streaks of crankcase oil over both forearms. He went back inside and put on a new shirt. Then he looked at the watch Reed had left by his bed. It was nine a.m.

The weekend unrolled ahead of him, empty. Earley guessed he could go to the clearcut and split out some rounds; he could pick up some volume and speed on his own, get the numbers back up. But his heart wasn't in it. All he could think of was Zan and Reed, wrapped in each other's arms. And Margie, who'd probably cried herself to sleep last night after he'd dropped her off down the street from her trailer. He remembered the look of contempt on Vern Gillies' face when he'd asked for the dimes and figured he probably deserved it.

Earley poured more coffee and looked out the window. He could see peaks and ridges he hadn't seen clearly for months. It wasn't a day to be working in mud.

Steelheads, he thought. I'll go fishing. The thought made him happy. He got out his tackle box and picked out a small stash of bobbers and aeroflies. He took down his favorite rod, threw a one-handed cast into the living room and hooked one of Reed's socks on the first try. He packed up a couple of sandwiches, tossed an orange and some nuts in a day pack, grabbed his waders and left.

The sunshine changed the whole landscape. The blue sky and firs were so bright that the colors seemed fake, like a Koda-chrome postcard. The air smelled like spring. Earley rolled down the window and let the wind roar through the truck as he sped down the coast road. The mouth of the Hoh would be rushing with meltwater, perfect for steelhead. The turnoff was just up ahead, past the sign for the Rainforest Trail. Earley had never been up there. Last fall he had given a ride to a couple of backpackers from New Zealand who'd raved about it.

"You lived here how long, mate?" said one. "And you've never done the trail?"

"Change your whole life, it will," said his friend. "It'll blow out your socks."

The Rainforest Trail sign loomed up, and Earley impulsively turned the truck towards it. Why not? he thought. I could do with my whole life changing around about now, or at least with my socks getting blown.

The approach road was long, and the trees started changing as soon as he turned off the highway. Instead of the towering trunks of Douglas fir, cedar and spruce, there were moss-covered hardwoods, their low branches trailing green veils and stream-ers of clubmoss. The damp ground was matted with horsetails, ferns and vanilla leaf, no bare space anywhere. It looked fertile and lush, a north country bayou.

Earley pulled into the parking lot next to the trailhead, which was empty except for a couple of Park Service trucks and a VW Bug. He stood in front of a big wooden map, gazing at distances and elevations. Avalanche warnings above Glacier Meadows, he read. Hard to believe, with the air warm and springy, but high elevations were treacherous. Earley went back to the truck for his gear. He figured he'd hike the first five or ten miles along the Hoh River and go fishing somewhere high up in the backcountry. He could take the wool army blanket he kept in the truck and bed down in one of the shelters if he had the urge. No one on the planet would know where he was, or care if his hike took him one day or two. No strings, he thought. Fuck it.

He strapped the blanket and fishing pole onto his day pack and started the trail at an easy lope. The groomed path was wide, with considerate wood slabs laid into the muddiest sections. Like a sidewalk, he thought. Piece of cake.

The trail started climbing alongside the Hoh River gorge. The water had turned a weird silty gray; it was moving so fast it looked like it was boiling. If there was a river that led to the Underworld, Earley thought, like in those old myths, that'd be just the right color. He fingered the Buck knife he wore on his belt and wondered if bears had come out of their caves yet. The winter was losing its grip, ice yielding to mud. The earth oozed beneath his stride, crusting his boots.

A few miles farther up, Earley ran into two older hikers on their way back down, Sierra Club types with collapsible cups on their rucksacks and loud cheery voices that called each other Mother and Pop.

"Great day!" said Pop, grinning, and Earley said, "Beautiful," hoping it sounded like something he meant. Mother smiled at him indulgently. Mated for life, Earley thought as they passed him by. Some people found that. He wouldn't be one of them; too much of his life had already gone by. *This is no way to live.*

This is *really* cheering me up, he thought, great plan. But hard on the heels of that thought came another that pleased him: that Zan and Reed weren't mated for life either. Earley didn't know how he knew this, he just did, had known it the moment he saw them together.

What was missing? He couldn't imagine how Reed, or any man for that matter, could help falling in love with Zan, unless he was worried that she'd be too much for him. And why wouldn't Zan fall for Reed? He had a big dick, he was smart, he played musical instruments. His family had money, even if he didn't. Reed didn't talk about his parents' wealth—had, in fact, changed the subject abruptly when Earley asked him what his father did—but it seeped out in his stories of sailing, of summers on Cape Cod and in the White Mountains. He was even good-looking, Earley supposed, in a way women went for: straight nose, even teeth and those startling, Paul Newman blue eyes. He was as fair as Zan was dark; they looked great together.

But somehow—and this wasn't just envy talking, he told himself—the two of them didn't catch fire. Earley couldn't say why; it was something he sensed, like the whiff in the air that lets dogs know on meeting which one is the boss. For all of Reed's moony-eyed pining, for all the way Zan threw her body against his and kissed him all over, something between them was not what it should be. Zan knew it too; there was a desperate cling in the way she touched Reed, as though if she ever let go of his body, he might float away.

Earley was doing a god-awful job of getting them out of his mind. Work would have been better. The whine of the chainsaw, the ache of the hard, steady rhythms would numb him, where walking through all of this beauty stirred everything up. Margie's voice echoed in his head, asking him, "How come you don't have a girl of your own?" A big healthy animal, she'd called him, and he figured that was about right. A Clydesdale horse. Reed was a thoroughbred, high-strung and flighty. Zan was one of those things from *Fantasia*, half horse and half pinup girl.

Earley noticed a strange smell in the air, not the primordial scent of wet earth and decay that hung in the rainforest air, but something harsh, acrid. He rounded a bend and thought, oh. Yes, of course. The forest ahead was charred and black, even the standing trunks torched by a forest fire. Nature's clearcut. It must have been recent; the underbrush hadn't come back yet. A few months from now there'd be fireweed budding, and western hemlock cones would release their seeds into the troughs of dead logs left behind by the fire. It would all cycle back, but now it was lifeless and eerily silent.

Earley craned his neck up as he walked through the burn zone, wondering which trunk the lightning had split, although it was equally likely that some irresponsible hiker had tossed down a Marlboro. People fucked up the earth every day. He stepped off the trail and his boot crunched on something. He looked down and saw vertebrae in the ash. Each bone was tiny and fragile. What had it been? Earley wondered, squatting to peer at the blackened remains. Then he spotted a deer skull, so tiny it looked like a toy. The fawn must have been born and died here, he reckoned, too new on its legs to outrun the flames. He thought about taking the skull with him, hanging it up on the wall of his bus, but decided to leave it where it belonged. He stepped away quietly, feeling a rawness like smoke in the back of his throat.

A few miles past the burn zone, the trail widened into a meadow. Right in its center, arching over the green grass in every direction, was a massive bigleaf maple. Every inch of its gnarled trunk was covered in moss, with trailing streamers that hung from its branches like yak fur. Off to one side, Earley spotted the Happy Four Shelter, an open-front lean-to of weathered wood planks. He wondered if Mother and Pop had slept up here last night, spooning together in matching blue sleeping bags.

The shadows were lengthening. Earley wished he had paid more attention back down at the trail chart to where the next shelter was, and how low the avalanche danger began. Glacier Meadows had an ominous ring to it. He figured he had about two hours till dusk. He could either pack on up the trail and see where luck brought him, or bushwhack down to the river and try to catch something for dinner.

He decided on dinner. The gorge was steep-sided and he missed his caulks. Reed had done well, he thought, scrambling around in those hiking boots all week long. Could it really be only one week since Earley had picked him up outside Bogachiel, in that ridiculous poncho? He wondered what he'd have been doing right now if he hadn't stopped to give Reed a ride. Probably cutting up stumps, ignoring the weekend because it was just like the rest of the week. He certainly wouldn't be clambering down to the Hoh River, clutching a fishing pole. Or zoning out picturing Zan with her shirt off. Both of those things were good things, he decided, baiting his hook.

Earley walked into the river. The chill of the water forced air from his lungs, made his blood rush and tingle. He fished until sunset, and just when he'd started to feel like an idiot, he hooked a beauty. It jerked his line, fighting for life, but he stayed on top of it, letting it thrash and swim till it had played itself out. He watched it gasp, supple and silvery, drowning in air, then gutted it out with his Buck knife and started back up the gorge.

It was dark by the time he got back to the clearing, and the air was much colder. He built a fire in a circle of stones in front of the grandfather maple and let it burn high and hot. Then he set his steelhead onto a flat rock and left it to bake on the coals. He hadn't thought of packing a plate or fork, so as soon as it cooled enough not to burn him, he picked it up whole in his fingers and chewed the charred flesh off the bones. It was possible he had once eaten something that tasted as good, but he couldn't think when.

He looked up at the sky. Clouding over already, but he could make out a few stars. Reed would probably know what the names of them were. Earley threw the bones into the flames and sat licking his fingers, feeling like some sort of caveman. The moon cleared the trees. It was practically full, and he realized he'd lost track of it during the weeks of unending rain. In Georgia you knew where the moon was. Earley remembered being a kid, lying flat on his back in the scraggly grassed clay of his tiny backyard, staring up at the moon to a soundtrack of neighbors' TV sets and family fights, his mom hollering and slamming doors, his dad hollering louder and breaking them open. How long had it been since he'd spoken to them? Had they given up wondering where he'd washed up, were they even alive?

Zan's parents were both in the army. He hadn't expected that, still couldn't line it up with his picture of who she was. Nothing about her was straight or obedient; she must have thrown off some serious sparks with a dad in the Officers' Club.

Earley poked at the fire with a stick and sent up a flurry of cinders. He was at it again. Well, so what. She *was* on his mind. Maybe he was on hers.

The sound Earley woke up to was like nothing that he'd ever heard before, a magnified, bellowing snort. He rolled over and peered out the front of the lean-to. Elk. Twenty or thirty head of Roosevelt elk, grazing under the huge moss-draped tree in the half-light of dawn. A dusting of new snow had fallen, icing the tips of the fir boughs, and Earley's first thought was of reindeer at Christmas. The bugling sound echoed again, this time with a clatter of antlers. Earley spotted a huge old bull at the edge of the herd, head lowered, shaking his rack at a young male whose antler sockets were empty and newly raw. What is he doing down here with his harem, Earley wondered, and why hasn't he shed his antlers yet? Bulls were supposed to stay solo in winter.

The bull elk had scented him. His head jerked up, alert, as

he sniffed the air, checking for danger. The young male abandoned his challenge and the rest of the harem stopped grazing and froze in place, waiting for signs. After a moment, the bull shook his antlers and lowered his head.

Earley worked his way up to a sitting position, moving with caution so he wouldn't spook them. He slid his feet into the boots he'd left next to his bedroll, and slowly unfolded himself to his full height. The bull stamped and snorted again and then dipped his chin, as though he were granting permission.

Earley moved quietly into the herd, feeling the elk shift their big steaming bodies around him. They stayed at a distance, aware of his every move, but they didn't bolt. Up close they were startlingly solid, bigger than cows, with furry black necks and creamy saddles around their asses. Earley had never been so close to anything wild before. He had no idea why they were allowing him among the herd, or, for that matter, why he'd had the urge to walk into its center. That big bull could probably kill him; his antlers were longer than Earley's arms, and the prongs looked like spear points. They stared at each other. High up in the tree, a raven clattered its wings and let out a harsh croak, and the herd scattered suddenly, racing past Earley and into the woods. He stood rooted, feeling his heart pound. It didn't seem possible that they had vanished so fast; it was almost as if he had dreamed them.

Earley shivered. The sunrise was back under clouds, and the wet air felt raw. He built a new campfire, wishing like hell he'd brought coffee or even a tea bag. He heated his metal canteen and threw a couple of orange peels inside it to steep. It didn't taste too bad. He wolfed down the orange and the rest of the cashew nuts, all he had left. Then he rolled up his blanket, stomped out the embers and headed out.

The hike back seemed shorter, though his left foot was bugging him something fierce. Maybe because it was mostly downhill, or simply because he was heading somewhere that he'd been before. Earley was starved by the time he got down to his truck. It took a few tries to turn over, so he let it warm up while he unlaced his left boot to see what the damages were. The heel of his sock had split clean through. Damn Kiwis were right, he thought, grinning: the Rainforest blew out my socks.

Earley swung down Route 101 to the mercantile outside Kalaloch and picked up an extra-large coffee, a Slim Jim and two Hostess cherry pies. He paid the whole bill with dimes. This is the life, he thought, unwrapping the pies with his teeth as he drove north and washing them down with sweet coffee. He fiddled around with the radio dial till he came to a station with half-decent music. Then he turned off the highway and started the long climb towards home. He hadn't passed a single car.

"On this neeeeew morning," Earley sang along with Bob Dylan, bouncing along the deep ruts that led up to his bus.

Even after the radio signal fuzzed out in a flurry of static, the words echoed in his head. He could barely remember how grim he'd felt yesterday morning. So what if some guy who was working for him had spent last night with a woman he wanted? Earley had climbed up a mountain, eaten a fish with his bare hands and stared down a bull elk whose rack was the size of an armchair. It was a new fucking morning, goddamn it, and he was the master of all he surveyed.

Earley jammed the truck into high gear and careened through the last couple turns. He coasted around the bend into his clearing and pulled up short. Next to the bus was a twenty-year-old maroon Volvo with a curtain of beads hanging from the back window. It had to be Zan's.

TEN

Zan was sitting right there at his table, wearing a man's plain white T-shirt and jeans. She leaned back and smiled as Earley came in. "Catch any?" she asked. Earley realized that he was holding his fishing pole.

"One," he said. "Ate it last night." He set down his day pack and blanket roll, nodding to Reed, who was stir-frying some kind of curry that made Earley's eyes water. He spotted a Sunday paper and several new bottles of spices on top of the counter, next to a tall pile of library books. It had never occurred to him Forks had a library.

"You went fishing overnight? Where did you sleep?" Reed turned, wooden spoon in hand, as if he was accusing Earley of something. The spoon was new too, Earley noticed. Reed was upgrading his stuff. It annoyed him.

"Some shelter," he muttered. "Halfway up Olympus."

Zan looked at his head, where it grazed the low end of the bus's curved ceiling. "You don't fit in your house," she said.

"What can I tell you?" said Earley. "I'm not an indoor kind of guy." He kicked off his boots, aware of his mud-crusted, threadbare wool socks. His sore foot was throbbing. If Zan hadn't been there, he would have boiled up some water and soaked it in epsom salts, but he didn't want to look like some wacked-out old fogey. He reached into the cooler and took out a beer.

"Are there any more of those?" Zan asked.

Earley twisted the cap off his and handed it to her. He'd meant to be a gentleman, but he was moving too fast: the head foamed out over his hand and spilled onto Zan's T-shirt. "Jesus wept," he mumbled, ears flaming. "I'm sorry."

Zan laughed, taking hold of the bottle and tipping it into her mouth. "Don't sweat it," she said. "It's not Fiorucci." Earley wasn't quite sure what that meant, but she didn't seem mad at him. He opened a beer for himself and sat down at the table. He tried not to stare at the wet spot the spill had made, right over Zan's nipple.

"What were you doing halfway up Olympus?"

"I went for a walk," Earley said. Why did he always roll out these boneheaded comments when he was around her? Of course he had gone for a walk; did she think he'd fly? "It was nice out," he added, as if that would help. Just shoot me, he thought. Put me out in the pasture and drill a hole clean through my brain. I won't miss it.

Zan traced the rim of her beer bottle, shaking her head with a rueful half-smile. "Jesus wept," she said. "I haven't heard that since I was in grade school."

"What is it, some Southern thing?" Reed asked. He was juicing a lemon.

"Shortest verse in the Bible," Zan drawled, her accent pitch-perfect. She glanced back at Earley and answered his question before he could ask it. "Four years in Biloxi."

"Did you move around a lot?" Earley asked instead.

"Yes." Zan picked up her beer, subject closed. Just as well. He didn't want to get into the whole Vietnam thing, his kid brother's medals, his own failed attempt at enlisting in high school. Later, he figured, or better yet, never. He wondered why people tried knowing each other by telling their pasts, when it was the future they wanted to learn. What would it gain him to find out where Zan had grown up, what shreds of the South they might have in common, or anything else that had happened before she'd wound up in his midnight-blue bus near the Suhammish Clearcut, with beer on her left breast and two men who wanted to fuck her?

Damn, he thought, jamming his beer bottle into his mouth, I've been in the room with her all of five minutes. If she ever stays overnight, I'm dead meat.

"Are you hungry?" Reed asked, pulling plates off the shelf.

"I could eat," Earley answered. "It smells mighty excellent."

"What happened to that chicken I bought?" asked Reed.

"Died in the sun," Earley told him. "I gave her a good Christian burial."

Zan laughed and reached for her beer. Earley noticed the muscles that twitched in her forearms. He wondered how long she'd been treeplanting, what else she had done for a living. A lot, he bet, and some of it none too savory. There was that past thing again. Couldn't people do any better than this?

"Reed talked about you all weekend." Zan fixed her dark eyes on Earley. "He thinks you're a god among sawyers."

"I'm the best one he's worked with," said Earley. "Doesn't narrow it much."

She smiled. "You've still got ten fingers. You can't be that bad."

Earley didn't tell her about the five-inch scar on his thigh where his chainsaw had bucked up and gashed him a few years ago.

It was hot in the bus with the stove cranked for cooking. He wanted to shed his wool shirt, but the longjohn top he had on was a mass of holes, not to mention the probable stink. He got up from the table and sidled past Reed in the tight galley kitchen. "'Scuse me, lil' dude," he said, laying his hands on Reed's shoulders, "passing through."

He went back to his room, peeled off the spare layers and picked up a sleeveless ribbed undershirt, the kind his old man called a wifebeater. Let Zan stare at *his* chest for once. You're being a bastard, he said to himself, but he didn't care. If Zan had no guilt about flirting right under Reed's nose, why should he? Earley looked at himself in the darkening window. He didn't look bad with his mouth closed, he reckoned. He paused for a moment, then pulled the wifebeater over his head.

Reed's chickenless curry was spicy as hell. Earley had knocked back two helpings, and he felt like the roots of his hair were on fire. There was sweat running down from his scalp to his forehead. He noticed that Zan's face was flushed, and felt vaguely annoyed that Reed's wasn't, even though he'd shaken hot sauce all over his rice. Earley swallowed some more beer and rolled the cool bottle against his cheek. Reed was kicked back, relaxed, one arm draped around Zan. He was telling some story about hanging out with the treeplanter gang, doing mushrooms with Young Nick and Robbo and trying to hunt grouse with rocks. Apparently this had upset the vegetarian contingent, even though they'd come back without even a grouse feather.

"Cassie was crying her eyes out," said Zan. "She says hi, by the way."

Earley must have looked blank, because Zan raised her hand to the back of her neck. "Long blonde braid?" Oh God, yes. The wafty one. Cassie for casserole. Why was she sending him messages?

"I get the feeling she liked you," said Reed, as if reading his thoughts.

"Big time." Zan met Earley's eye. "She asked me if you had a lady."

"He's got 'em stacked up like cordwood," said Reed. "A pussy in every port."

"Hardly," said Earley. Zan's eyes didn't leave his. She seemed to want more of an answer. Was she trying to match-make for Cassie, or using her friend as a shield to get more information herself? Earley wondered if Reed had told her about Margie. He sure as hell hoped not. "Tell Cassie I eat cow for breakfast," he said.

"Beast," said Zan. Her laugh was so dirty that Earley blushed. She pushed her seat back and stood. "I'd better get back down that mountain while I can still see it."

Reed's face fell. "You're not staying over?"

Zan shook her head, stretching. "Got work in the morning. But now that I know where you live, I can come back next weekend. All right?"

It could have just been the angle she stood at, but Earley could swear she was looking at him.

The week seemed to drag on forever. The rain clouds squatted back down on the mountain and stayed there, filling the clearing with fog. Earley dreamed about Zan every night. Or maybe they weren't even dreams, just feverish, half-asleep trips to the fantasy zone. He was so full of lust that he felt embarrassed whenever he stood next to Reed. Eating breakfast together was almost unbearable; Earley felt as if Reed could see inside his head, where an X-rated slide show of Zan was on permanent rerun. He took to chewing his toast on the run as he did morning chores, drinking coffee right out of the thermos as they wound their way up to the clearcut.

They were working together so well it was hard to believe Reed was new at this. He was unfazed by the weather and worked like a dog, so eager to please that it broke Earley's heart. Those pale skinny arms had more sinew than he had realized; Reed could keep swinging that mallet all day. It was easy to picture him running a marathon, pumping himself past exhaustion and into the zone. If he fucks like he works, Earley thought, Zan's already got some kind of love machine. Why is she looking at me?

But she was. No two ways about it. When he'd come back out of his bedroom wearing that wifebeater, Zan had stopped talking mid-sentence and stammered. All during dinner, her eyes had roamed over his muscles as if she was licking the sweat off them. Earley had loved her for being so obvious.

She was on his mind all the time. By the time Friday rolled around, Earley was hopeless. He kept trying to picture the weekend, and banging his head on the fact that Zan would be sleeping with Reed. If he could just figure out some way to get her alone. Yeah, right, he thought, in a thirty-foot bus. And what would he do if he could? Tell her that she was all over his fantasy life? Try to fuck her when Reed wasn't looking? Any move he might make was ridiculous, doomed. Not making a move, lying still in his bed while she made love to Reed, was unthinkable. The only way to get out of this halfway intact was to sleep somewhere else tonight.

Margie, he thought. Forgive me.

Margie wasn't at home. Earley cruised by the Shamrock on his way into town, and when he spotted her orange Pinto in the parking lot, he parked and went in. It was the kind of bar where men started drinking at ten in the morning and sat there all day without speaking. A staticky TV set flickered in one corner, next to a dusty stuffed bobcat; the St. Patrick's Day cut-outs had been on the wall for a decade at least.

Earley spotted her right off the bat, in a booth near the juke-box, sitting across from two broad-backed men in plaid shirts and dark caps. One was Harlan, the other was Gus Ritchie, the asshole who'd skimmed Earley's paycheck when he was a rookie. It figured those two would be friends. Margie was wear-ing a tight turquoise sweater, with her rusty hair clipped up on top of her head in an off-center ponytail. She'd put on a lot of eye makeup, light blue on the lids and dark stripes underneath. The two men were arguing loudly about some timber sale Har-lan was scouting, and Margie was moving a straw round and round in her piña colada without drinking any. She looked up and saw Earley. Her eyes widened, then darted towards Harlan.

"So what do we do then, ship logs to the Japs?" he was shouting at Gus. "We get fucked either way!" The roll of flesh under his ears was the color of beef.

Margie lifted her hand to her hairclip and let her hair loose, using the movement to shake her head "no" with her eyes fixed on Earley's. Then she turned away, picked up her piña colada and drained it dry. There was no way to tell whether she was just warning him off or still pissed at him.

"What do you want?" snapped the iron-haired barmaid. A couple of COs from Clallam Bay Prison turned on their barstools and glowered at Earley. So did Harlan.

"Nothing," he said. "Just looking for someone who owes me some money." He turned and walked back through the door, passing under the mounted stuffed rump of a deer, some hunter's idea of humor. Earley wished someone *did* owe him money; he couldn't see how he'd get much of a buzz off a handful of dimes, not to mention a place he could spend the night. Damn it all, Zan was in *his* bus. Why was he the one skulking around like a stray?

Because she's balling Reed, he reminded himself with a grind of his teeth. His front tooth, the gray one, was aching again. When was the last time he'd been to the dentist, he wondered, or any professional anything? That time in the ER when he'd sliced his leg open, what was it, four years ago? Five? Was it possible he'd been a shake-rat for five years?

Christ, Earley thought, a sixth of my life. He didn't know what that might mean, but it sounded bad. Stuck. Getting old. He passed Harlan's black crew truck, plastered with NRA decals, and fought back the urge to piss on his tires.

The Cedar looked friendlier. Earley swung open the door on a loud blast of laughter as somebody finished an off-color joke. He made a quick scan of the faces along the bar and was surprised to see Scoter Gillies perched on a stool at the far end. Damn, he thought, no free motel room. But Scoter might pick up the tab for a drink or two. Earley ambled over and leaned on the barstool beside his.

"So they're letting you out in public on Friday night?"

"Scary, huh?" Scoter grinned. His yellow front teeth overlapped at the bottom. "Bud's breaking in a new night clerk, so I traded shifts. Let *him* miss all the action."

"*Is* there any action?" Earley surveyed the room. It looked pretty much like the usual suspects; the few women there were all twined around husbands.

"Hope springs eternal in the tit," Scoter said.

Earley laid a big hand on his shoulder. "So what are we drinking?"

"Whatever you're buying. You owe me for two goddamn towels, you hick. Think my boss doesn't count every night?" Scoter signaled the bartender. "Jack Daniel's."

"I'm, uh, not in a Jack kind of cash flow this moment," said Earley. "I was hoping that you'd do the honors."

Scoter's sneer looked a lot like his father's. "No way am I carrying your sorry ass tonight."

"I can't carry yours either, my man. No hard feelings." Earley thumped Scoter's shoulder and got up to leave.

"I might purchase a bit of that Maui, though," Scoter said. Earley paused. There were a few joints in a Band-Aid container under the seat of his truck, but they weren't his to sell. Reed wouldn't mind if he smoked one or two, though, so why would this be any different? A couple of joints was a small price to pay for an evening alone with Zan. *In my goddamn bus*, Earley thought. *With my woman. Or should be my woman. I don't owe that lucky prick anything.*

"Two Js," he told Scoter. "Five bucks and a shot of Jack. Back in a flash."

Earley went out to the truck, slid the two joints into a used Slim Jim wrapper and went back inside. "Here," he said, handing the Slim Jim to Scoter, "eat hearty."

Scoter bought them both shots and schooners. Earley knocked back his bourbon and chased it with Oly draft, licking the froth from his mustache.

"Your old man was telling me somebody's after some acreage up around my way. You heard any grapevine on that?"

"I know nothink," said Scoter, imitating the fat guy on *Hogan's Heroes*.

"Too true," Earley said. "But if you were to pass on a rumor . . ."

"There aren't any rumors," said Scoter. "Not about Royalton, anyway. Not about two thousand acres of virgin Doug fir to the west of Suhammish."

"Two thousand acres? What access?"

"I don't have a clue."

"Don't dick with me, Scoter. I live up there."

"I wouldn't dick with you on a bet, Ritter. That's all I know." Scoter waved at a few of his millworker buddies as they came through the front door. They came over and sat with him. One of the mill rats got onto some endless story about a half-Indian trawler captain who'd practically drowned his whole crew off of Teahwhit Head, and Earley took off for the pool room. He paused in the doorway, remembering his first view of Zan leaning over her cue in that spill of light. A curly-haired guy in a cowboy hat nudged a ball into the pocket and straightened up, looking at Earley. He seemed to be puzzling out where they'd met before.

"Hey, aren't you Zan's friend? I mean, like, her friend's friend?"

Earley figured that was about the size of it. "Yeah," he drawled, eyeing the pitcher of beer on the table. "My name's Earley Ritter."

"Robbo," the guy in the cowboy hat said. "And this here is Nick."

Young Nick had unbraided his hair and removed the hawk

feathers, probably a smart move if he wanted to walk through the Cedar without getting punched out by some redneck. Or by an actual Indian. "We've met," Earley said.

"Herbal tea," Young Nick nodded. He looked ill at ease clutching a pool cue, as if one of his mythical tribesmen might spot him and say he'd sold out. Robbo bent over and shot, dropping the cue ball straight into the corner.

"Out," he said to Young Nick. "Three for three." He emptied his beer mug and looked up at Earley. "You play at all?"

"Sure, if you want to go four for four. Rack 'em up." What he really wanted was some of that beer, but there was a protocol. First lose at pool, then hang with the victor. The losing part wouldn't be hard; Robbo looked serious. Earley went to the rack and chalked up the longest cue as he shoved in two quarters. The balls clattered down and Robbo corralled them into a plastic triangle, lifting it carefully.

"Your break," he said. Earley hitched up the back of his jeans and circled the table. He placed the cue ball just a hair to the left and got into position, aware of Robbo's and Young Nick's eyes on him. As he drew back the cue, he saw Cassie wending her way from the ladies' room. She was wearing a crocheted vest over a peasant blouse, a long skirt made out of a split pair of blue jeans and Frye boots whose heavy heels accented her slouching gait.

"Oh, hi," she said, her voice rising in that uncertain lilt she had, as if nothing she uttered could stand on its own two feet.

"Hey," Earley nodded, and bent down to break. Cassie

pulled over a stool and sat watching them, taking sips from a bottle of unfiltered apple juice. Earley wondered which one of the guys was her date. Her spaciness went with Young Nick's, but Robbo, with his tangled curls and fleshy mouth, seemed to have more on the ball. It didn't take him too long to ream Earley at pool, and just as he'd hoped, Robbo thumped on his back and asked him to sit at their table. Young Nick poured him a beer.

"Here's to the earth," he intoned. "To the spirit of hops."

"John Barleycorn must die, man," said Robbo.

Earley was dying to ask him about his grouse-hunting technique, but he didn't want to send Cassie off on a tear. "You folks are planting some nasty terrain up there," he said instead. It seemed safe enough, but Young Nick launched into a rant about clear-cutting raping the earth, wrapping up with his girlfriend's commitment to Greenpeace and how she was, even now, sailing off to save whales from extinction. Earley didn't point out how few whales lived in clearcuts; these things were connected in Young Nick's mind, and Young Nick was buying the beer. Hell, maybe they *were* all connected. He thought of what Scoter had told him and winced at the thought of two thousand shaved acres. "How long have you been planting trees?" he asked Robbo.

"Two months," said Robbo.

"Me too," Cassie chimed in. So they *were* an item. But Cassie was looking at Earley with a flushed, eager gaze; she'd already asked Zan whether he had a lady. Was this some kind of treeplanter chick thing, sitting next to your lover and flirting with somebody else? Cassie did share a tent with Zan. Maybe she'd been taking notes.

Robbo kept talking. It turned out he was just out of high school. He'd grown up in Tacoma, had gotten his steady girl pregnant, married her fast and was trying to make some quick money before he became a dad. "It's pretty heavy," he said. "But I'm up for it. Gotta save money, though. I shouldn't even be feeding the pool table. I've got to save up for like diapers and cribs and stuff."

"You're propagating the species," said Young Nick soberly. "You're in your sowing phase. Sowing trees, sowing your seed."

"Reproduction," said Robbo, "here's to it." He raised his glass. Cassie blushed again, looking at Earley. Well, that answered that. She wasn't with either of them, and she *was* flirting with him. He rolled it around in his head for a moment. Going home with her did have a certain allure: he could get drunk for free, get rid of his blue balls and even wind up with a free place to sleep—in Zan's tent, of all places, while she was in Earley's bus. Cassie was willing, that much was clear. It was all there for the taking.

But something had changed since he'd fallen for Zan. Earley had always been willing to go with the flow, to settle for less if less was what came his way. He thought of that song that went, "If you can't be with the one you love, love the one you're with," and looked over at Cassie. She wasn't bad looking. A little anemic, but nothing a couple of steaks couldn't fix. She had pale blue-gray eyes and a longish, straight nose, a thin dancer's body. She could have passed for Reed's sister.

Young Nick got up to buy the next pitcher and asked whether anyone wanted a slice of pizza. "It's white flour and all, but I do like my 'za," he said.

Robbo and Earley said sure. Cassie shook her head, arms folded over her chest. "I'm a vegan," she told Earley. "I don't eat any product that comes from an animal, living or dead."

Earley pictured himself hunkered over the campfire, chewing charred trout off the bone. This could be a deal-breaker. "The way we treat animals is, like, a mirror," said Cassie. "Who gave us that kind of empowerment over their lives? I'm not judging you or your choices, I just think we should try to evolve beyond all that aggression. You know?"

Earley nodded, his heart sinking. Cassie shifted around in her chair so her leg brushed against his. He noticed the way she kept touching her hair, as if someone had told her that it was her best feature. Earley looked at Cassie, trying to make himself want her, but he just couldn't find it; his whole nervous system was wired for Zan. He couldn't bring himself to make love to her just out of convenience. Margie was different; they'd hung out together already, he liked who she was. And even though lately she seemed to be hoping for more, the fact she was married to that redneck shit put a limit on things.

Earley wouldn't be promising something he couldn't make good on. Cassie was melting in hope, like a big pat of butter.

Which she wouldn't eat, Earley thought, and that clinched his decision. If he was going to let her down, better to do it right off the bat. He excused himself and went to the bathroom. When he came back out, he walked straight through the crowd at the bar, fully aware he was being a coward by not even saying good-bye, that she'd see the back of his head looming over the much shorter guys he was passing. So be it. If Cassie thought he was a snake, she was probably right. Earley was heading back home to the woman he loved, even if he walked in on her loving the one she was with.

ELEVEN

Earley's lone headlight bounced over the unpaved road. It wasn't exactly raining, but a drizzle filmed over the windshield, obscuring his view. He turned on the wipers. It smeared and got worse, so he turned them back off and kept driving. The dark road seemed longer than usual, and his truck seemed to wobble and lurch over every exposed root. Shocks must be going, he thought, adding that onto the list of repairs that he couldn't afford.

He thought about Robbo, nineteen or whatever he was, hoarding his quarters for baby supplies. Earley had only himself to support, but instead of making him feel lucky, like it was supposed to, that thought suddenly made him feel barren, alone on the planet. Maybe a baby wouldn't be all that bad.

Someone to love you helplessly, whose very existence would tie your life to a woman's in ways that could never dissolve. Reproduction, Robbo had said, and for that one moment he'd known something none of the rest of them knew: that being a man meant more than just fucking and losing and fucking again. Maybe those planters were on to something, walking around in the mud like Johnny Appleseed. Earley made his living carving up other men's leftovers. Thirty years from now there'd be a forest where Robbo and Young Nick and Zan had been working. What would his legacy be? Shorter stumps.

He was up at the clearing. He pulled alongside Zan's old Volvo, facing the midnight blue bus. He cut the ignition and sat for a moment, unsure of himself. There was a faint glow of light from the midsection windows: if a candle or oil lamp was burning, they weren't asleep. What would it feel like to open the door on the sounds of Zan and Reed in full rut? Earley gritted his teeth. He'd made his decision back there in the bar. They weren't going to drive him away from his home.

He got out and slammed the door loudly. Fair warning, he thought; no surprises. He pissed on the base of a hemlock, then circled around the far side of his bus, stumbling over some beer bottles, sending them rolling, but keeping his balance. I'm losing my drunk, he thought. Not fair.

He swung himself onto the tailgate and through the emergency exit. The bus was warm, fragrant with woodsmoke and some kind of incense. He popped a cassette in the tape deck and peeled off his clothes as Santana played "Black Magic Woman." One of Reed's favorites. So what.

Earley climbed into his bed and lay listening. Over the chords of the song, he heard murmuring voices. They were talking again. No. It was just Reed's voice, rising and falling. He's reading to her, Earley realized. He's lying in bed next to Zan's naked body, and *reading*? Maybe it's some kind of college boy foreplay. Maybe he's running his hand up and down her thigh as he reads, or stroking her belly, her bush. . . . Earley's hand slid down into the bulge of his longjohns. He closed his eyes. Better than nothing, he thought as his hand started moving. I'm here, Zan, right here.

Three sounds hit his ears at once: breaking glass, "Jesus!" and a shriek of pain. Earley was out of bed instantly. He strode through the bus and pulled down the Mexican blanket, not stopping to think about privacy. Reed's bed was on fire. Flames leapt from the bedding, from shards of the hurricane lamp. Zan's hair swirled through the air, its black ends alive with fire. She was screaming as Reed tried to beat it out.

Earley threw the striped blanket on top of them both and lunged into the kitchen, grabbing the dishpan on top of the counter. He sloshed water over the bed, recoiling as dishes flew out with the soapsuds, shattering under the weight of a cast-iron frying pan. Jesus Christ, he thought wildly, I could have killed someone. Smoke hissed from the sheets. He grabbed hold of a pillow and dived for the bed, trying to smother the last flames. Reed threw him the blanket.

And then it was over. The air smelled of singed hair and lamp oil. Earley rocked back on his knees, his breath heaving. He looked up at Zan. She was nude, her eyes huge. The fringe of her long hair was kinky, uneven. Reed reached to comfort her, but she ignored his hand.

"You okay?" Earley asked.

She nodded. "You're bleeding."

He looked at his hand, where the cut glass had nicked him, and wiped it across the wet sheet. "Well, you can't sleep on this mess," he said, trying without much success to stop staring at Zan's naked breasts. She was staring right back at him, not even trying to hide it. Reed must have felt it as well; he was standing between them, nude, like an animal frozen by two sets of oncoming headlights. His eyes flickered towards Earley's erection, which, Earley realized, had started to poke through the slit of his longjohns. Embarrassed, he shifted the fabric and got to his feet, gazing down at the smouldering mattress.

"You better take my bed," he muttered.

Zan took a step forward, placing her hand on his chest. "You too," she said.

Earley looked over at Reed, who looked paler than ever. He didn't protest. Earley could feel the blood rise to his ears as he looked back at Zan. He was hers.

Zan led them both back to Earley's room. The sheets were thrown back from the futon, a disheveled mess. The tape was still playing. Zan turned towards Earley, her nipples just grazing his chest. She reached down to peel off his longjohns. Earley tried not to catch Reed's eye as she lowered them down his legs, her hands roaming over his buttocks and hipbones.

"I don't think . . ." he started, then trailed off. He didn't know what he didn't think.

"It's all right," said Zan. She knelt at the edge of the mattress. "Lie down," she said, turning to Reed. She was the only one who seemed to know what to do, so they both obeyed her. Reed lay on the outside edge of the bed, Zan in the middle. She took Earley's hand, guiding him onto the mattress right next to her. The three of them lay stiffly, side by side. Earley didn't know what to do with himself. He was dying to touch her, but what about Reed?

Zan seemed to know what he was thinking. She lifted his hand and placed it on her ribcage, guiding his fingertips towards her breast. Earley's breath seemed to freeze in his lungs. He felt like a teenager, faced with forbidden fruit. Go on, her hand told him. It's yours. His palm traveled upwards, cupping her breast. He heard her sharp intake of breath as his thumb found her nipple. Her skin was so warm it felt feverish.

"Earley," she whispered, her lips nuzzling into his shoulder. He could feel the sharp edge of her teeth, the tip of her tongue on his bare skin. She wanted him, no doubt about it. And he wanted her—God did he want her—but there was Reed, lying next to them in the dark while he felt Zan up. I would have punched me out by now, Earley thought. What is he thinking?

Zan traced his lips with her fingertips, and he kissed the

palm of her hand. His tongue found the pulse in her wrist as her hand traveled over his cheek, the rough beard on his jawbone. He could feel Zan responding, how ready she was. Her breast seemed to swell in his hand. They were moving in silent slow motion, alert to each other's cues, fully aware that each move they made might be the one that would push things too far. He knew they were crossing a boundary—had already crossed it, in fact—and that nothing they did now was safe.

Earley slid his hand downwards, caressing the curve of Zan's belly, and bumped against Reed's fingers lying there. He pulled back instinctively, but Zan wouldn't let him go. She rolled into his embrace, turning her back on Reed, caution behind them. She kissed Earley full on the mouth, twining her limbs around him like a vine. He pressed himself into her body. Her mouth opened into his, hungry and warm, as her hand slid between his thighs, cupping his balls. Earley forgot about Reed. He forgot about everything. Nothing mattered but this; there was nobody else on the planet.

He arched up to enter her, rising on both arms. Zan moaned as he slid inside, plumbing her depths in slow motion. She rose up to meet him, her legs sliding over his back as she drew him in. They were a perfect fit.

Sweet Jesus, Earley thought. Oh my sweet Lord. This was what men and women were made for. They were moving together as if they'd been practicing all their lives. Earley remembered the words from the Bible: he knew her. Not just her body, but *her*, her whole essence. Her sadness. The tough little girl she'd

been, with bruised knees and elbows, hating her father for calling the shots. The lovers she'd run from. Her rootlessness. That
she would never have children. Earley didn't know how he knew
this; he just did, and he knew that Zan knew the same things
about him. He could feel his heart swell in his chest. It was all
he could do not to blurt out, "I love you."

Zan's hands roamed over his body, exploring the gullies and
ridges of muscle, the stray black hairs ringing his nipples, the
sharp, bony knobs in the groove of his spine. She found the
long chainsaw scar on his thigh, and her thumb stroked its
edges, as if she were trying to heal the old wound.

Earley suckled the join of her shoulder and neck. He could
taste her burned hair. He blessed Zan for knocking the hurricane lamp over, starting the fire. Fate or accident? It didn't
matter. She'd found her way to him, and he was inside her, was
filling her, spreading his seed.

Zan rose up beneath him, twining her arms around his neck
and pressing her mouth onto his as he came. In all Earley's
years of lovemaking, no woman ever had done that before. They
kissed you before or long afterwards, as you were getting your
breath back, a sort of a thank you note. This was the first time
he'd felt someone's tongue fill his mouth at the exact moment
that he filled her, erupting in wave upon wave of sensation, a
shuddering, heaving surrender.

He lay breathing on top of her, all tension gone from his
body. I could die now, thought Earley. I wouldn't miss anything.

Zan lay beneath him, gasping for air. Earley noticed the tears squeezing out of her eyelids and wondered if she always cried, if she'd done that with Reed.

Reed. For the first time in what seemed like ages, Earley remembered that they weren't alone. Reed had rolled to the edge of the futon, where he lay with his back to them, curled in a fetal position. Zan must have remembered at just the same moment. She stretched out a hand and touched Reed on the shoulder blade. He didn't move.

Earley rolled off as Zan moved towards Reed, murmuring, spooning, caressing him. He didn't respond, and then suddenly he was on top of her, pumping with hard, angry thrusts.

Earley tried not to think of the size of Reed's penis, whether Zan liked it more than his. He was on overload. He'd never been in the same bed with another man, let alone one who was fucking the woman whose sweat was still glazing his skin. The whole mattress shook with their groans. Earley felt every jolt in his body. He would have given his soul to be someplace else. Anyplace. Deep in the woods. But leaving the bed didn't seem like an option. Reed had been able to take it; he should do the same. Or should he? There wasn't a road map for this.

Zan, he thought. Alexandra. My Zan. All this time he'd been dreaming about her, and now they were lovers. Jesus, the way she'd moved under his body; that heart-stopping kiss as he came. As they both came. He couldn't imagine how Reed could bring her as much pleasure, just banging away like that, as if he was running the forty-yard dash and the only thing that made any difference was crossing the finish line. Fuck Reed, he thought, squeezing his eyes closed to shut out the evidence that Zan was doing just that, about two feet away.

I can't take much more of this, Earley thought, I'm going to kill him. He stared at the cracks in the roof of the bus and remembered the trailer in Waycross, his folks going at it, and later, his sisters Judene and Sue, sneaking home boyfriends, while he and his brother lay wedged in their bunk beds, surrounded by rattling walls.

Zan cried out, a sharp yelp that could have been passion or pain. That dick of his could do damage, thought Earley. The bastard. Reed moaned and was still.

Earley stared at the ceiling, his mind flooded with questions. Who were they now? How would they talk to each other? The whole world had changed, changed forever. A clot of dark clouds shifted over the moon, and the shadows of fir branches, wind-tossed, made flickering patterns above his head. He felt Reed roll over, away from Zan's body. The tape player clicked and turned over, ready to start again. Earley reached out and shut it off, feeling the silence surround them like smoke.

Zan sighed a long sigh, satiated, at peace, her tangle of hair spreading out on the pillow. She reached out for Earley's hand, then for Reed's. Earley exhaled and surrendered. The three of them lay side by side in the darkness, breathing the same air in three different rhythms, until they were lulled into sleep.

TWELVE

"So are we swingers now or what?" Reed asked the next morning.

"Definitely or what," Earley answered, relieved that Reed had decided to play it light. His eyes ached. He didn't know whether it was from the stale smell of smoke or because he had barely slept, tossed by strange dreams and the uneven rhythms of two people snoring beside him. Once he'd awakened to find Zan curled tightly against him, her cheek on his chest. A little while later she'd woken him up as she thrashed in her sleep, rolling over to nestle with Reed.

"I loved it." Zan smiled, stretching her arms. "I should burn beds more often." Earley glanced over at Reed, who looked as uncomfortable as he was feeling himself. In the gray light of day it was hard to believe they had shared the same woman and slept in the same bed, one on each side of her body, like mismatched andirons.

"How did the fire start?" Earley asked, and as soon as the words left his mouth, he realized he didn't want to know what sudden, passionate movement had sent the hurricane lamp flying.

"I bumped into the table," said Zan. A teasing half-smile played over her lips as her eyes met his. Earley's heart lurched. Was she trying to tell him she'd done it on purpose, so she'd have an excuse to get into his bed? Maybe she had. He could picture Zan doing a lot more than singeing a mattress to get what she wanted.

He glanced over at Reed to see if the same thought had crossed his mind, but Reed was setting the coffeepot back on the woodstove. His bare foot knocked over the book he'd been reading to Zan. They had found it as soon as they got up that morning: a collection of poems by some Spanish guy, splayed open and soaked with dishwater. Reed had retrieved it, blotting its pages and fanning it open in front of the stove as Earley and Zan knelt by the blackened mattress, picking up stray shards of china and glass. Zan reached for a dagger of glass by the pillow, but Earley got to it sooner. She touched his hand, next to the gash he'd ignored last night.

"You ought to put something on that," she said.

"I 'spose." Earley savored the warmth of her fingers. He didn't hold much stock with Band-Aids. Cuts healed when they got good and ready. If it still looked bloody the next time he fired up his Husqy, he'd strap on some duct tape to keep out the sawdust.

Zan's dark eyes looked moist, like a spaniel's. "Thank you," she said, lifting his hand to her lips. Reed came in from the kitchen. He frowned when he saw Zan bend over to kiss Earley's cut. She's tasted my blood, Earley thought; what are you going to do about that? He threw the sharp glass in the cast-iron skillet.

"This thing's compost," he said, jerking his head towards Reed's bed. The long splash of lamp oil had seared a diagonal path through the sheet and into the mattress's foam core, exposing its heavy coiled springs. "You'll never get rid of that smell."

Reed nodded. "Where am I going to sleep?"

The question hung in the air, fully loaded. Reed looked up from the mattress to Earley. So did Zan. He could feel both their eyes on him, waiting. Would this be the way that they talked about what had just happened, and where it would go from here? Earley didn't feel ready to take it on. He needed some pondering time, and a pot of strong coffee. "We'll figure it out," he said, rising, his head nearly touching the roof.

They made French toast for breakfast. Zan cracked the eggs two at a time, like a short-order cook, while Earley sawed raggedy slices of bread with his Buck knife and Reed stewed some apples and berries in syrup, steaming the windows. Moving around in the bus's close spaces seemed tighter than ever, a tango of arms and thighs brushing against one another, not always by accident. Even when she was doing something as mundane as throwing the eggshells and coffee grounds into the compost can, Zan's every move stirred the air between her and Earley, still heavy with sexual musk. If Reed wasn't standing in front of that stove, he thought, we'd never make it to breakfast. I'd bend her right over the table. Zan caught his eye as if she shared his thoughts. Later, her gaze seemed to promise. We'll find the right moment.

Reed ladled the steaming fruit onto their French toast. They carried their full plates outside and sat down on the circle of upended cedar rounds Reed had dubbed Woodhenge. The mist was beginning to lift off the mountains in vertical wisps, like ghostly question marks.

"Looks like it's gonna burn off," said Earley. "We might see some sun today."

"That'd be a change," said Reed, chewing.

We're discussing the *weather*, thought Earley. Well, fine. It was easier. Maybe they just wouldn't get to Reed's mattress, and Zan would return to his bed by default.

"Is there someplace in Forks that sells mattresses?" Reed asked.

Scratch that for a fantasy. "Sometimes they show up at Sally Ann's," Earley said. Reed looked confused, so he added, "The

Salvation Army." His mother had called it that, just like the rest of the neighborhood. A way of preserving their dignity, Earley supposed, of pretending they weren't in need of salvation, cut-priced.

Zan shook her head. "Sally Ann's," she said, "Jesus wept, Earley. Y'all are the genuine article."

Earley drained the sweet dregs of his coffee and picked up the pie tin that held his French toast. "Might could do with a couple new plates while we're at it."

"And a new hurricane lamp," said Zan, meeting his eye again. This time Reed noticed. He pursed his lips.

"When do you need to get back up to planters' camp?"

"Oh, a couple of hours ago." Zan gave a cheerful shrug.

Reed looked surprised. "Since when are you planting on weekends?"

"We missed a few half-days last week when the wind was too high. Just Nick thinks we're falling behind."

"So you need to go back there right now?"

Zan reached over to spear a fried apple off Earley's plate and dredged it through Reed's maple syrup. "Don't sweat it," she said. "I think we're officially outside the rules."

Earley and Reed carried the mattress deep into the woods. Zan stayed behind to wash dishes, giving them ground, Earley figured. Neither one of them said anything for a long time, and

Earley kept wondering who'd break the silence, and how. He stared at Reed's back as they crashed through the underbrush, bearing the unwieldy mattress like prey. The sound of their footfalls seemed amplified.

The mattress was heavier than it looked, with a coiled-spring and batting construction beneath the foam rubber. The smell of singed foam and lamp oil was acrid. That fire was no accident, Earley was sure of it now. Zan had wanted him so much that she'd been willing to burn herself—Reed too, if need be—so they could be lovers. Granted, she probably hadn't planned to set fire to her hair; the flames had leapt out of control, but the fact she'd been willing to risk her own skin to be with him made Earley feel dizzy with longing.

"Is this going to biodegrade?" Reed asked as they wrestled the mattress between low-slung branches.

"Sooner or later. The moss'll take over."

"We're all gonna turn to moss sooner or later," said Reed, shifting the weight onto his other shoulder. "But foam has a half-life of three thousand years or some shit. This is going to be here when the rest of this forest is thirty feet under. Or paved. Or whatever they're up to by then." He was sounding a bit like Young Nick at the Cedar, thought Earley. Maybe they read the same library books.

"Sometime in the Upper Paleolithic, mankind took a really wrong turn," Reed was saying. "We've lost touch with the knowledge we had as a species."

Probably true, Earley thought, but in cave days, when a man took another man's woman, they didn't eat breakfast together and chat in the woods. They went at each other with clubs, and the stronger man won. That was the knowledge we had as a species.

They'd come to the edge of a steep ravine. The drop was precipitous, as if some giant axe had sliced straight through the earth, leaving tree roots and boulders exposed to the air. The dry gully below wound down towards the creek where they went to haul water. The sound of its waterfall rumbled beyond the trees, low and insistent, like thunder. "Kiss it good-bye," Earley said, and they heaved the mattress over the side, sending down showers of gravel.

Reed took a step forward, watching his former bed tumble and crash on the rocks below. "See you in three thousand years," he said. The toes of his Gore-Tex hikers were right at the edge. One push, Earley thought. Just a brush of my arm, and I'd have Zan all to myself. Accidents happen out here in the woods. Who would know?

I would, he thought, and turned back towards the bus. Back towards Zan.

She was heating a big tub of water on top of the woodstove. "Would you cut my hair?" she asked Reed as they came inside. "This burnt stuff stinks."

"Sure," he said, startled. "I'll do my best."

Zan turned to Earley. "Do you have a pair of sharp scissors?"

"Damn straight," Earley said. He stretched over Zan's head and took his tackle box down from the ceiling rack. He set it onto the table and opened the lid. Reed surveyed the twin trays of lures: spin'n'glos, hoochies and spoons, an assortment of flies. He touched a concoction of red thread and duck down.

"Did you tie these yourself?"

Earley shrugged. "It's a long, boring winter." He lifted his copy of *Dot's Tide Guide* (*Bigger the Dot, Better the Fishing*) and took out a few pairs of scissors, fanning them out. "Choose your weapon."

Reed picked a long pair of needlenose shears. Earley opened them, checking the edge with his thumb, and sat down with a whetstone and chamois. "They're already sharp," he said, feeling the urge to defend his tools, "but a new edge cuts best."

He and Reed hauled the washtub outside, sloshing the front of their jeans with hot water. Zan sat on a stump round, gazing at Earley as Reed draped a motel towel over her shoulders. That wicked half-smile of hers made him feel naked all over again.

Reed dipped a tin pitcher into the tub, slowly pouring the warm water over Zan's head. He squeezed some shampoo on the palm of his hand and massaged it into her scalp, drawing her hair up into a froth of white lather. Earley was struck by how different she looked without her familiar mane. Her eyebrows were bristling and black, and her neck looked surprisingly powerful, supple and arched like the throat of a deer.

Zan closed her eyes, leaning back into Reed's caress. Earley felt a hot stab of envy. He wanted to bury his hands in that lather, to make Zan his own. He had a brief, vivid image of Reed flying over the edge of that ravine and landing spread-eagled on those jagged rocks. I could have, he thought. We were standing right there.

Earley headed back into the bus and busied himself with the woodstove. This was no way to be thinking. Reed was his buddy, his partner. He followed Zan all the way up here from Frisco, Earley reminded himself, scraping grease off the griddle; he ought to be throwing *me* over a cliff. How could he lie there last night with his back turned and just let it happen?

He looked back out the window as Reed bent down, scooping his pitcher back into the washtub. The sun caught the flow of the sparkling water as he poured it tenderly over Zan's head. Earley imagined himself in Reed's place. Go on, *kiss* her, you moron, he thought, and just at that moment Zan arched her head up to give Reed a kiss. Reed dropped the pitcher and straddled her, thrusting his tongue in her mouth.

Earley took a step backwards and knocked over Reed's drying book. He cursed, then crouched down on his haunches to pick it up. *Love Sonnets of Pablo Neruda*. The pages were still

soaked and starting to ripple in front of the heat. Earley hung
it up over the clothesline, between pairs of holey wool socks.
He didn't know what else to do with himself, so he took down
the rest of the laundry and put it away. He refilled and trimmed
all the lamps, replacing the one Zan had broken, and opened
the windows to air the place out. He couldn't resist looking out
at the stump. Reed was standing behind Zan, snipping away at
the fringe of her hair as if nothing had happened. Earley
picked up the canvas sling and went out to the woodpile to
refill the kindling bin.

Reed stepped back and looked at him. "Does this look
straight?"

"Please say yes," Zan said without turning her head.

Earley looked. "It's a mite bit shorter on this side." Reed
snipped again and he nodded. "That's good."

"All done," said Reed.

Zan slid the damp towel off of her shoulders, shaking off
stray clumps of hair. "Do you have a mirror?"

"There's one on the truck," Earley said. He couldn't help
noticing how wet the front of her T-shirt was. Zan walked over
and bent to look into the side mirror.

"Christ," she said, "I look like Arlo Guthrie."

Not with those tits, Earley thought, remembering the way
they'd swelled under his fingers. He imagined himself peeling
off that wet T-shirt and taking Zan right on the ground, in the
moss and pine needles. He wanted to see her body in daylight,

to map every cranny and curve of her skin. He wanted to taste her, to lose himself in her saltwater essence, to make love for hours. Instead he said, "You look nice."

They went back inside. Reed handed over the scissors and Earley put them back in the tackle box. Zan picked up *Dot's Tide Guide* and thumbed through its pages. "What day is today?"

"Saturday," Reed answered.

"I meant the date."

Reed looked at Earley, who didn't have much of a clue. He never kept close track of time; weather made more of a difference in his life than numbers and dates. Fridays in Forks were his one indicator of where in the week he was, and more than once he'd rolled into the Cedar on the wrong night. "First weekend in April, I guess. Just after the equinox. Could be a hell of a spring tide. What does it look like?"

Zan ran her thumb down the chart. "Big dot. The biggest."

Earley looked over her shoulder. "No shit. There's a minus tide at 3:20 this afternoon. Want to roll out to the beach and dig geoducks?"

"Hell yes," said Reed. "What are geoducks?"

"Clams," Earley said. "Major clams. The giant sequoia of clamdom."

"I make a mean chowdah," said Reed.

"We catch one of these puppies, and you've got a pot full. They weigh about ten pounds apiece. And they dig really deep, so there's just about three tides a year you can go for them."

"Excellent!"

"I've never been to the beach up here," Zan said.

"Well, you've got a date," said Earley.

"Two dates," said Reed.

Zan looked from one to the other, then grinned. "Lucky me."

That was as close as they came to discussing it. Earley didn't know how, when or why, but it seemed Reed and Zan had agreed he was part of their couple, a "we" of three people. The idea that he could make love to Zan without losing his friendship with Reed seemed too good to be true, but he wasn't complaining. The three of them got in his pickup and headed due west, towards the ocean.

THIRTEEN

Earley drove towards La Push. Kalaloch and Ruby Beach were closer, but their surf was too rugged for bay-dwelling geoducks. There was a sandspit not far from Rialto Beach that ought to be perfect, and if they struck out, they could walk straight across it and dig razor clams in the breakers. Either way, they'd wind up with a good pot of chowder. Earley had turned up three shovels of varying sizes and outfitted Reed with a scarred pair of gumboots. Zan would have to make do with industrial Hefty bags over her work boots, duct-taped onto her jeans to stay up.

As soon as they got down the mountain, Reed flipped on the radio; he'd memorized just where the static zone ended. The college station from Olympia was playing the Allman Brothers. "Lord, I was born a ramblin' man. Tryin' to make a living and doing the best I can . . ."

Reed whooped and cranked the volume. "It's the Shake-rat National Anthem!" They all sang along at the top of their lungs. Zan sat in the center, her right arm draped around Reed. She leaned her head against Earley's shoulder, and a spurt of irrational joy surged through his veins like a drug rush. It was all he could do to keep steering.

How in the world had he gone from the way that he'd felt at the Cedar last night, lower than shoe leather, to this bliss in a few short hours? It wasn't just sex, although that had been pretty ecstatic; he'd had good sex with Margie, and still felt alone in the world. What buoyed him now was a sense of belonging, a feeling of being a part of some larger design. Earley didn't know how to define it and he didn't care. It was enough just to be in this truck, bombing down the coast road with the wind pouring in through the wide-open windows, Zan's cheek pressed against his warm shoulder and Reed, rocking back and forth, drumming on the truck's door as he hollered about being born in the back of a Greyhound bus. This is as good as it gets, Earley thought. This is what I've been missing.

There was no traffic on the approach road. In the summer, it would have been full of families and old folks in Winnebagos, driving out to pose photos in front of the seastacks. But all they passed now was a family of Quileute Indians packed into a sagging Chevette. Reed waved and they looked at him like he was crazy.

They crested a ridge and caught their first view of an endless horizon. Reed yodeled and whooped. He grabbed hold of the roof and stood up through the window, his whole torso cantilevered out over the road. Earley leaned over Zan and grabbed him by the waistband. "That door's gonna fall off, you moron!"

"Who needs fuckin' doors?" Reed hollered. "We've got us an ocean!" He leaned out farther over the gravel. Zan grabbed hold of his legs, helping Earley to haul him back into the seat. Reed thumped back down into her lap, slamming against Earley's arm. Earley swerved wildly and came to a long, screeching stop in the oncoming lane. The air smelled like burnt oil and brake fluid.

Reed grinned like a madman, his face flushed from wind and adrenaline. "You must've left your damn brain where the Lord lost his shoes," Earley drawled, and the others cracked up. Zan kissed the back of Reed's neck and turned towards Earley, opening her mouth to his.

They heard the breakers before they could see them. A jumble of driftlogs was heaped at the edge of the parking lot. Seagulls and arctic terns flapped and squawked overhead, and the wind smelled like seaweed. Earley pulled on his waders and turned towards Zan, who was eyeing the black plastic bags with distrust.

"Are you sure these'll work?"

"So long as they don't fall down." Earley picked up his thick roll of duct tape as Zan slid one leg into a bag. Then he knelt at her feet and gathered the plastic around her leg, unrolling a spiral of tape as he worked his way upwards. Her thighs were strong, muscled and meaty like haunches.

"I think you should know I'm enjoying this." Zan's voice sounded throaty.

"You and me both," he said, rolling the tape between her upper thighs, where the denim was worn thin as tissue. Reed came around the side of the truck, wearing Earley's big boots. He watched for a moment, suppressing a frown, then reached into the back for the buckets and shovels.

When Zan's legs were both wrapped, they set off for the beach. Earley dropped back to let Reed walk beside her. He was feeling this out step by step; taking turns seemed the right thing to do. As they crested the tangle of weather-bleached logs, the sound of the breakers got suddenly louder.

There it was: the Pacific. A couple of steep, jagged seastacks loomed up from the shallows. Reed stopped in his tracks and said, "Whoa."

Earley could second that emotion. He hadn't grown up around ocean—the Atlantic was less than an hour from his door, but he'd seen it just once, on a drunken joyride halfway through high school—and he still got a feeling of awe every time he looked out at that massive expanse. It made him feel puny and grand all at once, the same way he felt when he looked at the Milky Way, or Mount Olympus. Reverent. That was the word for it. Something that he'd never felt in a church, not in all those years he'd been dragged by his mother, who hated it too, or his Gramma Mulvaney, who'd swayed with the Power and spoken in tongues.

"Like a Chinese painting," said Reed, gazing out at the mist-shrouded seastacks, and Earley realized where he'd first seen those improbably vertical, tree-capped silhouettes: on the wall of the Happy Panda in Waycross.

The tide was way out, exposing a long strand of pebbly, dark sand. There were a couple of clamdiggers way down the beach, at the waterline. Reed started towards them, but Earley shook his head. "They're digging for razors," he said. "We're after the big game." He nodded his head towards the wide, brackish bay where a flatwater creek emptied into the ocean.

"What are these mega-clams called again?"

Earley sounded it out for him. "Gooey-ducks. And if you think the *name* is weird, wait till you see them."

The beach was rough going. They clambered over driftlogs and boulders with highwater stripes of popweed and barna-cles. The packed sand was littered with crab shells and waxy, wrist-thick whips of bull kelp. Gulls dropped shells onto rocks and dove after them, wheeling and shrieking and stealing each other's meat. Earley carried his poacher's spade over one shoulder, with a bucket dangling down like a hobo's bindle. Reed did the same with his long-handled shovel. Zan lagged a little, shifting her camp spade from hand to hand and complaining the bags on her feet were too slippery. Earley offered his arm, but she shrugged him off. "I'm not Rapunzel."

They reached the bay side at last. Earley walked along the wet muck at the edge of the tide flat, patient and slow as a heron. "What are you looking for?" Reed asked.

"The right place to dig."

"Well, I know *that*. How will you know when it's—"

He broke off midsentence as Earley waded into a thicket of eelgrass and bent down to pick up a white, empty shell, twice the size of his hand.

"Holy shit!" said Reed.

Earley smiled. "That's nothing," he said, handing over the shell. "Picture this with a fourteen-inch neck sticking out."

"No way," said Zan.

"Seeing is believing," said Earley.

They fanned out and searched through the eelgrass for telltale pocks in the sand. "Is this one?" Zan asked. Earley shook his head.

"Bigger." He found one himself and began to dig.

The other two followed suit. Zan bent down over a likely pock, scrabbling away with her camp spade. "Wish I had my hoedad," she said. "I could *move* this crap."

Reed swung his shovel up, strumming it like a guitar. "If I had a hoedad, I'd hoe it in the mo-or-ning . . ."

"Very funny," she said, flipping up more wet sand.

Reed put down his shovel and started to dig again. "How far down do we go?"

"Two, three feet," Earley answered. His own hole was that deep already, with no sign of clams. He moved to a new spot and started again. So did Reed, and then Zan. They dug till their arms got tired, moving crabwise along the spit, leaving a long chain of empty holes. Zan put her shovel down first.

"This is like treeplanting, minus the trees."

"Clamdigging minus the clams," said Reed.

"They're down there," said Earley.

"Yeah, right," said Reed. "This is some P.T. Barnum–style hoax of yours, Earley. We're digging for Bigfoot."

"You know what they say about big feet," said Zan, stretching out on a log. "Wake me up if you find any fourteen-inch necks."

Earley was irritated, not so much at their jokes, but the two of them ganging up. He kept right on digging. "Give up if you want," he said. "I'm eating chowder tonight."

"Do they sell cups at the Cedar Bar Lounge?" said Reed.

Earley dug faster. The sand under his shovel had spurted. "I'm on one," he said. Water refilled the hole as he scooped out the heavy wet sand. He could see the black neck tip, the wrinkled tan meat. He jammed the blade of his poachers spade down alongside it and rocked on the handle hard, heaving the geoduck upwards. Then he grabbed the thick shell in both hands and turned to face Zan and Reed, hefting it up to his crotch. The neck dangled down like a porn star's cock.

"Jesus Christ," said Reed, staring.

Zan cracked up. "It's bigger than yours!"

Earley waggled the clam back and forth so the neck swayed and bounced. "It's not the meat," he said, "it's the motion of the ocean." He added a bump and grind. "Who wants to touch it?"

"I'm getting my own," said Reed, fetching his shovel.

"Me too," said Zan.

The temptation to say "I told you so" was overwhelming, but Earley resisted. He scooped up a bucket of seawater and set his clam in it to rinse off the sand. All three of them dug for another half hour without turning up any more geoducks. The sun had dipped low in the sky and the tide was beginning to come back in. Earley suggested they move to the surf and dig razors. "They taste better anyway."

"You go," said Reed. "I'm going to get one of these suckers."

Earley looked over at Zan. "I could do surf," she said, meeting his eyes. This was just what he'd hoped for: finally, a chance to be with her alone. He nodded, feeling the roof of his mouth go dry.

"Meet us back at the truck before dark," she told Reed, and kissed him. Earley picked up his bucket and both of their shovels. They set off across the spit, casting long shadows over the pebble-strewn sand. Zan walked fast, trying to put some distance between them and Reed, Earley figured, or hoped. He wondered what she must be thinking right now. Women mystified him at the simplest of times, and nothing about this was simple. He slung his spade up on one shoulder and loped after Zan, grateful that she wasn't asking for small talk.

The sun was red-orange and the clouds were beginning to glow from behind. A couple of shearwaters skittered over the wave tips, veering around the tall seastacks. The gray waves licked at their tide stripes. The wind off the ocean picked up and Zan shivered, wrapping her jacket tighter around herself. Earley would have offered his wool shirt, but he didn't want to be told that she wasn't Snow White. Southern girls went for that gentleman stuff, but Zan was a different breed. It wasn't some Women's Lib thing she was trying out, either. The need to prove that she could fend for herself ran much deeper than that; it was fierce and defiant, and made Earley long to protect her. An instinct he'd have to suppress, or she'd kick his butt.

Where had she come from, this woman who walked just ahead of him, keeping a maddening distance? She seemed to skim over the sand dunes, while Earley sank deeper with every step. He wanted to close up the distance between them, to learn all her secrets and tell her his own. The strength of his longing amazed him. He didn't know where to begin.

"There's a fishing boat out there," he said, squinting at the horizon. Against the bright disc of the sun, he could make out the dark silhouette of a gillnet rig between the red running lights. "He's heading for harbor, see? Red right returning."

"What do you think he's returning to?"

"Dinner," said Earley.

Zan punched him. "I'm serious."

"So am I. Fishermen eat." Zan's brows knit together. She

wants me to say something more, Earley thought, and it's not about fishing boats. Maybe she's hoping that I'll be the first one to talk about us. The realization touched him and frightened him: Zan wasn't as confident as she gave out. She was edging alongside the subject, wondering, as Earley was, where they would go from here. He stared at the gillnetter, hoping the right words would come to him.

Zan followed his gaze. "Think he lives by himself?"

"Not if he can help it," said Earley. "Most people don't."

"You do." She looked up at his face. "Can you help it?"

Earley squirmed, digging the toes of his boots into sand. "I'm not good at people," he mumbled. "Anyway, I don't live by myself anymore."

"I noticed," said Zan. She threaded her fingers through his, and the warmth of her skin on his made Earley's heart pound. They were standing alongside a tide pool, a miniature world ringed with mussels, anemones, barnacles. A wine-red starfish was clinging to one of the boulders. Its shape was so perfect it looked artificial.

Zan took a deep breath, like a diver about to plunge over a cliff. "I couldn't wait one minute longer," she said. Earley looked at her, suddenly thick-tongued. She lifted her hand to the scar in his beard, and he noticed her fingers were trembling.

"Since the moment I saw you," she whispered. "That night in the bar."

"Me too," Earley said.

"I mean, I don't believe in fate and that garbage, but if I did . . ."

"I'm about to believe in all sorts of stuff I don't believe in," said Earley. He put his hands on Zan's hips, drawing her closer. "Do you give a damn about razor clams?"

Zan shook her head. "But I do give a damn about Reed," she said. "You can't even imagine how much he means to me, Earley. He's one in a million. We can't shut him out."

"I won't," Earley promised. And lifted her right off her feet.

FOURTEEN

"How do you *clean* these things?" Reed stared down at the two geoducks on the sideboard. "This is a Freudian nightmare."

"Slit the skin off the necks and mince them," said Earley, secretly pleased that Reed's geoduck wasn't as big as his.

Reed picked up the knife. "I may vomit."

"You want me to do it?" Zan asked.

"No," said both men at once. She looked affronted.

Reed laughed. "It's a guy thing."

"You got that right, lil' dude," Earley grinned at him.

"Pardon me while I put on my mascara," said Zan.

"Put on Otis Redding," said Earley. "These clams could try a little tenderness."

"So could I," said Zan. She grabbed a beer and walked back to the tape deck.

Earley and Reed exchanged mystified looks. Earley shrugged and Reed picked up his knife. "The first of the geoduck martyrs," he said.

Earley turned towards his room. Should I follow her back there? he wondered. Zan seemed to need soothing for something, though he was hard-pressed to say what. He thought of her kneeling on his bed, sorting through his shoebox of tapes, and the thought of her touching these bits of his history made his heart swell. "Since the moment I saw you," she'd said on the beach, and he realized she hadn't finished that sentence. Since the moment she'd seen him she'd . . . what? Been in love with him? Wanted to fuck him? Or neither; she might have meant something else altogether. Whatever she'd meant, she was on his bed, and if Reed wasn't standing right there with a knife in his hand, he would have gone back in a heartbeat and laid her across it.

All the way home he'd been wondering where Zan would sleep tonight—if she decided to stay, he reminded himself; she'd already missed one day of work. Reed had no mattress, though he'd muttered something about making do with the couch cushions till he could pick one up. Earley's bed was the logical place, but he knew something other than logic would make this decision, and that he could blow it by acting too eager. He'd just have to bide his time, see how the tide ran.

Earley turned over a geoduck shell in his hands. Ten-pound clams, oldgrowth cedars with trunks thick as silos, twenty-foot seaweed: no wonder he liked the Pacific Northwest. Everything here was outsized. Earley's big body was in perfect scale with this landscape; he fit. His bus, on the other hand, felt close and cramped with three people inside it. He could feel every movement the other two made: Zan flipping open the tape deck, Reed's hand rocking a cleaver over the clam necks.

"Want me to chop onions?" Earley asked, moving closer. Reed gave him a knife as Zan turned on "Pain in My Heart."

"That was some wicked good chowdah," Reed said in his best Kennedy accent, as he leaned back and rolled a cold beer bottle over his forehead. The woodstove had fogged up the windows, and he had stripped down to his T-shirt to cook. Earley noticed that Reed's arms were starting to look a bit ropier, though still pretty scrawny for someone who split wood all day.

"Have thirds," he told Reed. "We've got gallons."

"I'm done. How about you, Zan? More geoduck soup?"

Zan shook her head. The tape deck in Earley's room flipped over again, and she pushed back her chair. "That's enough Mr. Pitiful."

"Change it," said Reed. "Earley's got other tapes. At least four of them."

"Fuck you, I've got ten at *least*."

"Black Sabbath does not count as music. Neither does Aqualung."

"Fascist," said Earley. "You just don't appreciate metal."

"I'd rather listen to you play the chainsaw," said Reed, tipping back his beer. Zan came back from Earley's room with the guitar.

"Play something," she said to Reed, holding it out.

"I don't really feel like it."

"Play something bad," Earley said.

Reed reached back and flopped the guitar in his lap. Without stopping to tune it, he strummed a few loud minor chords. "There is . . . a HOUSE . . . in New Orleans . . ."

"Dig it," said Earley, and joined him. "They CAAAAALLL the Rising SUNNN!"

"You sound like a pair of coyotes," said Zan.

Earley threw back his head and howled as Reed kept on singing, "It's been the ruin of many a poor boy . . ."

". . . and GAWD, I kno-ow I'm one." Earley's voice rose in a falsetto whoop, as Reed slammed a last chord. They both cracked up. Reed slapped Earley five.

"Listen to you, big man, you're a regular John Fogerty."

"I can shatter an eardrum," said Earley.

"You got the *gift*, man. Bred in the bone."

"It's that Southern thang," Earley drawled. "All that hog-callin' out thar in the cotton fields."

"All that poon in the cotton fields."

"That too, lil' dude." They slapped five again, laughing. Earley reached for his bottle and noticed that Zan's smile looked pasted on.

"How do you get any work done?" she asked, and he realized she felt left out.

"We shut up," Earley said. "No singing in the clearcut."

"That's right," said Reed. "Deadly serious. Men at work." He played a quicksilver run of notes, then stopped abruptly and wiggled his fingers in the air.

"Stiff," he said.

"That makes two of us," Earley said, running his hand down Zan's arm. She shook her head.

"Save it." She picked up the chowder bowls.

"Leave those," said Reed. "I'll wash them tomorrow."

"I'm just getting rid of the live stuff." Zan banged the bowls down on the counter.

She's pissed about something, thought Earley, wondering why she'd rebuffed him. Was she upset that he'd hit on her in front of Reed? Or she just didn't dig Eric Burdon? Whatever the problem, he'd better make nice or she'd walk out that door.

"The live stuff?" he echoed.

"That's what Lester, the cook at my first greasy spoon, used to say."

"Where was this?" Earley asked, gazing at her in rapt fascination. It wasn't that much of an act; he wanted to hear every detail Zan offered about her life.

She paused for a moment, as if she wasn't sure that she wanted to answer. Her eyes glinted with something that could have been pain. "Sweetwater, Texas."

"You *have* hit the hot spots."

"The army can pick 'em. I sat out Saigon, though."

"How'd you manage that?" Earley was drinking this up.

"I left home. My folks went to Vietnam, I went to Baja." Zan slammed a lid onto a pot full of leftover salad and stuffed it into the cooler. "Hitched a ride on the back of a draft-dodger's Harley. I turned sixteen in Cabo San Lucas."

"I didn't know that," said Reed, with an edge in his voice. He sounded resentful that Earley had gotten her talking so easily.

"Sixteen in Mexico. What did you do about money?"

"I lived," said Zan. She picked up Reed's beer bottle, draining the dregs. Earley waited for her to say more, but she didn't.

"Hard times," he said softly. Zan shrugged.

"It was better than 'Nam." She looked at Earley. "How'd you get out of the draft? Reed lucked out with his lottery number."

"327," said Reed.

"4-F," said Earley.

"4-F?" Zan looked incredulous. "*You?*"

"Too tall," Earley mumbled. It still made his ears burn; his kid brother had come home with medals, and he'd been turned down. True, Earley had tried to sneak in underage, but the part that still stung was the sergeant who'd sneered at his gangling limbs and told him to go home. "And skinny. I looked like a lamppost."

"Not anymore," said Zan, eyeing his biceps.

"A decade of moose work'll do that," said Earley. "I'm not a teenager."

"Neither am I," said Zan. She stood between him and Reed, setting a hand on each of their shoulders, as if she were completing a circuit. "I'd better get rolling."

Reed looked devastated. "You're not going to stay?"

"Can't afford to get fired." She stroked both their shoulders. "So who's going to kiss me goodnight?"

Reed darted a quick glance at Earley, then got to his feet and pulled Zan into an open-mouthed kiss, mashing his pelvis against hers.

The heat rose in Earley's throat. He stood, looming over them both. Zan twisted towards him and met his kiss hungrily, rising up onto her toes. She drew them both into a three-way embrace. Earley could feel her warm breath at the base of his neck, and Reed's on his shoulder.

"Next weekend," she whispered. And left.

FIFTEEN

They woke to the sounds of fierce growling, a loud crash of metal on metal. Earley was out of bed instantly. "What is it?" said Reed, sitting up on the couch.

Earley reached up to a rack in the roof of the bus and pulled down his rifle. "Where'd you put all that clam trash?"

"Out back, in the compost," said Reed, his eyes wide in the moonlight.

"We've got us a bear." Earley jammed in a cartridge and went outside, feeling his nuts shrivel in the cold air. There wasn't much light, but he could sense movement behind the shed, in the grove of young hemlocks where he and Reed dumped their perishables. He raised the gun to his shoulder, cocked it and shot.

The sound echoed off distant cliffs, seeming to hang in the air. He could feel the sharp tang of gunpowder inside his nostrils and throat, and he heard heavy thrashing and footfalls through underbrush. He stood frozen a moment until the sounds stilled, then shivered. He went back in, ducking his head.

"Did you get it?" Reed asked.

Earley shook his head, holding his rifle in front of him like a militiaman. "Shot at the sky. I just don't want her coming back night after night."

"What makes you so sure it's a she?"

"I'm not. Could have been a young male."

Reed was staring at him. His eyes moved to the rifle in Earley's hands. "Why do you have that?" he asked. "Do you hunt?"

"Every now and again," Earley said, hoping Reed wasn't about to go off on some East Coast liberal tear. "When I'm hungry and broke." He didn't mention shooting Dean's toaster oven. Reed was standing as still as a tree, and Earley suddenly felt very naked. He put the gun into its rack and turned to go back to his bedroom. The shadows of branches and moonlight played over Reed's body, highlighting the bulge in his underwear. Earley swallowed and edged past him, feeling uncomfortable.

"Go back to sleep," he said.

. . .

Reed spent the rest of the night on the couch and woke up complaining that his back hurt. Welcome to my world, thought Earley, who'd had a backache for a decade, no matter what surface he slept on. He couldn't help thinking Reed's whining was bogus. And even if Reed was such a wuss that his back hurt from spending one night on a couch, was this really about that, or did he just want a new mattress so he could screw Zan with some semblance of privacy? Just thinking about it pissed Earley off.

After she'd left them last night, he and Reed had gone through the usual motions of evening chores—scraping the dishes, discarding the compost, throwing logs into the woodstove and damping down its chimney—but they'd both been wired pretty tight. The bus was so silent that when a fir bough unburdened a fresh load of rain on the roof, they both jumped. Earley was hyperaware of how close Reed was standing, and kept shifting around in the bus's cramped spaces to keep a slight distance between their two bodies. He still found it hard to believe that they'd shared the same woman and slept side by side, but he couldn't see any advantage to talking about it. Way he saw it, he'd finally gotten Zan into bed, and the one thing that mattered was getting to do that again and again. If Reed wasn't trying to punch him out, so much the better; it spared him from having to flatten the guy.

Earley had never liked getting in fights. He was big enough and strong enough to break someone's head without even trying, and the bloodlust and gloat that boiled up inside him when he started to punch freaked him out; he could feel himself turning into his old man. Though he had to admit he'd enjoyed slamming Dean in the face when the time was right. He wondered if Dean's lip had healed. Dean was probably too cheap to go to the ER for stitches, so he might be walking around with a souvenir for the rest of his life, his mouth curled into the permanent sneer of his parting shot, "Loser."

Takes one to know one, thought Earley. Dean had loserdom written all over him. He was younger than Earley, just turned twenty-five, but you could already tell he was going to wind up as one of those red-faced, loud middle-aged men at the Shamrock, with a couple divorces under his belt and a gut swelling over it, cursing women for having his number. How could I ever have hired him? Earley wondered. I must have been desperate.

He glanced over at Reed, who was reading a week-old newspaper, frowning at headlines about the Khmer Rouge and the oil crisis. Different species, thought Earley. He tried to imagine what Reed would be like twenty years from now, and couldn't come up with a picture. He wouldn't be cutting up stumps in the woods, that's for damn sure, or living in some cast-off schoolbus. Sooner or later, he'd come into money; this hardscrabble life was just something to play at, a working-class hat to try on in front of a gilt-edged mirror. Fortunate Son, Earley thought, and the words of the chorus drilled into his head: *It*

ain't me, it ain't me, I ain't no fortunate one. He thought of himself twenty years down the road. Christ, he'd be practically
fifty. Hard to imagine that he'd still be living like this, and
equally hard to imagine he wouldn't. The usual trappings of
fifty—a wife, couple kids, a home with a yard—seemed like
somebody else's life. Probably wind up a few barstools from
Dean, he thought. Losers Anonymous.

He wondered if Zan thought he was a loser. No way, he
decided. She'd wept in his arms as she came. She made love to
me first, he reminded himself, and made Reed wait for seconds. Not only that, but she grabbed my hand on the beach
and told me that she'd been in love since the moment she saw
me. Earley was sure that was what Zan had meant. Granted,
she might not have used the word "love," but what else could
have led to "We can't cut out Reed"? I'm in, he thought, looking at Reed again. I'm in solid, and your days are numbered.
Maybe Reed already realized where they were heading, and
that's why he hadn't protested when Zan made her move. It
was share her or lose her, and Reed had shut up and accepted
his fate. Look at him sitting there reading, thought Earley. He
knows.

"I'm going to bed," he said, peeling off his undershirt. Reed
looked up from his paper, his pale face haloed by lamplight.
He seemed to be trying to think of the right thing to say. After
a moment he gave up and looked back down, biting his lip as
he turned the page.

. . .

"Can I borrow the truck?" Reed asked after work the next day.

This was a first. "What for?"

"I want to go check out that Salvation Army. My back is a mess."

Whiner, thought Earley. He scooped up Reed's mallet and froe in one hand, slung them over his shoulder and picked up his chainsaw. "I'll go with you. We can score some new groceries while we're in town. I can't deal with chowder all week."

Reed didn't look pleased, but he nodded. I bet he was planning to sneak up to Zan's, Earley thought, feeling smug that he'd headed that off at the pass. They bumped down the hill side by side in the truck. As soon as they got within range of the highway, Reed snapped on the radio, grumbling his way down the dial as they gunned towards Forks. "'I Honestly Love You.' 'The Way We Were.' Why is this schlock on FM?"

"Turn it off, then," growled Earley, but Reed didn't let up.

"This is what people are paying to hear while this country collapses around our ears. 'The Hustle.' I mean, shit, why *not* live in the woods?"

Earley said nothing. He stubbed out his Drum roll and reached for the dial, just as Reed landed on the Olympia station. "Friend of the Devil" was playing.

Reed whooped and bounced out of his seat. "Stop the truck."

"What?" Earley stared at him.

"Pull over! Now!"

Earley did. Reed jumped onto the shoulder while the truck was still moving and knelt at full length, touching his forehead to the ground like a supplicant. "Grisman!" he yodeled. A log truck roared past with a huge blast of wind and an indignant blare on the air horn. Reed leapt up and hurled himself into the jetstream, dancing across the white line as the taillights swooped past. "DAWG IS GOD!" he yelled, waving both hands.

Earley stepped on the gas pedal, revving the engine. "You're out of your gourd."

"So's everybody worth knowing." Reed beamed as he got back in, cranking the volume. "Listen to that mandolin. That is some tasty picking."

Earley didn't bother to tell him that he had no clue which set of twangs was the mandolin. "Shut the damn door," he said. Reed swung it closed, looping a bungee cord over the handle and threading its hook through the broken hinge.

"Fixed it," he smiled. "Did you notice?"

The air in the Salvation Army smelled of mildew, detergent and Pine-Sol. Earley and Reed walked past racks full of kids' jackets and wilted shoes to the back of the store, where the furniture was. There was only one mattress, a double with yellowing stains and frayed edges. Reed frowned. "This looks like somebody died of TB on it."

"Maybe they did. It's probably been sterilized."

"Pass," said Reed. "Is there anyplace else?"

"Sure," Earley said, "in Seattle, Port Angeles, Sequim . . ."

Reed nodded. "I can make do on the floor."

Earley wondered if Zan could. He certainly hoped not. "Let's check out the dishes," he said, stomping towards Housewares. "We need some fine china."

There were more choices here. Reed picked up one plate of turquoise Formica and a second of dark brown ceramic with bright yellow flowers. "Wedgwood or Havilland?" he asked.

"Door Number Two," said Earley. "That first number looks like it fell off the roof of a HoJo's."

They went to the counter with three of the brown flowered plates. "These are part of a set," said the thin, dour woman who worked there. "You can't break up sets."

"We only need three," Earley said.

"It's a set of eight plates."

"We don't know eight people," said Reed. "Besides, how do you know there isn't some family of five out there somewhere who doesn't want *these* three?"

"I won't break a set," said the woman, her nostrils pinched.

"Oh come on, live a little," said Reed, leaning forward.

"Forget it," said Earley. "Who cares about plates?"

"I do," said Reed. "I care about everything." He turned back to the woman at the counter. "Do you take donations?"

She looked suspicious. "Why?"

"I'll take the set." Reed went back and returned with the

other five plates, setting them onto the counter. The woman
punched register buttons, glad to be rid of them.

"That'll be six dollars and forty-four cents."

"Thank you," said Reed. He gave her the money, handed
three of the plates to Earley and turned to go.

"What about these?" the woman demanded, pointing at the
other five plates.

"Donation," said Reed. "Take it off of my taxes."

"You don't actually *pay* taxes, do you?" asked Earley as they
drove to the store.

"Good question," said Reed.

"'Cause we're way off the books. Gillies' mill is cash only,
and not much of that. Unless you've got some trust fund back
home to report."

Reed looked out the window. Bull's-eye. What the fuck was
he doing here anyway, breaking his balls in the rain for a couple of nickels, when he had a stretch limo parked at the curb?
He claimed he'd come up to Forks looking for Zan, but he
hadn't done much about staying with her when he found her—
if Earley hadn't just happened to need a new splitter, Reed
would have been off to Alaska that same afternoon, with his
thumb in the air like a tramp. What the hell was his problem?
Spoiled brat, Earley thought, doesn't know when he's got it
good. Well, at least he can pay for the groceries.

"What did you say your old man does for bucks?" Earley

knew he was picking a scab, but he couldn't resist. Reed glared at him.

"What do you care?"

"Is it a secret?"

"Of course not, it just doesn't make any difference," said Reed. "He's a judge. Ran for Congress last year and lost."

Congress, for Christ's sake. "You vote for him?"

"He's a Republican," Reed said dismissively. "What does your father do?"

"Works at a paper mill. If he's still breathing."

"Paper?" Reed lifted his eyebrows. "And you cut up trees?"

"It's a living," said Earley. "You cut up trees too, at least *this* week."

Reed stared at him. "This week?"

"Come on, man, you're halfway through college. You're not going to stick with a shit job like this and you know it."

"Are you going to fire me?"

"Why would I do that?" said Earley.

"Got me," said Reed, his voice tight and bitter. He reached for the radio dial.

Earley laid his hand over it. "Leave it off."

Reed opened his mouth to say something, but bit it back. Go on, thought Earley, glancing over at him with those damn flowered plates on his lap, pick a fight with me. Show me what you've got for balls. Last night he'd felt sorry for Reed, been relieved not to get in a mix with the guy. Now he was itching to pop him one. What had Reed done to get under his skin like this? Nothing, he thought; Reed's just being himself. And I want to kill him.

It was going to be like this all week, Earley bet. Both of them knew Zan was coming on Friday, and who she would sleep with was anyone's guess. It was hard to believe they'd all wind up in the same bed again, even if Reed didn't manage to scare up a comfortable mattress. Earley didn't want to share Zan; he wanted her all to himself. Reed knew it, too—that was why he was sulking about getting fired. Watch your back, white boy, thought Earley. I'll pull her right out from under you.

They parked at the FoodMart and did a quick shop. Earley picked up a couple of steaks, breakfast sausage, Coke, bean sprouts, three six-packs. Reed paid with a traveler's check. They stopped at the post office and, at Reed's insistence, the library. When they got back in the truck, Earley clicked on the radio.

Reed looked at him. "I thought you didn't want music."

"I changed my mind." Earley put on a country station. They listened to "Wasted Days and Wasted Nights," then "Daydreams About Night Things."

"It's always the same three chords," said Reed.

"So?"

"So nothing. It's just how it is. That's why you can sing along with a country song you've never heard before."

"How come you quit playing music?" Earley turned his head, looking right at him. Reed's eyes went opaque. Muscles twitched in his jaw.

"Wasn't good enough."

"Sounded damn good to me."

"Maybe I didn't quit. Maybe I'm resting."

"You're fucking your hands up for sure."

"They're my hands." Reed clicked the radio onto a different station.

"What the hell are you doing?"

"I can't take John Denver."

"I like this song."

"Fine," snapped Reed, clicking it back. "He's all yours." He stared out the window, his chin on his fist. Earley turned up the volume. They were approaching the turnoff for Bogachiel campground. Earley could have used a good shower, but he didn't want to get naked with Reed after sharing a bed with the guy. This was all just too strange for a Georgia boy. People were fooling around in all sorts of weird combinations these days, but that wife-swapping Plato's Retreat stuff seemed utterly foreign to Earley, not just kinky but kind of pathetic. If you knew how to do the real deal, if you really made love to a woman, there was no need to be messing with extras. He wondered what his brother Darrell would say if he found out that Earley had been in a three-way. There'd been a pair of ash-blonde twins in the trailer park down by the swamp when they were teenagers, and Darrell and Earley had jerked off to whispered fantasies about fucking them both in the same bed, but Sueleen and Trish were both girls. That was *Playboy* material. Darrell would freak at him sharing his futon with Reed.

Darrell had always had kind of a wild side—he'd ridden a Harley and gone with black hookers—but when he got discharged from 'Nam with two-thirds of his arm, he had married a girl from church, popped out three babies and settled down flat as a board. He thought Earley was nuts. Nuts to leave Waycross, nuts to move north, nuts to live out in the woods like some damn hippie scum. His one visit to Forks had been a disaster, and they'd dropped out of touch, except for a two-year-old Christmas card photo of Darrell's three girls, his name signed in his wife's schoolteacherish writing. I miss him, thought Earley. I miss my brat brother.

He looked back at Reed, who was younger than Darrell by three or four years, but could otherwise pass for a sort of kid brother. Earley had broken him in, taught Reed all he knew about woods work. They'd moved a few tons of raw cedar in all sorts of weather and hung out for long, easy hours, drinking beer, playing music, cracking each other up, fixing dinner together or—this was rarest and best—doing nothing at all, just enjoying the fact that the other was there, without needing to say a damn thing. I don't want to lose that, thought Earley. I want him *and* Zan.

It sounded impossible, but what was the obstacle, really?

Reed wanted the same thing as he did, he'd swear to it. Zan wanted them both. Or did she? Earley had to admit that he didn't have much of a clue what Zan wanted. She was a glorious mystery, like a macaw swooping down on a feeder of sparrows. He couldn't imagine how she had wound up in these rain-soaked woods, breaking her back in anonymous labor, as far off the map as a person could get. It was almost as if she was trying to lose herself. What was she running from, so hard and fast?

Just be grateful, he thought, turning off the main highway and onto the spur that led up to the blue bus. You'll see her on Friday.

SIXTEEN

Earley stood on the dock next to Reed and Zan, watching the Winslow ferry slide into its slip with a backwash of engines. It slammed into the barnacle-crusted wood pilings, which creaked and groaned as if they would collapse.

They were on their way to Seattle to buy Reed a mattress. They could have found one in Sequim or Port Angeles, closer to home, but all three of them liked the idea of taking a road trip. They'd spent Friday night together on Earley's big futon, and as Zan and Reed thrashed and panted beside him—she'd taken Reed first, this time—Earley had decided that letting Reed have his own bed wasn't such a bad thing after all. There wasn't a doubt in his mind now that Zan would continue to sleep with them both, and if Reed had a place to make love to her one on one, well, so would he.

Not that he minded as much as he would have imagined. In fact, Earley had to admit that their lovemaking turned him on. It was like watching a porn flick that stroked all five senses. Even when he closed his eyes, he could hear, smell and practically taste their two bodies mating, could feel the occasional lingering brush of an arm or leg over his skin. By the time Zan was ready for Earley, he felt like an iron bar. He slid in deep and then nearly withdrew, over and over until she was frothing beneath him, willing to go wherever he took her, all his. When he woke after midnight to find Zan curled into his chest, her cheek resting over his heartbeat, with one leg tossed carelessly over Reed's ankles, he knew it for certain: she wanted them both, but she wanted him more. The least he could do for poor Reed was to get him a bed.

The ferryman lowered the ramp, and dozens of people streamed off the ferry. Like chum salmon spawning, thought Earley, feeling his height as the crowd eddied past him. He laid one hand on Zan's shoulders and the other on Reed's. "Let's go," he said. They dashed through the aisles between tam vinyl benches and burst through the doors to the upper deck railing. The Puget Sound fanned out before them, with the rolling green humps of the San Juan Islands off to the north and the high Cascades, crinkled and snow-covered, rising behind.

It was a car ferry, but they were going on foot to save money. They had stashed Earley's truck in the parking lot of the Pentangle Cafe, where they'd chowed down on pitas and listened to three local women playing a jazz brunch. The drummer was black and athletic, the pianist petite with a blonde frizz of hair, and the flutist so pregnant she looked like her water might break any minute. Earley watched her sway, mesmerized. "That takes some guts," said Reed. "Shame she can't play better."

"They sound pretty decent to me." Earley bit off a loose chunk of falafel, licking the hummus that stuck in his beard.

"C minus. The drummer's got half a right hand, and that piano chick owns some Thelonious Monk records. The babe with the belly should go back to her high school marching band," Reed said. "What time is our ferry?"

"We'll make it," said Zan, glancing up at a clock screened by spider plants. "You sure you don't want to drive onto the car deck? What'll we do with the mattress?"

"Carry it on," Earley said. "We can pick it up on our way out of town." He hadn't been to Seattle in a few years, but he thought he remembered a couple of department stores near the ferry dock. No way was he paying to transport his truck, or driving in big-city traffic. The mattress was just an excuse; the point was to have an adventure.

They'd started the day in high spirits, stopping for hot homemade pie in a roadside joint just north of Forks and enjoying the waitress's growing confusion as Zan nuzzled a different partner each time she came over to top off their coffees. They'd sped past the teal green waters of Crescent Lake and stopped for an impromptu skinny-dip in a fern-covered hot spring that Earley knew, just east of Marymere Falls. They were high as three kites, splashing each other and laughing at everything anyone said. Reed climbed up the cliffs and cannonballed right between Earley and Zan, whooping and sending up waves of hot spray. Earley was filled with a spiraling joy he could barely contain. It was rare enough to feel this kind of connection with one other person, but what were the odds against three people being so happy together? Blessed, he thought. We just got blessed.

The ferry was moving away from the dock. It churned past a tidy marina, steaming out into the channel. Earley stared out at the manicured beachfront homes that lined Bainbridge Island, each with its own private dock. The wind whipped through Zan's and Reed's hair as the boat picked up speed. "Keep an eye out for killer whales," Earley said. "They like to swim around ferries."

"We used to whale-watch off the Vineyard," said Reed, watching a sailboat yaw past them. "That sloop needs a spinnaker, big time."

"Hey, Earley," Zan pointed. Two roofers were clambering over the tar-paper roof of a newly built house, nailing up cedar shakes. "You might have cut those."

"I might indeed," Earley said. "Looks like they found a good home." It was a two-story clapboard with classic proportions, a skylight or two and a wraparound deck overlooking the water. The builders had left a nice rim of young hemlocks around the newly seeded lawn. Lawyer with kids, he thought, two-income couple. Gas grill on the deck and a golden retriever. The Normals.

"I'm freezing." Zan shivered. "Let's go inside."

"There's a snack bar." Reed looked up at Earley. "I'll get you both coffee."

Earley shook his head. "I'm fine where I am."

Reed slipped his arm around Zan as they headed inside. Earley heard her laugh at something Reed said and wondered if it was a crack about him. He leaned over the green guardrail, watching the house and its roofers recede. He'd spent half his life cutting wood and he'd never lived in a home that was made of it. There was a cleared site near his bus, overlooking the waterfall, where he dreamed about building a cabin someday. If he ever had someone to build it for. He thought about Robbo, bringing his paycheck back home to his wife and new baby, and wondered if he'd ever have that. Not likely, he thought, not the way things were heading. Margie Walkonis had asked him why he didn't have a girl of his own, and what had he done? Switched from one who was married to one who was sleeping with two guys at once.

Well, fine. Some people sank roots in the ground and some didn't. It wasn't like marriage was such a great thing; take a look at his parents. Earley figured that anything he carved out in this life would be better than what he'd been dealt. At least there was nobody screaming at him every minute or whupping his butt. He'd gotten out. He was his own man. He headed inside and let Reed buy him coffee.

Earley couldn't believe how bizarre the Seattle waterfront seemed to his eyes, like an outpost on some distant planet. Safety-orange monster cranes hunched over shipping containers and tankers. The Space Needle stuck up between glassfront skyscrapers and crisscrossing highways. Cars zipped back and forth on the Alaskan Way Viaduct to a pounding soundtrack of backhoes, jackhammers and diesel roar echoing off the cement. As they followed the crowd off the ferry, alongside the crush of exiting cars, Earley fought back the urge to press both hands over his ears. How could anyone in his right mind live with so much commotion? He reminded himself that he'd lived in Atlanta for years before drifting up north, that this level of din had seemed normal to him. He guessed it was like walking into the Cedar on Friday night after a week in the woods—or like using a chainsaw. You noticed the noise for a while, then you didn't. Some switch in your brain simply turned off, or went into overdrive.

Zan and Reed seemed to have snapped into city mode, walking faster and talking in loud, brassy voices, excited and flirty,

like kids on a date. Earley slouched in their wake, feeling out of
place. "Let's get the bed taken care of and then we can cruise,"
said Reed. "Where are those stores you were talking about?"

Earley couldn't tell one city block from another, but after a
few false starts, they found a department store that sold furniture. They rode an escalator to the third floor, passing rows of
washing machines, gas ranges and vacuums till they found the
beds.

"May I help you?" A trim salesman with a combed mustache
appeared out of nowhere as Reed read a tag. He wore glasses
and spoke with a slight air of challenge, as if the three people
before him looked likely to shoplift a Castro Convertible.

"We want a mattress," said Reed.

"What size?" asked the salesman.

"Double," said Reed at the same time that Earley said, "Twin."
The salesman looked from one to the other.

"You can't fit a double behind that couch," said Earley.

"So let's move the couch."

"To where?"

"Anywhere," Reed said. "I want a double."

"Twin."

"Double," said Zan. "Reed's buying it."

"Fine," Earley said. "He can take it away in his backpack."

"What's that supposed to mean?" Reed demanded.

"It's my bus."

"It's my bed."

"Do you folks need a minute?" the salesman asked.

"No," said Reed. "I want a firm double mattress. Got one that fits in a backpack?"

The salesman's brow wrinkled. "Our camping department might have some inflatables."

"Bingo," said Reed. "I can raft down the Hoh River when Earley gets rid of me."

"Fuck it," said Earley. "Just buy your damn double. We'll fit it in somehow."

"You bet we will." Zan slung her arm around Reed.

Oh, so now I'm in the doghouse, thought Earley. That's great. That's just great. "I'll meet you outside," he growled, turning before Reed could argue. He clumped through the Housewares department and circled around to the down escalator, riding past floors of men's suits and cosmetics. A blonde who was spritzing after-shave samples stepped towards him, smiling, took one look at Earley's expression and stepped back without a word. He stomped past a wall of TV sets, all playing a promo for *Charlie's Angels* with three girls in pantsuits whipping hair over their shoulders as they posed with guns. The electric doors swung open for him, and he went outside, gulping the sour, gritty air like a drowning man.

The front of the store had window displays full of mannequins in prom gowns, shag wigs and pastel tuxedos. Earley slumped on a lamppost and rolled up a smoke. The smell of the traffic was making his head hurt. Why had he thought this was going to be fun? He would have been happy to spend the whole day at that hot spring.

He squinted out at the harbor and wondered why he'd been so pissy with Reed. Especially in front of Zan. He didn't give all that much of a damn how the mattress would fit. The couch was a piece of junk anyway; it could rot in the rain for all Earley cared. It was more about who got to make the decisions. And it *was* his bus. One alpha dog to a pack, he thought. That's how it works.

Zan came out first. "How could you do that to him?" she demanded.

Earley did not feel like hashing this out. "All I said was the bus is too small."

"Yeah, well, maybe it is. Maybe we both ought to leave you alone."

Earley looked at her, stunned. That "we" was a poison dart. With one syllable, Zan had redrawn the lines: two of us, one of you. He stared at his boots. He'd never known how to respond when a woman got on him for being a jerk. Some guys could talk their way out of this stuff; he just sank. I can't work things out with *one* other person, he thought, forget about two. It was simpler to live in the woods by himself and avoid all this crap, stick to what he could handle.

Simpler, but not what he wanted. Earley imagined himself waking up in his bus every morning and eating his own lousy cooking in silence, driving up to the clearcut alone, without

Reed by his side, sinking into bed every night with no dreams about Zan, no chance of them making love ever again. I can't give this up, he thought. No.

He looked over at Zan. She was one of those women who looked even sexier when she was angry, her dark eyes on fire. "I'm sorry," he mumbled.

She softened at once. "This is hard on him, Earley. Reed isn't blind. He's got to know what's going on with us."

There it was again. Us. Only this time, she'd made Earley part of the two, not the one. "*I* don't know what's going on with us," Earley said.

Zan looked as if he had hit her. It was just a split second, but Earley could tell he had touched a raw nerve.

"If you don't know," she said, "then it's not going on. My mistake." She looked out at the harbor, her mouth a straight line. What was she trying to tell him? That she was in love with him too? Then why the hell didn't she come out and speak the words outright, so they could both celebrate? Why was she still hanging on to Reed, taking his part against Earley, insisting that Reed get a mattress with room for two? Earley tried to remember that only a few hours ago he had felt blessed by their threesome. My head's going to burst, he thought. I'm going to splatter my brain cells all over that window of tuxes. I've got to get out of this stinking city.

Reed strode through the electric door, waving a credit card sales slip. "They're open till six," he announced, his voice oddly bright. "We can pick it up on our way home. What's the happening spot in Seattle?"

"Got me," Earley said. "The ride on the ferry is my main event."

"Don't be such a slug. Let's at least prowl around a bit, case the joint. Come on, pick a direction." Zan looked at Earley, then pointed left.

"Cool." Reed took off in that strange, lifting walk of his, without even looking to see if the others would follow. He led them down Yesler Way, towards Pioneer Square. It seemed like a marginal neighborhood, a lot like the ones where Earley had shacked up in Atlanta and Houston when he first left home. He wondered why buses and ferryboats always disgorged you in some part of town that nobody wanted to visit.

A man in a gray trenchcoat stood outside a gated-up dry-cleaners muttering, "*Rolled* smokes, weekend smokes. Pass me by, you won't get high."

"Wanna bet?" said Reed, turning to Earley. Earley grinned, wondering if Reed was holding. I'm probably too paranoid to light up a squiff in the city, he thought, but it surely would help take the edge off. Reed stopped in front of a faded brick building.

"Look at *this*!" The storefront was lettered, in stickers that looked as if they were intended for use on a mailbox, NORTH-WEST BIGFOOT MUSEUM. The window was blocked with tan shelf paper, on which several newspaper clippings were posted, along with the legend, FIND OUT THE TRUTH! ADMISSION $3.00.

"Check it out, World's Largest Collection of Actual Photos and Plaster Casts! This is a must-see. My treat."

You sure can find ways to waste money, thought Earley. "I'll wait outside."

"Me too," said Zan.

"Come *on*, where's your sense of adventure? I want to Find Out the Truth."

"I already know the truth," Earley said. "I want a cigarette."

Reed looked so disappointed that Zan said, "Oh fuck it, let's go."

"What the hell," Earley said, and they followed Reed in.

The man at the counter looked up from his paperback mystery. He had a squared-off salt-and-pepper goatee but no mustache. He looked like an Amish nerd. "Three?" he said, his voice rising as if he could barely believe his good fortune.

"Yes, *sir*," said Reed, counting out nine dollar bills. Earley noticed that they were the only customers. He wondered who paid for the rent on this place.

"Let me know if you have any questions," the man with the goatee was saying.

Reed nodded. "Have you seen him?" he asked in a conspiratorial whisper.

"Never close up," said the man, "but my wife was abducted when we were out camping. She spent forty-eight hours with a Bigfoot clan near Lake Wenatchee."

Uh-huh, Earley thought, they're called bikers. He watched

Reed pore over the "Who Is Sasquatch?" display, a wall full of blurry enlargements of black-and-white photographs. Most of them looked like your basic gorilla suit, obscured by some well-placed underbrush. Zan was standing in front of the "Artist's Rendition of Family Grouping," a primitive painting of several dark, hairy Bigfeet hunkering outside a cave. "It's my tree-planting crew," she said. "Look at Just Nick." Reed hooted and clapped.

"Spitting image," he said, and moved on to a table which featured a man's loafer, a size 19 EEEEE basketball sneaker and an "actual cast" made of plaster of paris.

"This is so extravagantly fraudulent. Look at this thing. It's a swimming flipper with toes. You can practically read the word Speedo."

The man with the goatee was frowning, his brows knit together. Earley had the impression that they were invading his personal Lourdes. The guy was a wacko for sure, but he was a true believer in *something*. Maybe people just wanted to think that they might be related to something bigger than they were, something that hadn't been tamed. "I'm ready to roll," Earley said. "How about you?"

"No way in hell," Reed grinned, gleeful. "I want to find out Why Scientists Haven't Found Bones . . . Yet."

Earley went out for a smoke. It annoyed him that Zan had stayed in the museum with Reed. This triangle thing was a pain in the ass, he reflected. You just couldn't stop keeping score. Earley figured he had the edge in bed; Reed had it everywhere else. Especially here, in the city, where money did most of the talking.

He twisted the ends of his cigarette paper and looked up and down the street. Bleak, like the neighborhoods he'd lived in when he first left home. Narrow alleys and cobblestone streets, winos sleeping on benches. He spotted a neon cross over the Bread of Life mission and shuddered. I'd kill myself first, he thought.

The window next to the Bigfoot Museum belonged to a shoe repair stall, which was closed for the weekend. Earley peered through the glass. The cramped stall was just wide enough for a cobbler's bench, every inch of available space crammed with shelves of old shoes, tins of polish and boot-blacking, stained wooden lasts. In a cage in one corner, a mangy capuchin monkey huddled next to a 40-watt bulb. I'm with you, bub, thought Earley. His feet hurt from walking on concrete. It was hard to believe there was earth somewhere under that pavement, that all this had been oldgrowth woods just a couple of lifetimes ago. Things get used up, he thought. We walk around thinking there'll always be more, but there isn't. He'd heard people talking about this at Gillies' mill, that the woods around Forks were getting logged out; in another few years there'd be nothing to clearcut. A couple of pulp mills had already shut, and timber prices were down in the basement. End of an era, he'd heard people say, boomtown heading for bust.

Earley wondered if he'd have to figure out some other way to support himself sooner or later, and couldn't imagine what that might be. One thing for sure, he thought, lighting a match: he would never move back to a place where his feet didn't touch the earth.

SEVENTEEN

Reed and Zan came out of the Bigfoot Museum arm in arm, laughing. "Well, that was unique," said Reed, grinning. "We've found out the truth. What's next?"

"How about a beer?" said Zan.

"Bingo," said Earley. "A beer and a place to sit."

Reed looked around and then pointed across the street, towards a go-go bar decked out with window-length streamers of tinsel. "How about that place over there with the Totally Nude Live Girls?"

"No," said Zan.

"Oh come on, it'll be a hoot. There won't be any girls in there like you."

"They're exactly like me," Zan said curtly. "I won't give those club owners money." Reed looked at her, chastened. So he hadn't known that about her, thought Earley. He'd guessed it as soon as Zan told him how young she was when she left home. How the hell did Reed figure an underage girl with a C-cup put food on the table? Must not have come up much in Marble-head, Earley figured, trust funds and all that. He wondered how Reed's father would feel about his son and heir dropping out of college to live in the woods with an ex-go-go dancer. And me, he thought. Purebred white trash to your fortunate son.

"I could go for a totally nude live Bigfoot," he said to let out the tension.

Zan punched his arm, grinning. "You *are* a live Bigfoot."

"Should I get totally nude?"

"I dare you."

Earley shrugged and started unbuttoning. "What do I get?"

"Mm," said Zan, flicking her tongue. That was all Earley needed to hear. He dropped his wool shirt on the pavement and started to peel off his undershirt. A couple of businessmen looked at him, startled, and veered to the opposite sidewalk.

"You're going to get busted for streaking," said Reed.

"Would you bail me out?"

"No way in hell."

Earley grinned and reached down to unzip his fly. He eased his jeans down to his hipbones, then paused with his hands on the waist of his briefs, aware of heads craning in passing cars. "I don't think Seattle is ready for my Mount Olympus."

"Coward," Zan smirked.

Earley shrugged and dropped his jeans down to his ankles. The cool air felt good on his skin. He wouldn't have dreamed of exposing himself at, say, the Cedar Bar Lounge, but he didn't know a damn soul in Seattle. There was something delicious about standing here in city traffic and flashing his dick at the skyscrapers.

"Pull up your pants," said Reed. "You'll get arrested." Zan whipped her head around anxiously, scanning the street for police cars.

"Me and Jim Morrison," Earley said, bending to grab his jeans.

"And look at what happened to *him*," said Reed, watching Earley get dressed.

"Let's get out of here." Zan seized his arm. "I need a drink." She looks worried, thought Earley, wondering why; Zan was the one who had dared him to strip, and now she was digging her fingernails into his arm, looking frantic. They ducked down a side street and started to wend their way back up First Avenue. There was nothing but warehouses and a few second-hand stores.

"I don't get it," said Reed. "We would have passed twelve bars by now if we were in Boston. What's wrong with this town?" They were passing a glass-fronted pawnshop with signs hawking prices for guns, tools, kids' bicycles. Reed stopped in front of the window. "That's a Gibson," he said. "Sunburst finish with f-holes."

Earley followed his gaze. It was a teardrop-shaped instrument, smaller than a guitar. "What is that, a mandolin?" he said, guessing; he knew it was one of the things that Reed played.

Reed nodded. "I wonder what poor bastard had to put his axe in hock. If that sounds half as sweet as it looks, it's not one I'd part with unless I was desperate."

"Try it," said Earley.

"Why?"

"Why not?" said Zan. "Want me to dare you?"

Reed shrugged and walked into the pawnshop. A muscle-bound black man with several gold necklaces looked up from his racing form. "Can I see that mandolin in the front window?" Reed asked.

"Point me at it," the pawnbroker said as he lurched towards the window. His back was the size of a fridge, and he had a few bluish tattoos on the backs of his hands. I wouldn't mess with that dude on a bet, Earley thought. I bet he's done time.

"Right next to the SG Ferrari," said Reed. "Um, that bright red electric. " He winced as the pawnbroker grabbed the mandolin by its neck and handed it to him. Reed flipped over the price tag that dangled from one of the tuning pegs, then tested the double strings one at a time. He sat on a $35 desk chair to tune up.

It took a long time. Zan lost interest and started to browse through a rack of used clothes. Earley's eye roved over the weapon case behind the counter. There were some fine-looking hunting knives.

"Look," said Zan, "girl clothes." She was holding a red dress in front of her body, and Earley realized he'd never seen her in anything other than jeans. The dress had a low neck and wide, filmy skirt; it looked like something a fifties starlet would wear. "How much is that?" said Earley. He wanted to see her dressed up in it, to fumble with buttons and zippers and peel that red fabric away from her skin.

"It'd go great with my treeplanting boots," said Zan, hanging it back on the rack. Reed finished tuning and started to play. He picked out a gypsyish tune that sounded heartbroken and plaintive, then rose into a vibrating wail and a wild run of fast-picking. Earley stared as Reed's fingers raced over the fretboard. It sounded like three men were playing. Reed's eyes were squeezed shut and his head angled off to the right, so the cords in his neck stood out. He didn't seem to be breathing.

Reed finished the tune and his body relaxed, as if he were leaving a trance. "Sweet sound," he said, plucking a string.

The pawnbroker squinted at him. "Ever see that movie *Deliverance?*"

"That was a banjo," said Reed. "Different mammal." He laid the instrument down on the counter and walked towards the door.

"You don't want it?" the broker said. "Give it to you for a hundred and twenty."

"I'm not in the market," Reed told him. "But thanks."

"Why the hell don't you—" Zan started, but Reed was already outside on the street. She sighed and went after him. Earley went too, with a nod to the pawnbroker. We didn't earn that dude any more gold chains, he thought. What a weird life, selling castoffs that people want back. A cement mixer drove past, its rear chamber grinding.

"That guy doesn't know what he's got there," said Reed. "That instrument's stenciled *The* Gibson; it's got to be prewar. Worth eight hundred, nine hundred easy."

Zan stopped in her tracks. "And he's letting it go for a hundred and twenty? Right back." She turned towards the pawnshop.

"Don't," said Reed, grabbing her arm.

"It's my money. What if I told you I wanted to go back and get that red dress?"

"I'll buy it for you," said Earley. "Come on." He moved Reed's hand off Zan's arm and led her back into the pawnshop, holding the door open for her like a Southern gentleman. Reed clumped in after them, frowning.

"Don't put that back in the window," Zan said to the broker. "I'll take it." He laid the mandolin onto the counter and went to the window to pick up its case. Earley turned to the clothing rack, hoping the dress didn't cost too much. He picked up the hanger and flipped the tag over. Reed watched, a strange smile on his face.

"So Zan's buying something for me, you're buying something for her . . . I guess I buy something for Earley. What floats your boat, man?"

"How about that Bowie knife there with the scrimshaw?"

Reed took out his wallet. "How much?"

"Shit," Earley said. "I was kidding."

"Three hundred," the broker said. "It's a collectible. Numbered and signed."

"Out of my league," said Earley.

"I'll take it," said Reed, his voice clipped. "You take traveler's checks?"

"I don't want it," said Earley. "That's way too much money."

"I don't want a mandolin," Reed said. "But Zan's buying me one."

"Reed?" Zan sounded worried.

"What? Early Christmas. Or call it a birthday. We all do have birthdays," said Reed. "This'll give us something to remember each other by. Zan can dress like a hooker, Earley can stab me, and I'll write a ballad about it."

Zan's arm swung around like a club, her fist landing under Reed's chin with a crack. He staggered and fell against Earley, who caught him instinctively.

"Jesus!" said Earley. Reed moaned.

"Did I break his jaw?" Zan asked.

"Don't think so," Reed mumbled.

"Too bad," said Zan. She turned and walked out of the store, slamming the door so hard the glass rattled.

Earley helped Reed to his feet. "You okay?"

"I guess."

Earley turned to the pawnbroker, who stood frowning, his massive arms folded. "Doesn't look like we're going to be buying anything."

"What are you, kidding?" said Reed. "I'll pay for all of them. *And* buy the drinks at someplace that has ice." He seemed almost giddy as he rubbed his jaw. As though he's just landed some blue-collar Merit Badge, Earley thought, ten points for brawling. He's lucky that Zan was the one who punched him; *I* would have broken his jaw, not to mention the rest of his body. He looked outside, wondering if she was all right. Fuck Reed and his wallet, he thought, I'm going to take care of her.

Zan was walking away very fast, heading back towards the ferry dock. Earley caught up with her at the next light. She kept her arms folded across her chest.

"Leave me alone," she said.

"I'm not doing anything," Earley said. "I'm just here."

Zan didn't look at him. "Give me a cigarette."

Earley reached into his pocket and gave her a loosely rolled Drum. "It's not a thing of beauty," he said, clicking his lighter a couple of times till it sparked. Zan leaned into his hands and lit up. Earley watched her drag deep and send smoke through her nostrils. "I didn't know you smoked."

"Used to," she said, and her whole face dissolved into tears. Earley drew her against his chest, folding his arms around her as she shook with sobs. Her breath was uneven and ragged, but she didn't make a sound. Earley was struck by how small she felt. He was so used to being a head or more taller than people that it barely registered most of the time, and Zan looked so strong that he thought of her as a big woman. But standing with her in his arms, on a street corner next to the sewer grate, he suddenly felt as if he were trying to comfort a child.

"Damn," Zan said. "Damn. I hate crying." She fumbled to drag on her cigarette once more, then dropped it into the gutter and leaned against Earley, her shoulders still shaking, her face burrowed into his wool shirt. He wished she'd make noise. She was crying the way people cry when they've had too much practice in keeping things secret. It sounded as if it must hurt her throat, swallowing back so much feeling. Who did this to you? he wondered. Who hurt you so much that you can't even show it, and how can I get you to trust me? He wrapped his big arms around Zan's heaving body, trying to still her. She flinched and drew back.

"It's okay," Earley mumbled, knowing that he sounded lame, but what else could he say? He'd been trying to work his way up to "I love you," but he knew that this wasn't the moment. He wondered what Zan would do. Kiss him with all her might, push him away, send a roundhouse to *his* jaw? He had a wild impulse to blurt it and see, but he was afraid it would backfire. He didn't think he'd ever felt so many different emotions at once. It was like coming into city traffic fresh out of the clear-cut, more input than he could contain. "It's okay," he muttered again to the top of Zan's head, "it's okay."

He felt an arm slide over his back. Reed was hugging them both. Earley felt Zan's body stiffen, but Reed didn't let go. He just stood there in silence, his arms around both of them. Earley looked down at the top of his head, which was only an inch or two higher than Zan's. It made him feel strange, being hugged by a man, even though Reed was now pressing his lips into Zan's hair and drawing her closer.

"I'm so sorry," Reed said. "I'm an asshole."

"I want to go home." Zan's voice sounded shaky.

"Let's have that drink first. I could use one."

"How's your jaw?"

"It hurts."

Earley was starting to feel uncomfortable, standing right there on the street with the two of them clinging to him like a mast. He took a step back, extricating himself. "Let's look for a bar on Bainbridge, or better yet stop at the Cedar," he said. "I want to get out of this city."

"Me too," said Zan.

"We have to pick up my mattress," Reed said, looking at Earley.

"Fuck," Earley said. "Then let's get it and split on the next ferry out. I've had it."

Reed reached down and picked up the shopping bag that he

had left on the pavement. So he *did* buy that crap, Earley thought, and he had such an urge to break Reed's jaw the rest of the way that his fingers curled into a fist. The thought of Reed buying that ivory knife, dropping three hundred dollars to prove a point, pissed him off big time. They could have lived off that money for weeks.

Earley stormed off towards the store, and the other two followed in silence. No two against one happening *now*, Earley thought. They each kept their distance so fully that somebody driving past might have assumed that they were three strangers.

No one spoke until they reached the department store. "It's back at the loading dock," Reed said. He reached inside his jacket and took out the yellow receipt. They went around to a wedge-shaped parking lot behind the store and went in through a swinging glass door. Reed gave his receipt to a clerk, then spotted a plastic-wrapped mattress leaning against the wall. "There it is."

"That's a twin," said Zan.

"That's what I paid for."

Earley looked at him, puzzled. Zan shook her head angrily. "Jesus, Reed! You can't even give yourself what you want."

"Earley was right. A double won't fit with the couch."

"Earley's *always* right, isn't he, Reed? He's a god." Zan's voice was pointed, accusing. Reed took a deep breath. He seemed to feel both their eyes on him.

"What are you talking about? He's a natural born fool. Aren't you, big man?"

"Uh-huh, and with shit taste in music," said Earley, relieved Reed was kidding around again. Maybe things would go back to normal when they left Seattle.

Apparently Zan didn't think so. "Babies," she said. "Little boys playing games." She glared at them both with what looked like contempt, though Earley had the peculiar, split-second sensation that she was about to start crying again. What was the matter with her?

He picked up the mattress and swung it up onto his shoulder. "Let's get this damn thing on the ferry," he said.

But that didn't go smoothly either. Earley carried it up the raised ramp, with its tin-roofed corner housings like prison guard towers. The man who stood next to the gate taking tickets said, "You can't bring that mattress on board."

"Why not?" said Reed. "The boat is half empty. It leaves in five minutes and you've got, what? Six people on board?"

"A hundred and thirty-nine," said the man, pursing his lips.

"And what's the capacity?"

"You can't carry on furniture."

"Want me to buy it a ticket?" asked Reed. "Or charge us as if it's a car and we'll drive it on board."

Earley let go of the mattress and stomped up the boat ramp. "Hey!" said the man. "You can't leave that there!"

"Would you like it?" said Earley. "We can't take it onto the ferry. Store's closed, so we can't take it back. What do you want us to do with it? Maybe you've got a back room in your office, and some Mrs. Asswipe who wants to shack up with you."

Reed burst out laughing. The man was dyspeptic. "You hippies think you own the planet. You think you can just break the rules, make a mess for the rest of the world to clean up. Well, you can't. You're no different from anyone else."

"I'm aware, sir," said Earley. "May we take our mattress?"

"Get out of my sight." The man turned his back on them, punching tickets for a small gaggle of Japanese tourists. Earley picked up one end of the mattress and Reed and Zan shouldered the other. They walked up the ramp.

"That was *classic*," said Reed. "I'm aware, sir!"

Earley shrugged. "It worked." The ferry let out two long, low, mournful hoots. They carried the mattress onto the upper deck, set it down under the wall-mounted canvas firehose and lifeboat instructions and went to the rail, looking out at the Sound as the boat churned away from the city. Good riddance, thought Earley. He looked south towards the vivid green whaleback of Vashon Island and the broad cone of Mount Rainier, its snowy flanks starting to tinge with sunset pastels. The Japanese tourists leaned on the rail, snapping pictures.

A triple-decked cruise ship steamed past them, her navy blue smokestack adorned with the North Star and Big Dipper of the Alaska State Ferry. Zan slipped her arms around Reed. "Look at that, Reeder. You were about to ship out on that thing."

"And look how much I would have missed." Reed brought Zan's palm up to his swollen jaw, then pulled her into an open-mouthed kiss. The wind twined their long hair together, Zan's dark and Reed's blond. Earley envied Reed being able to kiss Zan without having to bend his knees and crane his neck downwards; he'd never been face to face with a woman unless he was lying on top of her. He stared down at the wake that churned under the boat, roiling and gray as the Hoh in spring melt.

Zan let go of Reed and went to the mattress they'd left on the deck. She lay down on her back, with her head in its center, and patted both ends. Reed trotted over at once, like a puppy. Earley paused. If I don't stay in this, I'll lose her, he thought. He remembered the way Zan had sobbed in his arms, how he'd wanted to tell her right then and there that he loved her. Just let it play out, he told himself. Stay on the ride.

He glanced back at the tourists, popping their flashbulbs and chattering in Japanese as they posed in trios and pairs against pink Mount Rainier. Souvenir this, he thought, stretching across the mattress beside Zan and Reed. The three of them lay side by side on the tiny striped rectangle, watching the sunset set fire to the sky.

EIGHTEEN

The Cedar was hopping. Earley was used to the Friday night, blow-off-your-paycheck crowd, but Saturday was even busier. There were a lot more couples, and some of the wives were gotten up fancy in skirts and stiff hairspray, forcing their husbands to two-step in front of their bar buddies. Scoter Gillies was down at the end of the bar, getting plowed with a couple of Quileute mill rats and Clay Johannsen, a hollow-cheeked Vietnam vet who still wore his dogtags and shaved his head, even though now he flew choppers around the Olympics instead of the Mekong. Clay's black T-shirt had faded to khaki. He hunched at the end of the Cedar's long bar like a vulture guarding a carcass instead of a bottle of Colt 45 and a double shot of tequila.

The men's heads swiveled towards Zan as she passed. Earley couldn't resist laying his hands on her shoulders as he steered her back to the pool room. All the tables were full, so they leaned by the cue rack while Reed went up front for a pitcher.

"Glad you're here?" Zan asked, twining her fingers through Earley's.

He nodded. "I'll be even gladder when we get back home. I'm not a city guy."

"You know exactly where you belong," said Zan. "Most people don't."

"Where do you belong?" Earley asked. He liked holding her hand like this. It felt so old-fashioned and innocent, like a couple of teenagers on a first date.

"There." Zan jerked her head towards a booth, where a couple of loggers were standing up, pulling on raingear. "Let's grab it before someone else does."

Earley stepped towards the two men. "Y'all done here?"

"All yours," said the first man, eyeballing Zan with such obvious envy that Earley gave him a spontaneous pat on the back.

"Thanks, man," he said, folding his big frame to fit onto the leatherette bench. Zan sat down across from him. "You didn't answer," he said.

"Answer what?"

"Where you belong."

"Yes I did." Zan laid both her hands on the knotty pine table.

Earley noticed how battered her knuckles were, a darkening crack across one of her nails. "Here," she said. "This is where I belong right this moment. I don't stay anyplace long, Earley. I don't know how."

I could show you, he thought, gazing into her eyes. Stay with me. Live with me. Love me forever. But all he could manage to ask her was, "Why'd you leave Berkeley and move up here?"

Zan's eyes went wary. "What did Reed tell you?"

"He didn't." Earley remembered the stricken look on Reed's face when he'd asked the same question. He'd assumed Reed was pained by the way Zan had ditched him, but the sudden, raw edge in her voice made him wonder if there was more to it. He remembered how anxious she'd looked in Seattle. "Was there some other guy?"

Zan sat back. "Not until you," she said quietly.

Earley's heart lurched. Was she trying to mess with his head, change the subject, or was she about to confess how she felt?

Zan picked up a salt shaker, twisting the cap. "I wasn't expecting this either." She looked right at Earley, unguarded, her eyes searching his. "I was so glad to get hooked up with Reed again. Falling for you was the last thing I had in mind."

Earley drank in her words. Zan had told him she'd fallen for him, out loud in a public place. That was almost as good as "I love you" in bed. He had a mad urge to propose to her on the spot. He didn't care who she was or what she had done. If she was in love with him, nothing else mattered.

"Zan," he breathed, reaching to take her hand. She looked over his shoulder and smiled. Reed had come back with their pitcher. He set it between Zan and Earley and plunked down three mugs, still wet from the dishwasher. Earley slammed his back into the bench. Would he ever get more than five minutes alone with her?

"Oly," said Reed. "It was that or Coors pisswater. This town could do with a shipment of Heineken." He slid onto the bench next to Zan and started to pour, angling the pitcher and glass so the head wouldn't foam. He handed the first mug to Zan, then poured one for Earley and one for himself, lifting it up in a toast.

"To Bigfoot," he said. "Long may he wave."

"To us," said Zan, touching her mug to Reed's. Earley raised his arm, banging his mug against one, then the other.

"Us," he said, looking directly at Zan.

They were most of the way through the pitcher when Earley saw Zan look behind him. The next thing he knew, there were hands sliding over his eyes. He caught a quick glimpse of magenta nails, but even without that he would have recognized the cushiony warmth of her breasts on the back of his neck.

"Margie," he answered, before she could finish "Guess who?"

"Quick on the draw," Margie smirked. "Can I sit?"

Earley was taken aback. Margie was always so careful, especially here at the Cedar, where Harlan's logging crew cronies hung out. "Yeah, sure," he said, wishing she wouldn't. But Margie had already plopped herself down on the bench. Earley slid down to make room for her, bumping his knees into Zan's underneath the booth.

"'Scuse me," he muttered.

"For what?" Zan asked, acid.

"Introduce me to your friends," Margie said, giving Earley a mock-playful swat.

Earley looked at Reed first. It was easier. "This here is Margie Walkonis. And this is—"

"Oh yeah, you're the guy with the weird pants. We met at the laundromat."

Reed's face was as stony as Zan's. Earley finished up quickly. "Reed Alton, my splitter. And this here is Zan."

"Anne?"

There was glacier ice frosting her eyes. "Alexandra. I go by Zan."

"Okay." Margie's tone had a fuck-you-bitch shrug. It was clear as a bell what was going on. Margie had seen Earley sitting on one side of the booth and Zan and Reed on the other, and jumped to the likely conclusion that they were some couple he knew. What would she think if she knew the truth? Earley tried to imagine the look on her face. Shocked disbelief with

a little contempt mingled in there, he reckoned. More or less
the way Earley himself would feel if he heard that, say, Clay
Johannsen was having a three-way. He tried to imagine sharing
a mattress with Margie and Harlan, and practically shuddered.
Why was it any different to shack up with Zan and Reed?

The conversation had screeched to a halt. A couple was
fighting behind them, and some duo moaned on the jukebox.
Earley stepped in. "So is Harlan away?"

"Harlan who?" Margie said, reaching for Earley's beer. "He
finally ran off with that truck slut. Nineteen years and not even
a goddamn *note*. Oh, and Amber moved in with her boyfriend.
So you can come in through the front door tonight." She tipped
back his beer mug and drained it.

Earley winced inwardly, darting a look at Zan. Her eyebrows
were knit into a straight line. Margie plunked down the beer
mug, so hard it rattled. It wasn't her first. "I'm a free fucking
woman," she said, then corrected herself. "A fucking free
woman."

"A free fuck?" Zan suggested.

Margie looked her in the eye. "That's right, Anne. You got it."

Earley didn't know whether to flee to the men's room or sell
ringside seats. He couldn't believe Zan and Margie were having a fight over *him*, but what else could it be? They'd known
each other exactly two minutes. Earley turned towards Reed
for a reality check and noticed that Reed's smile looked pasted
on, hostile. The side of his jaw was a little bit puffy where Zan

had socked him. Dangerous woman, thought Earley. It turned him on. So did the knowledge that Zan cared enough to get jealous. But what was he going to do about Margie?

"Harlan's a scumbag," he said in an effort at gallantry. "Always was."

"Nineteen years," Margie said. "We eloped from the prom." She sloshed beer from the pitcher so fast it foamed over the top of the mug and spilled into her lap.

"Damn," she said, squirming. "My new pantsuit." Her voice sounded broken, forlorn. Earley knew he should do something, get paper towels or offer to drive her home, but he just sat there. I guess I'm a bit of a scumbag myself, he thought, watching her blot the peach fabric.

"Go powder your nose," said Zan.

Margie stopped dabbing and turned to her. "What the hell is your problem? My husband runs off with some slut and you're *dumping* on me? What kind of a woman are you? If you think this won't ever happen to you, you're dead wrong. There'll always be somebody younger, ready to grab your man. See how you like it when *you* get ditched." Margie stood up unsteadily. Her breasts were exactly at Earley's eye level. "You know where to find me," she said, and walked off without saying good-bye.

Zan leaned across the table towards Earley. Her eyes were intense. "If you ever go through that chick's front door, I'm gonna mince you for chowder."

Earley didn't like her tone. "You get two lovers, but I don't?"

"Not if one of them's her."

Earley sat back and folded his arms. He had half a mind to get up and go after Margie, leave Zan stranded right there at the Cedar Bar Lounge, where she said she belonged. But then she'd be with Reed, who could easily charge a motel room and treat her like royalty. Earley would lose the round. "I'm a big boy," he said, meeting Zan's eye. "I can decide what to do with myself."

"Let's go home," said Reed, standing. "It's been a long day."

Zan's gaze did not stray from Earley's. "Sure," she said, "let's."

Reed's new mattress got stuck in the doorway. He and Earley bent it nearly double and wedged it through, cursing and knocking a few Mason jars to the floor as they wrestled it in through the kitchen. They dropped it behind the couch, panting. The clear plastic wrapping was shredded and wet. "Let's take that off," said Zan, dropping down onto all fours and ripping at it with her hands.

"It can wait," said Reed. He knelt down behind her, pressing his groin to her buttocks. "I can't." Earley was shocked to see Reed so aggressive. His own dick got stiffer, as if for a duel.

"Neither can I," he said, reaching to unzip, "and I won that bet."

Zan turned towards him with a wicked grin. "Damn straight,"

she said. "You get a one on one." She got up and went into the kitchen.

"Where are you going?" said Earley.

"Massage oil," she called back. "Go light up a candle and take off your clothes."

"Shit," said Reed. "Just because I didn't whip it out on the street."

"It's a man's world," said Earley. "Excuse me while I get massaged." He stepped into his bedroom, closing the Indian curtains behind him. He went to the nightstand and lit a thick candle, then peeled off his clothes and arranged himself on the futon. Face up, he decided, let her get the full effect. He settled himself on the cushions, resting his head on his hands so his elbows fanned out and his biceps looked bulky. His penis stood up like a spar tree. He lay back and listened for footsteps. Why was she taking so long? Had she stayed in the kitchen to make out with Reed? This whole thing was driving him crazy.

Zan parted the curtains. She'd put on the dress from the pawnshop. It was a little too big for her, gauzy, the backlit red fabric so sheer that Earley could see the silhouette of her body right through it. "Jesus," he said, staring. Zan smiled and held up a bottle of almond oil.

"Dress on or off?" she said.

"Either," said Earley. "Both." Zan set the oil down alongside the mattress, her eyes roaming hungrily over his body.

"Off," she said. "Don't want to rip it." She knelt down beside him and turned her back, lifting her tangle of hair to one side.

Earley rolled up to a sitting position, sliding the long zipper down in a slow tease along her bare skin. He could see every knob of her spine in the candlelight, the oblong dark mole in the small of her back, the swell of her buttocks.

"Thanks," said Zan, rising and turning to face him.

"Where's Reed?" he asked, suddenly noting how quiet it was.

"He went out for a smoke," said Zan. "Wouldn't you?" She slid the red dress off her shoulders, then took a step forward and let it drop down to the floor. She was naked beneath it, as he knew she would be. She's playing on me like a harp, Earley moaned to himself, and I don't give a damn.

"Roll over," said Zan, as she knelt down and squeezed a few drops of the almond oil into her palm. Earley did, turning his head to one side on the pillow. Zan moved onto the futon and straddled his back. Earley could hear her hands rubbing together, warming the oil. He held his breath, lying in wait for her touch.

Zan started out with the palms of both hands in the small of his back, moving upwards and outwards. Her oiled hands felt smooth and improbably warm as the candlelight flickered around him. The smell of almonds was heady. Earley sighed and gave in to her, closing his eyes as she worked away on his shoulders, kneading and releasing every sore muscle, caressing the wings of his shoulder blades, moving down the deep groove of his backbone.

How long had it been since anyone touched him with this kind of tenderness? Earley remembered his mom smearing Vap-O-Rub onto his chest when he'd had the croup, what would it be, twenty years ago? More. And a couple of girl-friends had given him backrubs, but nothing like this one. Zan's fingers were practiced and sure. She'd done this for a living, no question about it. Earley thought about how many skins she had had to touch, older men, fat men, men who had scared her, might even have hurt her, and it made him angry. He wanted to punish them.

"Christ, Earley, you're like a piece of sculpture." Zan's voice sounded husky. He could feel her warm breath as she bent over him, kneading the furrows and ridges along his spine.

"Whole lot of years cutting wood," Earley murmured, cheek pressed to the sheet. He could feel Zan's inner wetness on top of his buttocks; he loved how turned on he was making her, just lying still. "When do I get to turn over?"

"Now," she said, arching up so that he could roll over beneath her legs. Her hands traveled over his pectorals, down to his belly, his groin. "And this is the part that my customers never got," she whispered, sliding a warm, oily hand in between his legs. Earley's breath caught as she stroked his cock, tracing it down to the root, and then bent down to take him inside her mouth. Her lips slid over his foreskin, her tongue thrusting, flickering, making him groan out loud.

Zan was insatiable. Earley lay back as she pleasured him, licking and sucking as if she could not get enough of him. She's going to eat me alive, he thought, swallow me whole like a python. He could feel her tears damp on his thighs.

Without warning Zan shifted position and straddled him, angling the head of his penis against her own genitals. She circled above him and then slid down suddenly, bringing him so deep inside that he thought he'd explode. Her breasts bounced and swung as she churned up and down on him, clenching, releasing, making him hers. This is what it must be like for women, Earley thought, getting fucked. He liked the sensation, but not the idea; he wanted to be on top.

He arched his back and thrust upwards, asserting his own rhythm. Zan gasped and pushed back. Earley grabbed her hips, flipping her onto her back and plunging in, grinding his body against hers. Nobody's going to outfuck me, he swore to himself, pumping harder and faster. Not you, and not Reed.

Reed, he thought suddenly. Where the hell is he? Has he been outside in the rain all this time? And as soon as the thought formed, Earley knew without looking that Reed would be standing just outside the curtains, watching and listening and beating off. Good, he thought feverishly. Maybe we'll all come at once. Maybe Margie's at home in her waterbed, working some battery vibrator, dreaming of me. I can fuck you all. Open the earth and I'll fill it. I'll be the Paul Bunyan of fucking. He gathered himself into one fluid essence and shot it out so hard that Zan screamed.

Reed was inside the bedroom so quickly that Earley knew he'd been right. "Are you all right?"

Zan nodded, gasping, her cheeks soaked with brine and

her skin drenched in sweat. She couldn't speak. Neither could Earley.

Reed stared at their soaked, heaving bodies, their intertwined limbs. Then he dropped to his knees and curled onto the futon beside them.

"Don't leave me," he whispered.

NINETEEN

Earley slept fitfully, skimming in and out of dreams about ferryboats, knives and Vick's Vap-O-Rub. The sensation of warm hands caressing his chest was so real that it pulled him up out of a deep, swirling sleep, like a trout that's been hooked. The predawn light was muted and granular, still too dim to see anything clearly. An owl hooted low in the distance.

Earley shut his eyes, hoping to drift back into the warmth of that dream. In that borderless zone between waking and sleep, it took him awhile to realize there was a hand sliding, light as a whisper, over his thigh towards his hipbone. At first he thought he was still dreaming, but no, there it was, like a secret, a promise, a feathery touch that glided so lightly the hairs on his thigh prickled softly.

Earley's breath caught. He kept his eyes closed, reluctant to break the spell by admitting that he was aware of it. He could sense Zan's face, inches away from his own. Her breathing was even and steady. Was she caressing him in her sleep? A deep, private shudder ran through his whole being; he felt himself falling insanely in love. He had to look at her, he had to know.

Barely breathing, he turned his head, opened his eyelids a sliver and peered at Zan. She was sleeping, all right. Her dark eyelashes feathered her cheek, which was propped, Earley noticed, on both of her folded hands.

He must have tensed involuntarily; Reed's hand stopped moving at once. So he wasn't asleep, Earley realized. Holy shit.

Earley froze. He could feel his own heartbeat echoing inside his ears. What the hell should he do? If he moved or spoke, or did anything that made it obvious he was awake, he'd have to confront Reed. And what would he say? Why the fuck was your hand on my leg? Reed would deny it, or pretend he thought Earley was Zan in the dark. Maybe Reed *was* asleep, Earley tried telling himself, but it was no use. He knew full well that Reed wasn't sleeping; knew, too, that Reed realized that he had woken up Earley and was lying a few feet away from him, tense as a guy-wire, wondering how Earley was going to respond.

I can't deal with this, Earley thought. Not at five in the morning, with Zan fast asleep in between us. He was dying to get off the futon and out of the bus. But if he stood up now, he knew he'd be making a statement. I know what you're up to, you bastard; I'm not going to play.

Well, why shouldn't he make a damn statement? Reed was the one who had crossed a line; why did Earley feel guilty? His heart was still racing. If he stayed where he was, they could both still pretend he'd slept through the whole thing. Anything else would be tipping his hand.

Earley lay there in stunned indecision, hyperaware of Reed's every breath. The longer he waited, the harder it felt to speak up. By the time the wood pewees and warblers had started their dawn song, Earley had all but convinced himself there was no need to, that Reed hadn't actually touched him at all.

Zan made them both breakfast. She had no feel for the wood-stove: the bacon was dry as old bark and the scrambled eggs tasted like cotton. Even the coffee was awful. "Do they let you camp-tend?" asked Reed.

"They did once," said Zan, helping herself to more black-ened hash browns. She didn't seem fazed in the least by the way the food tasted. Earley loved her for being so matter-of-fact. He ate seconds of everything. Reed picked at his plate, though whether it was because the food was so lousy or he was still feeling self-conscious was anyone's guess. He still hadn't met Earley's eye.

"I'm going to go take a shower," he said, scraping his plate into the compost can.

Zan's eyebrows went up. "Where?"

"There's a waterfall down in the gorge," Earley told her. They'd started to use it the week before, though the water was still cold enough to raise goosebumps.

"Isn't it freezing?"

"Yeah," said Reed, grinning, "it's great."

"Macho man," Zan smirked.

Reed twisted his T-shirt, threw back his head and brayed, "STELLLLLA!" like Brando. Then he scooped up his towel and soap and headed off into the woods. Earley watched out the window as Reed slouched past the chopping block, stomping along in his unlaced caulks. He had to be normal. Didn't he?

Zan came up behind Earley, holding the coffeepot. "Heat that up for you?" she said like a waitress. He turned around, glad to be rid of his thoughts about Reed.

"Hey, we've got the place to ourselves for once. What do you say?" Zan was wearing one of Earley's wool shirts as a bathrobe. He slid his hands up her bare legs and over her buttocks, pulling her closer. She still smelled like almonds.

"Is that all you ever think about?"

"No," Earley said. "But it's high on my list."

Zan looked at him. "What do you dream about, Earley?"

You, he thought. And Vick's Vap-O-Rub. Neither of those

seemed to be the right answer. "I'll show you," he said and led her outside.

They set off down the path, sidestepping a widowmaker. Earley reminded himself he should come back and buck it up for firewood sometime. There was a sweet springy scent in the air that he couldn't quite place, some berry flower or Nootka rose that had opened out in the new sunlight. The woods seemed so lush these days, everything hurtling from bud into ripeness, plants growing so fast you could practically see them expanding, like stop-motion footage. The whole world was green.

They were walking in single file. Zan, who had never been back here before, led the way, with Earley, as usual, dogging her footsteps. They passed the steep cliff edge where he and Reed had thrown the charred mattress after the fire. Earley paused to look down at it, lying below among boulders and yellow-green skunk cabbage. It was soaked through with rain, the striped fabric already fading from white to damp gray. A short way beyond it, the path twisted off to the right, tracing a zigzagging switchback down the dry gorge to the creek beyond. Zan started to follow it down.

"No, this way," said Earley, guiding her onto a less-worn path that led off to the left, through a thicket of devil's club. He stamped down the thick, thorny canes with his boot soles, leading Zan deeper into the trees. He had to stoop frequently, holding back branches to keep them from lashing back at her.

"This is one hell of a back road," said Zan. "Where are you taking me?"

"Almost there." Earley stepped over the trough of a nurse log. He knew every step of this route, but he'd never brought anyone with him before. He led Zan through a cluster of red osier dogwoods and into a small, heart-shaped clearing. The sunlight streamed down, cathedraling through the tall fir trees. The air was so moist he could see dust motes swirling within every ray.

Zan stood next to him. "What am I looking at?"

"The cabin I'm going to build. Here's the front door." Earley stepped over a root and turned back to take Zan by the hand, ushering her after him. "Living room. The woodstove goes right where that rock is. Windows here, here, and a big one right here, facing the sunrise." He drew a big rectangle in the air, framing the peak of Olympus. "Sixteen-foot ceiling."

Zan's mouth crinkled into a smile. "Sixteen?"

"There's a loft bed up there, looking out at the mountain. And under the loft"—Earley paused for dramatic effect—"is the bathroom. Flush toilet, a deep sink with hot and cold running, and here, with a view of the waterfall after I thin out those hemlocks, the world's hottest, steamiest shower."

"Waterfall?" Zan said. "Is that what I'm hearing?" She stepped forward and stood on a flat shelf of rock, looking down. Earley followed her gaze. The green bowl of moss-covered rock was bisected by a white veil of spray that fell over the cliff and into the creek shallows. Reed stood in front of it, taking his clothes off.

Zan watched him bend to step out of his jeans. "Want to go down and join him?"

"No. I don't." Earley sounded a bit too emphatic, even to his own ears. "Can't we just be alone with each other? I'm sick of Reed."

Zan looked at him, nodding, her eyes impenetrable. "But I'm not."

They were gone a long time. Earley boiled water and washed Reed's thrift-store dishes, hating his guts. Maybe he ought to just fire the bastard; it wasn't as if he even needed a splitter at this point. Especially not one who groped him in bed. He willed himself not to revisit the scene from this morning, which hovered behind every thought, unignorable. But when he pushed that away, he was left with the sting of Zan turning her back on his cabin—his cabin!—to go off with Reed. What cabin? he thought as he hurled the gray dishwater onto the ground; it's nothing but thin air. I don't even own the damn land. Wanting something, even wanting it so much that the desire for it felt like a part of your body, as real as a leg or an arm, didn't mean you'd ever get it. Look how much he wanted Zan.

Maybe I'll go and stand under that waterfall too, he thought angrily. Show those fuckers who's boss on this hill. He set off

down the trail, noting the bright yellow flash of a warbler winging from tree to tree, some trilliums starting to bloom under-
foot. Could it really be only a week since they'd carried Reed's
mattress along this same path? So much had changed, and was
still changing, minute by minute. Earley took a deep breath.
He could hear the rush of cascading water as he stepped to the
rim of the gorge and looked down.

Zan and Reed lay in the mossy glade next to the creek, their
bodies pale against all that lush green. They were turned towards
each other like bookends, their faces just inches apart. They
seemed to be talking about something that made them both
happy. Reed's hand traced the curve of Zan's hip, moving up from
her thigh towards her hipbone. So it *was* her that he'd reached
for this morning. What a relief, Earley told himself, but there
was a hollowness inside his chest as he watched them together.

The splash of the waterfall buried their voices, but Earley
could see Zan was laughing at something that Reed had just
said. He wondered if they had already made love, or if this was
still foreplay. And then it occurred to him: maybe they weren't
having sex at all. Maybe they were just talking, enjoying each
other. Maybe Reed shared a kinship with Zan that Earley
would never have; maybe they were, in fact, soul mates.

So what did that make him? What he'd been so many times
to so many women, he figured: a muscular body to play with, a
big dumb fuck.

Zan reached for Reed's hand, kissing his fingertips one at a
time. Earley felt as if his heart would burst. There was some-

thing so tender in that simple gesture. I'll never have that kind of closeness, he thought. Not with Zan, not with anyone. Sex took you only so far. There were intimacies that went so much deeper, connections that made people realize they weren't alone in this world.

Earley blinked several times. Something seemed to have gotten in one of his eyes; it was watering freely. He felt like a creep standing up there and spying on Zan and Reed. I should go down and join them, he thought, or else take off and give them some privacy, but somehow his feet wouldn't move. Make me part of you, he thought to himself as he watched them together. Sweet Lord, let me in.

Zan took off for the planters' camp right after dinner, some kind of weird quiche made of tofu and kale. Earley was still hungry, so he boiled up a couple of hot dogs and washed them down with a cold Oly while Reed took out the compost.

"Want to play Go?" Reed asked when he got back, kicking off his boots.

"No," said Earley. Reed nodded as if he'd expected that answer. They went through their bedtime routine in charged silence, avoiding all physical contact, like prizefighters circling each other before they start sparring. The bus's cramped spaces seemed tighter than ever, and they both made a point of drawing the curtains shut tightly around their beds.

Earley lay still on his futon, remembering the whispery

touch of Reed's hand sliding over his thigh. He moved his own hand to the same place and noted the texture of sinew and hair, the hardened scar tissue where he'd been cut by his chainsaw. Reed had to have known whose leg he was touching. Why else was he acting so dodgy?

If he really grilled himself, Earley had to admit it had crossed his mind that Reed was a little too fond of him, not just eager to learn Earley's skills as a woodsman, but doting on his every word. But he'd set those suspicions aside when he saw the way Reed looked at Zan, heard him talking for hours about how obsessed he was with her. Earley had watched Reed have sex with a woman; he couldn't be gay. The fact that he *had* watched made Earley uncomfortable. He remembered the first night they'd met, that damn shower, the way he had noticed the size of Reed's penis. What did that make *him*? Had something been off all this time and he just hadn't noticed? Or had he played into it somehow or other?

It pissed him off, having to ask all these questions. His friendship with Reed had been effortless. They simply fit with each other, they'd gotten along since the moment they'd met, and now Earley found himself wondering why. The blueness of Reed's eyes annoyed him; his long ponytail made him look like a girl. Three-dollar bill, he thought. How did I miss it? And what am I going to do with him now?

The next morning wasn't much better. Reed went to the gorge for another cold shower. He came out of the woods with his hair dripping wet, singing "Midnight Train to Georgia," stopping short when he saw Earley loading the truck.

They drove up to the clearcut without a word. Reed drummed on his knees, then glanced over at Earley to see if it bugged him. Earley turned on the wipers. It wasn't quite raining, but banks of low clouds were hung up on the mountainside, shredding through treetops like cotton wool. They drove in and out of dense patches of cloud cover, fogging the view. Earley reached into his pouch for a smoke he'd rolled, fumbling with one hand to twist the ends tighter and light it. Reed moved to help him, but drew back before their hands touched. Good instinct, thought Earley. I'd flatten you.

Earley didn't look back as he strode up the mountain's bald face, clambering over clots of lopped branches, mudslides and scree. No more holding back, he thought; keep up or drop.

They were working so high up the mountain that it wasn't worth the time it took getting there. I've got to order that fly-out, vowed Earley. Next time he went into town he'd swing by Gillies' mill and set up a copter date with Clay Johannsen. They'd piled enough cedar to cover the cost three times over. But there were a couple of oldgrowth stumps high on the ridge that Earley wanted to tackle first, real old men of the forest, so broad that he could have parked his truck on them if he could have gotten it up the hill. Those cedars had been there

since men fought in armor. They might have topped two hundred feet. Not anymore, Earley thought. Now they're somebody's deck.

He got to the first of the giants and revved up his Husqy.
There was a lot of heartrot, but plenty to salvage if he cut
around the spault. Reed waited in silence as Earley bent over,
spraying them both with a cinnamon dusting of cedar as he
carved the first big block out of the stump. When he was finished, Reed lifted the block out, still warm from the saw blade.
He carried it to an adjacent stump, jammed the splitting wedge
into the soft wood and hefted his sledgehammer.

They worked all morning without a break, decimating the
stump and unearthing a big log behind it that might yield a
couple of cords' worth of shakebolts in spite of the rot. Earley
wanted to wear Reed down, like he had when they first started
working together. It annoyed him that Reed could keep up
with him now. He was sweating in spite of the drizzle. He
peeled off his wool shirt and set it on top of a log, working in
his damp undershirt. He was down to the heart of the tree.
The wood had changed color, the copper tones turning the dry
red of sandstone. Earley nosed his blade into the heartwood,
burning in hard. The saw sputtered, sending up plumes of
black smoke. "Shit," he said, cutting the engine.

Reed looked concerned. "Did you run out of gas?"

"Bar oil," said Earley, cursing himself for forgetting to refill
the reservoir. He could smell the thick fumes, and the metal

cap was hot enough to burn his fingers. Why hadn't he noticed it sooner? He'd run it to sludge.

"Is the can in the back of the truck? I'll go down if you want."

Earley shook his head. He could picture the lubricant can right where he'd left it, on the hood of the bus with their lunch. If you hadn't been singing that goddamn song, he thought, I would've gotten the truck packed up right. "Left it back home," he said, turning his back on Reed as he headed downhill by himself.

Earley twisted the steering wheel, swerving around a deep puddle that he hadn't noticed that morning. This road's getting worse every day, he thought, washboard and mud. He rounded a tight curve and slammed on the brake. He was nose to nose with a heavy black truck. Nobody drove on his access road, ever. Earley stared through the glare on the windshield and stiffened. The driver was Harlan Walkonis. Had Margie said something? Had Amber?

Earley's fists clenched and opened like heart muscles. There was a hunting rifle on the rack right behind Harlan's head. Earley reached backwards and unsnapped the sheath of the knife on his belt, just in case.

Harlan got out of his idling truck, reaching backwards to hitch up his pants. He probably weighed more than Earley, but he had the flushed, suety look of somebody who sat in a truck cab all day and a barstool all night. His eyes had a permanent squint, under tan brows that bristled like birds' nests. Earley pushed open his door and unfolded himself to his full six foot five.

Harlan peered at him. "Earl Ritter?"

Earley gave a nod, waiting for more.

"Do you own that trashed-out blue school bus a couple miles up?"

That wasn't the question that Earley expected from someone whose wife he'd been fucking. "What if I do?"

Harlan drew back his lip in a sneer. "Then you better get ready to drive it away, or we'll push it aside with a Cat. It's on Royalton land."

TWENTY

Reed was enraged. "They can't get away with that!"

"Who's gonna stop them?" said Earley, plunking the oil can on top of the stump. "A couple of shake-rats who don't have a pot to piss in, squatting on Royalton Timber's front yard? They don't give a shit about people like us. All they want is the timber sale."

"Two thousand acres of clearcutting? That's going to destroy the whole forest. Not just where we live."

"The Forest Service sold Royalton logging and access road rights to the parcel above us," said Earley. "They already own where I live. They can do what they want."

"And you're just going to lie down and take it?" Reed's voice was indignant.

"I'm gonna put oil in my chainsaw and cut up the rest of this log," Earley said. "Gonna earn my damn living, like always." He unscrewed the cap of the oil tank and jammed in a funnel, pouring the black liquid into his chainsaw.

Reed folded his arms. "And when the first bulldozer rolls up our driveway—"

"My bus has four wheels. I'll move on when I have to." Reed's eyes registered Earley's shift from "our" to "my," but he didn't let up.

"It's not a done deal yet," he said. "We can fight this."

"How?" Earley snapped. "Are you going to call up your daddy the judge? Maybe *he* can buy two thousand acres. Little dowry for you and Zan."

"Fuck you, Earley. You don't know the first thing about me." Reed grabbed his sledgehammer and stamped off. He's pissed at me, Earley thought. Good.

He yanked back the ripcord and nosed his saw into the giant log's heartwood, sending up twin sprays of brick-red dust. So much for that cabin with sixteen-foot ceilings, he thought. I'm going to be stuck in some portable can for the rest of my life. I'll never have anything that I can call my own. People like Reed thought they had the power to change things; Earley knew all too well it was hopeless. The world gave you nothing to work with except your own body. That was all you could count on. Behind him, Reed cried out in pain.

Earley swiveled fast, choking his saw. Reed was doubled in

agony, clutching his leg. "Shit, man. Oh, man." He was breathing hard.

"You okay?" Earley asked idiotically. Reed shook his head. "What'd you do, drop the wedge on your foot?"

"Hit my ankle," said Reed through clenched teeth. "With the hammer. I felt something crack."

Earley imagined the force of an eight-pound sledgehammer, swinging down in an arc from high over Reed's head to his anklebone. He sucked in air. "Let's get you off it." He guided Reed onto the chopping block, letting his injured foot drag in its boot. He gave Reed his canteen and made him take a drink. "Just sit still for a minute."

Reed nodded and drank some more water, splashing it over his chin. His face was flushed. "Shit," he said, blinking back tears.

"Can you move it at all?"

Reed screwed up his face with the effort. "Not up and down," he said. "There's about five different bones that slide over each other right there at the ankle. I fucked up bad, Earley. I'm fucked."

"Okay," Earley said, thinking hard. "Let's leave on your boot, that'll help hold it still. I'll fake up a splint and we'll get you on down to the truck, okay, buddy?" Reed nodded. Earley picked up the hammer in one hand, the wedge in the other, and knocked off a couple of splits from a shake bolt in two swift moves.

"I couldn't do that in a million years," Reed said. His voice sounded broken.

"What?" Earley didn't know what he was talking about.

"You're made for this work. I never will be."

"There's nothing so great about cutting up shakes," Earley said. "It's just work." He scooped up his wool shirt and knelt next to Reed, using its sleeves to bind the two wood splits on either side of Reed's ankle.

"That ought to get you downhill at least. Ready to try it?" Reed nodded. Earley got behind him and hoisted him into a standing position. "How's that?"

"I can make it," said Reed. "What about the tools?"

"Leave 'em. I'll come back tomorrow."

"Your Husqy?"

"I'm taking that." Earley picked up the saw by its handle and offered his free arm to Reed. "Come on, lean on me."

Reed did. They set off at a slow hobble. From the look on Reed's face, Earley knew every step was excruciating. He wondered if he should say something about how they'd fought, and decided against it. This wasn't his fault. He looked down at the miniature roof of his truck, at the vertical acres of slash piles and stumpage between them and it. What the hell was he thinking of, working so high? He remembered that time he'd fallen on top of his chainsaw and gashed his leg. His partner back then was a Makah Indian, Leroy Tatoosh, who had driven a jeep for a medical unit in 'Nam. Leroy's quick thinking had saved Earley's ass, but if they'd been working this high on the mountaintop, he would have bled to death. Flyout, he thought. I'll call Clay from the hospital.

"I've totaled this ankle before," Reed said, teeth gritted. "Tore a ligament running a marathon."

Earley winced. "Ouch."

"I finished," said Reed. "Four hours and ten. I just thought it was shin splints."

"Tough guy," said Earley.

"Not tough. Just stubborn."

"Same difference."

They'd come to the edge of a gully carved out by a fork of Suhammish Creek. No way is Reed going to get down that ravine, Earley thought. He looked left and right for an easier crossing. The creek cut a deep gash through the clearcut. The rains and erosion had choked it with tangles of branches, its steep sides precipitous. Reed set one foot onto the edge. Earley stopped him. "Hang on. I'll carry you down."

"I can make it."

"You fall down on that foot, you'll be roadkill," said Earley. "Take off your shirt."

Reed looked at him. "Why?"

"Gonna backpack my saw."

Reed unbuttoned his red chamois workshirt, the L.L. Bean number that had tie-dyed their clothes in the washing machine. He stood pale and thin in his T-shirt as Earley threaded a sleeve through his chainsaw handle and slung it across his back, tying the sleeves in a knot on his shoulder. He bent down next to Reed.

"Left arm over my shoulder," he said. "I'll try not to hurt your leg. Ready?"

Reed nodded, wincing as Earley slid one arm behind his knees, testing their bend. Earley paused for a moment, then stood up straight, swinging Reed's broken body up into his arms, like a bride crossing over the threshold.

"Codeine," said Reed. "This shit's better than Quaaludes." He was sprawled on the couch with his leg propped on cushions. Earley had driven him back from the local emergency room, where a tired-looking doctor had squinted at X-rays and told Reed he'd fractured some bone; Earley couldn't remember the name. A younger doctor had wrapped Reed's ankle in plaster of paris and sent him back home with a rubber-tipped crutch and a fistful of painkillers.

"I was never a 'Lude man myself," Earley said. "I like drugs you can smoke."

"Help yourself," said Reed, nodding his head towards the ashtray that sat on the low trunk between them. Earley picked up the joint they'd been sharing and reached over to Reed's bedside table for matches. Reed was reading a new book called *Riprap and Other Poems*. It was sitting on top of his instrument case.

"You know, you haven't played your mandolin once," Earley said.

"You haven't used your knife."

Earley stepped into the kitchen and took out his scrimshaw knife. He set an apple on top of the trunk table, halved it and speared a chunk. "Your turn."

Reed crunched up the apple and swallowed. "All right," he said. Earley stretched backwards and handed the instrument case to him.

Reed took out the mandolin, tuning its paired strings. "There's only one problem. I'm too stoned to play straight."

"Didn't stop Hendrix," said Earley.

"Yes it did. Big time."

"Oh, *that*," Earley said, relighting the roach.

"Jimi. Janis. Jim Morrison. End of an era."

"They were all younger than I am," said Earley. He took a deep toke, grateful the topic was music, not Royalton's timber sale.

"When is your birthday?"

Earley held the smoke in his lungs for a long time before he exhaled and said, "Sometime next week, I think."

"Hell, boy, how deep in the Okefenokee did you grow up? Don't you even know when your birthday is?"

"Sixth of May. I don't know what *today* is."

"The seventh."

Earley stared at him. "You're shitting me."

"No, man, I'm telling you true."

"I'm thirty?"

"Damn straight. Happy birthday."

Earley couldn't believe it. Thirty years old. He had thought that would bother the hell out of him, and here it had come and gone by without him even noticing. These milestones, these boundaries that seemed so significant, just didn't matter that much when you got right up next to them. It was all fluid. He took another deep drag on the roach, which was charring his fingers, and felt a sensation that rose through his scalp like lava. The room seemed to swim in a haze of warmth. The hurricane lamp at the edge of the room sent out pulses of light, like a lighthouse.

Reed tightened the last string and plucked it. "So what do you want to hear?"

"Play me that song again."

"What song?"

"The one that you played in the store." Earley could still hear the gypsyish wail of the tune. It had given him goosebumps.

"I don't remember it. I was just riffing."

"You made that *up*?"

"Yeah." Reed shrugged, as if it were no big deal.

"Make up something else. Something for me."

Reed looked at him. His eyes looked too bright in the lamplight. "All right," he said softly. Then he turned his head to one side, closed his eyes and began to play.

Earley leaned back as Reed's fingers slid over the fretboard, now fast, now dreamlike and wavery, coaxing a tune from the strings. The notes clustered and swam, swirling around them like eddies, like meltwater. Reed's lips parted, moving a little, as if he were making the strings vibrate with his own breath. I am really deep stoned, Earley thought. I feel golden. Like honey.

He gazed at the back of Reed's neck as he bent over his mandolin, at the pale, jutting knobs of his spine, lamplight catching the fine downy hairs like a halo. Earley's hand floated up from his lap and hovered in space for a moment. Then his fingertips came to a rest on Reed's nape, at the base of his ponytail. Reed stiffened at once. He stopped playing.

"Don't mess with me, Earley," he said in a choked voice.

"I'm not," Earley said. His fingers moved softly over the back of Reed's neck. What am I doing? he thought. He could feel Reed's pulse throbbing, the warmth of his skin turning gritty with stubble. He's a *guy*, Earley thought, this is weirder than hell. But he didn't stop touching him.

Reed put down his mandolin and turned towards him. The look in his eyes was like nothing that Earley had ever seen. It was love, pure and simple, but something more, something ashamed of itself and relieved and stark naked and painfully new. This is it, said Reed's eyes. This is what I've been trying to tell you.

"Earley," he whispered. And kissed him. Earley was shocked by the warmth of his lips, that they felt just the same as a woman's. His response was instinctive: he kissed back the mouth that was kissing his own. His hand slid around Reed's waist. Christ, he thought, feeling dizzy. I can't let this happen.

Reed pulled away from him, trembling. "I can't believe this."

"I'm having some trouble myself," Earley said.

"I've wanted to do that for so long."

"You have?" Earley looked at him, wary.

Reed gave a small nod. "Does that freak you out?"

"Well, yeah."

"Me too." Reed laid his palm onto Earley's chest, right where the fine hairs curled up from the scoop of his undershirt. Earley could feel his heart pounding. This was a trail that led over a cliff. He lifted Reed's hand off and handed it back to him. "Look, man, it's not like I'm . . . I don't know why I . . ."

Reed's jaw set. He looked down at the table and nodded. "We're both pretty high," he said in a flat voice, as if that would let them both off the hook.

"No hard feelings."

"No feelings at all," said Reed. "That's what the codeine is for." He looked so miserable that Earley wanted to hug him, but he was afraid it would just make things worse. When he'd carried Reed down from the scene of the accident, there'd been no question of what he should do, or what anything meant. He'd taken Reed into his arms as if it were the most natural thing in the world for men to take care of each other. A couple of minutes ago he had reached for Reed's neck with the same tender impulse; he'd kissed Reed right back. I want to touch him right now, Earley realized, feeling a hot pulse of danger. He turned his head slightly to look at Reed's profile, the gold fringe of lashes veiling his eyes, the taut cords that twitched in his jawline.

I want you. Earley tried out the words silently, feeling the roof of his mouth go dry. There would be no turning back this time, no second step on the brakes. Did he mean it, or was he just horny, stoned, lonely? *I want you,* he thought again, feeling the room pulsate. *Jesus.*

Reed turned, just as if he had heard Earley say it out loud. He reached out for Earley's hand, and when Earley didn't withdraw it, Reed bent down and kissed his fingertips, one by one, the same way that Zan had kissed his in the waterfall gorge. Earley remembered the desolation he'd felt as he watched from the edge of the cliff. Why the fuck not? he thought, feeling the warmth of Reed's breath on his skin.

He gathered Reed into a clumsy hug, drawing him closer. He was so much taller that Reed's face nestled into the base of his throat. Earley rested his lips on top of Reed's head, inhaling the thick musk of cedar dust, woodsmoke and work sweat that both of them shared. He could hear his own heartbeat. He hadn't felt like this since he was thirteen, when touching a girl was charged with equal parts peril and thrill, like a skydive. If Reed *were* a girl, Earley thought, I'd be on him like gravy on beef.

He slid his hand down Reed's back. "How's your leg?" he said.

"What leg?" said Reed.

"Want to go and lie down?"

Reed didn't hesitate. "Yeah," he said shakily. "Yes, I do." He swung his hurt leg off the couch. Earley helped him get up. Reed leaned up against him, hobbling towards the orange curtain. Earley drew it back.

There was his futon, sheets twisted as usual, bathed in blue moonlight. They stood for a beat staring down at it. Then they turned towards each other, madly unbuttoning and yanking off layers until they stood bare-chested in their jeans.

Reed twined his arms around Earley. There was no air space between their two chests, no breasts to cushion the contact. Their skins seemed to generate heat. Earley could feel himself sweating. His blood seemed to pulse with the flickering glow of the hurricane lamp. I'm getting a hard-on, he realized, and then, with a jolt: so is Reed. He took a step back. "Should I put on some music?" he asked.

"I don't need a damn thing," said Reed. "Except maybe your knife." Earley must have looked startled; Reed actually smiled.

"I don't think my jeans will fit over this cast," he said. Earley nodded, his heart pounding too fast. He imagined sliding his knife up the leg of Reed's blue jeans and slitting the fabric off him like opening an oyster. It turned him on.

He wrapped his arms around Reed's back, lowering him to

the mattress. He'd meant to get up and go back for his knife, but Reed wouldn't let go. He pulled Earley on top of his body, angling his cast to one side so that Earley was straddling his unbroken leg. Their mouths found each other, tongues twining like lovers. Earley could feel his body responding, some primitive part of his brain taking hold. And then he felt Reed's hand unzipping his jeans.

"Okay?" Reed whispered. Earley didn't answer. His breath caught as Reed's fingers took hold of his cock.

Earley closed his eyes. The glow of the hurricane lamp seemed to pulsate inside his eyelids. The room swirled to the rhythm of Reed's moving hand. A whirlwind of images flew past him, too fast to grasp: Zan's red dress. Her mouth. Margie's waterbed. Reed and Zan fucking. His brother. Zan's nipples. Zan clutching his back. Zan convulsing in ecstasy, bringing him with her. Zan weeping against his chest.

Zan.

Earley let out a low animal moan. He could feel something pressing against his thigh, hard and insistent. Reed's penis, he realized, straining against the blue denim. Earley's own inner pressure rose with it, volcanic.

God help me, he thought as he came.

TWENTY-ONE

Earley woke up with Reed's face on his chest. Christ, he thought. Now what? His mind was still bleary from smoking so much, but it didn't take too many brain cells to realize that he'd landed himself in a wide world of trouble. At least I've still got my pants on, he thought, as if that would absolve him of something.

Reed sighed in his sleep. What the hell am I going to do with this guy? Earley wondered. He's going to be useless for work with that leg, and the fucker is snoring on top of my nipple. He fought back the urge to shove Reed away; he wanted to get out of bed without waking him.

Earley reached for a pillow, then sidled away from Reed, carefully wedging the pillow where he had just been. He was most of the way off the futon when Reed flopped over suddenly, flinging his arm across Earley's hip. Earley pushed it away without thinking, then froze, sure he'd awakened Reed. Reed didn't stir. Relieved, Earley swung his legs onto the floor and unfolded himself towards the bus's low ceiling. He slunk to the kitchen, stepped into his unlaced boots and ducked out the front door.

The clearing was thick with mist, all the familiar landmarks obscured. Tree trunks loomed up into nothingness, low boughs receding in layers of scrim. Earley took a deep breath. He could feel the faint needling of sideways rain, misting cool moisture all over his skin. It was almost as good as a shower. He leaned back and closed his eyes, letting the miniature drops cool his eyelids. This was more like it. Now he was someone he recognized. Someone he knew how to be.

He shook his wet head like a dog and set off towards the twin hemlock saplings where he'd dug the latrine. In moments, the midnight-blue bus was swallowed by swirling fog. I could get totally lost, he thought, wending his way down the path that revealed itself only a couple of steps at a time. The thought pleased him. He imagined just walking off into the woods and never returning, living off berries and steelhead. He had his Buck knife and a good pair of boots; what more did a man really need?

Earley unzipped and took hold of his dick, stopping short at the memory of Reed's fingers doing the same thing last night.

And I came like a shot, Earley thought. What the hell does that make me?

Well, I didn't touch *his*, he thought savagely, pissing. He thought of the hundreds of times that he'd stood at a urinal next to some stranger and whipped out his joint without giving it two seconds' thought. Never again, he thought. Now I'll be wondering whether he thinks I'm a faggot. Earley stood still for a moment, listening to drops shift through boughs. Then he zipped up his fly and headed back into the fog.

The bus smelled like a Led Zeppelin concert. The stink of stale pot smoke hit Earley between the eyes as soon as he opened the door. He made extra-strong coffee and poured nearly all of it into his thermos, hoping he'd make it out to his truck before Reed even woke. The guy was on serious painkillers, codeine and Darvon, plus a few hits of the Thai stick that Earley had rolled to catch up with him. Maybe he'd sleep until noon. Earley knew he was being a coward, but he was willing to live with himself if it got him back into the clearcut. He craved a long stretch of solitude so intensely it felt like a thirst. Work would steady him, help clear his head. He smeared peanut butter across a tortilla and rolled it up hastily, grabbing some chips and a couple bananas. Then he heard a low groan from his bedroom. Damn. Reed was awake.

Earley had never been lucky with exits. He pictured himself

hunkered down behind Margie's propane tank and winced. Reed knew he was up; there was no graceful way to get out without seeing him first. Earley could hear sounds of thumping and shifting behind the orange curtains. He imagined Reed struggling painfully onto his cast, standing up to the sound of a door slam. Too harsh, he thought. I can't do that to him. "Need help?" he called back to Reed.

"Nah," came the answer. "I'm cool." Reed parted the curtains and flashed a shy smile. He hobbled out, steadying himself with a hand on the wall. He'd slept in his jeans, and they hung down so low that his hipbones stuck out like twin blades.

"How's your leg?"

"It sucks." Reed sounded cheerful. He scooped up a container of pills from the trunk and swallowed one dry. Then he looked in the kitchen and saw Earley's lunch on the counter.

"You're going to work?" Reed's voice came out strained, less accusing than hurt.

Earley squirmed. "Might as well. Gotta go get your tools before they rust. Thought I'd carve up the rest of that big monster log while I'm at it."

Reed didn't say a word. He looked down at the split-open apple, now brown, that was pinned to the table with Earley's knife. Earley continued, "I would've come in, but I figured you needed the rest more than anything."

"More than good morning? More than how are you feeling?"

"I already asked."

"How my leg is. I don't give a shit about my damn leg." Reed reached out for Earley's hand. Earley withdrew it.

"Look, Reed, I didn't . . . I've never done that before."

"Neither have I," said Reed. Earley nodded, relieved. So it was just something that came out of nowhere, maybe because they had gotten so stoned, or because they were both missing Zan. There was no need to put it in words.

"But I've wanted to." Reed said it quietly, staring down at his hands.

Something closed off inside Earley's chest. He wanted to beg Reed to stop, not to say any more, but it was already too late. The words had been spoken, the boundary was crossed. "You can't unconfess a confession," Earley's gramma had said to him once, many years ago, and he knew that Reed's words had burned into his brain in the very same way, that he'd still remember them years from now.

Reed looked at him. "Not just with you. There was this Portuguese kid on my track team, Fernando. We used to train distance together. We were buddies, you know, both had girlfriends and all, but I couldn't stop thinking about him, what it would be like . . . " He trailed off, staring out at the fog. "It's just always been there. Way down deep under everything else."

Earley did not want to hear about guys named Fernando. "But what about Zan?"

"What about her?" Reed asked, his voice tender.

"I thought you were madly in love with her."

"I am," said Reed. "You can be more than one thing at once."

Earley didn't answer. The picture he couldn't escape, of himself reaching out for the nape of Reed's neck, had leaped back into his head again. He felt dizzy, uprooted. Reed was still talking, he realized.

"Look, I spent two years living in San Francisco and didn't come out. You've got to figure this wasn't the top of my wish list." Reed was looking right at him, his blue eyes imploring. "It doesn't change who I am. I'm not going to wear feather boas and platform shoes."

"What do you call those?" said Earley, jabbing a toe at Reed's caulk boots, which stood on the mat by the door. Reed laughed. He thinks it's a joke, Earley realized; he thinks I'm okay with this. He swallowed hard as Reed stepped forward, pressing his cheek against Earley's wool shirt.

"When you carried me down off the mountain, you know what I thought? 'This is as close as I'll ever get. This is worth breaking my leg for.'"

"I'm not," Earley said. This was scaring him.

"Yes, you are." Reed's voice was fervent. He shook his head. "I can't believe that I'm saying this out loud. It's been in my head for so long."

Earley took a deep breath, extricating himself from Reed's arms. "Look, I don't know how that happened last night, but it was a one-time thing."

"Not for me," said Reed.

"Well, I'm not gonna do it again." Earley's voice sounded strident, even to his ears. "It's just not who I am."

"It's a part of you," Reed said. "The part that you don't want to look at."

"You got that right," said Earley. "I don't."

Reed's eyes traveled over his face. "Okay," he said quietly. "That's pretty clear. So I guess I just live with it." He limped towards the door.

"Where are you going?"

"I have to piss something wicked."

"Do it out the emergency door," Earley said. "There's no steps."

"I can handle the steps," said Reed. "Got to get used to this." He limped forward and Earley made room for him, turning away as Reed thumped down the stairs and pushed open the door.

"Fuckin' chowdah out there," Reed went on. "I can't see a damn thing." He stood on the bottom step, arcing spray into the fog. When he turned back, he still had his dick in his hand.

"What the hell are you doing?" snapped Earley.

"That's all the difference," said Reed. "Between me and the other three hundred people you've slept with."

Earley felt his blood rising, his hands stiffening into fists. "If you didn't have that damn cast on, I'd slam you right through that door."

"Do it," said Reed, raising both hands in surrender. His

penis stuck out of his jeans like a big veiny finger, pointing directly at Earley. I'm going to kill you, thought Earley. He thought of the knife on the table, the rifle stashed over his head, the edge of the gorge. A dangerous rage simmered under his skull; he felt like his father, about to explode any which way, and God help whoever was standing in range.

"I'm going to work," Earley said in a low growl. "Get out of my way."

They stood for a long moment facing each other, like gunfighters waiting to draw. Then Reed reached down and zipped his fly. Earley scooped up his thermos and left without saying good-bye.

Earley worked without pause, attacking the rest of the giant log. Then he picked up the mallet and froe Reed had left there the previous day and hammered the fragrant rounds, splitting off bolt after bolt, unrelenting. He worked till sweat poured down his face and his sides heaved. Fuck, he thought. Fuck. It's not helping.

How did it happen? he wondered, his mind swinging wild as he wielded the wedge-shaped froe, crashing it down into wood. The memories cascaded through his whole body: the taste of Reed's tongue and the warmth of his fingers, their sliding caress. But the image that seized him up most was of Reed hunching over his mandolin, freezing as Earley reached out to stroke his neck. I made the first move, he thought. Reed took it further, but I touched him first.

Earley shook his head, trying to dislodge the memory. Not in my wildest dreams, he thought. He'd been stymied to find himself sharing a bed with a man and a woman, but this was beyond any sense of himself that he'd ever imagined. He wasn't as shaken by what Reed had done—a hand job was nothing, just locker room stuff; any port in a storm—as by what he, Earley Jude Ritter, lifelong lover of women, had felt as he reached for Reed's neck. That was the part no amount of hard work could erase.

Earley shouldered the mallet and stood looking down over Suhammish clearcut. The afternoon sun was beginning to burn off the fog, so it lifted in vertical wisps, like an old-country vision of souls in flight, rising to judgment. Below him, the fireweed was starting to bud out in vivid pink spires. Earley loved fireweed for its willfulness, rising from ash and mud, the gashed land's first effort to heal itself. Next would come shrubs, alder, Douglas fir, hemlock and finally western red cedar, the climax species, the second growth. In a century even the sawed-off stumps he was leaving behind would be gone for good, reclaimed by moss and rot. No one would know this had once been a clearcut, that some sad pair of shake-rats had busted their humps on this mountainside, scraping a living from splinters of wood.

Nothing stays put, Earley thought. In a couple more days he'd have cut up the last of the oldgrowth stumps and bundled their cords for the chopper line. Clay Johannsen would carry them off to the mill, and Earley would never set foot on this ridge again. He looked to the west, where hill after green hill unrolled to the skyline. How many of them would be shaved down to mud by this Royalton contract? His road would be gutted by skidders and bulldozers, his clearing turned into a heavy equipment lot. Even the waterfall creek would be ruined, its clear water clotted with mudslides and slash.

Time to move on. Earley was sick of that phrase, not just of the words but of the whole notion of living his life as a ram-bling man. Rootlessness was its own sort of harness; he felt as tied down by the obligation to keep on moving as he would be by settling. Maybe more, he reflected, thinking about the cabin he'd wanted to build, with its view of Olympus. That would have been something new, at least, in a lifetime of mov-ing from one makeshift perch to another. He had a quick flash of himself as an old man, hunched over some knife-scratched bar, all jutting elbows and leathery fading tattoos. But I don't even have the tattoos, he thought. Too much commitment.

He thought of the words to that Joplin song Reed had been playing last night. *Freedom's just another word for nothing left to lose.* Guess I'm free, he thought glumly. In a few short weeks, he'd have to scratch out a new home for himself, to drive his bus into some other clearing, learn its trees, streams and gul-lies by heart and then, more than likely, move on again. Would Reed still be with him? Would Zan?

Zan. Earley's heart pounded harder as soon as he thought of

her. He wanted to be with her right now, to bury himself in her body and lick the salt tears from her cheeks as she came. She would still all the voices that plagued him, make him feel whole.

I need to get laid, he thought. Laid by a woman. Reed was stuck at the bus; there was nothing to stop Earley from driving up to the treeplanters' camp and striding right into Zan's tent. He could carry her off like a pirate, or take her right there, in the mud and straw. Zan was as carnal as he was, a restless appetite seeking release. Earley could still feel the rush of emotion that had surged through him the very first time they made love, the sensation of power and knowledge, of primeval mating, their two bodies fusing like some force of nature. Reed could never be those things to him.

He could feel the heat rise through his groin like sap through a tree. I want her this minute, he thought. I can't wait until Friday. He grabbed up his Husqy and started downhill.

His truck wouldn't start. Earley turned it over twice, checked the gas gauge, the fan belt, the clutch. He was cursing a blue streak before it occurred to him that he'd stuck the wrong key into the ignition. What a bonehead, he thought as he backed up, his tires spitting gravel and gouging out ruts.

The shadows were lengthening as Earley pulled out of the clearcut. He could picture Reed back in the bus, replaying the three tapes of Earley's he liked as he cooked up some goddamn elaborate dinner. Well, he could eat it himself. Earley stepped on the gas, bumping so hard over an old skidder track that his pickup lurched sideways and his rotten tooth sent a stab of pain up through his skull.

He wondered how Reed had been getting along on his cast all day long. Had he run out of wood? Could he make his way down to the creek to haul water? That path would be tough to negotiate on a crutch. Five years ago, when Earley had gashed his thigh with his chainsaw, the guy he'd been working with, Leroy, had stayed by his side like an army nurse till he was back on his feet. Men were supposed to take care of each other. Deserters were scum.

All right, Earley thought, then I'm scum. No big news there; just ask Margie Walkonis. My scum credentials are legion.

He sped towards the fork where the main road continued downhill to the highway and town, and his own muddy spur switchbacked up to the bus. If he kept going straight, he could be inside Zan's tent in less than an hour. Reed would be worried when he didn't show up for dinner, but Reed was a big boy; he'd cope. Even if he was hurt. Earley mentally kicked himself. Scum.

He was right at the fork now. His foot lifted off the gas pedal, hovering over the brake. I want her, he thought, and went straight down the hill.

Earley snapped on the radio at the exact spot where Reed had discovered the static died out, but there was nothing worth listening to, just hellfire and brimstone and Toni Tennille. The highway whizzed under his tires, and he realized he hadn't driven to town by himself since the night he'd picked Reed up hitching. He remembered how Reed had stood huddled up in his drenched poncho, the dazed way he'd stared when the pickup pulled over, his eyes wide and ghostly, as if he had given up hope.

It was strange to remember how green Reed had seemed at first glance, spacey and nervous and painfully young. If he hadn't lit up that reefer, thought Earley, I would have left him on the road outside Bogachiel campground and never looked back. I'd have taken my shower and gone to the Cedar, and Zan would have been there shooting pool. I would have met her all by myself. One man and one woman, like everyone else.

Earley pondered on this for a moment. He had to admit there were flaws in his argument, starting with not having had even *one* dime for a shower if Reed hadn't been with him. And would he really have had the raw nerve to walk up to the beautiful woman he'd seen bending over the pool table, when he was flat broke and stunk to high heaven, without even knowing her name?

Probably not, he conceded. He probably would have just sat on his barstool and fantasized, too awkward to hit on someone who was so clearly out of his league. Reed had brought them together. Just as Zan had brought him together with Reed.

He pulled his truck onto the shoulder, just past the curve where he'd picked up Reed. I can't do it, he thought. I can't leave him alone.

Reed was making spaghetti and meatballs, green salad, no fuss. He was wearing an old V-necked undershirt, ripped at the notch, and those loose drawstring pants he had worn to the laundromat, the ones Gladys Keneally called trousers. He had slit the right leg to the knee to make room for his cast. "How'd it go?" he asked, trying to keep his voice casual as he looked up from the chopping board.

"Fair." Earley sat on the driver's seat to unlace his caulks, jerking the straps off the boothooks one-handed. "Got the rest of that log we were working on bucked up and bundled. I'll drop by the mill and put in for a flyout next week."

"Take me with you," said Reed. "I've been doing a whole bunch of reading, and I've got some questions about this new clearcut they're trying to ram down our throats. We're right at the edge of the national park. That's protected land. There are watershed issues. I think we can still pull the plug on it if we get organized."

No way in hell, Earley thought; the last thing he needed was Reed rolling out some tree-hugger rant at Vern Gillies. And if anyone caught any whiff of an off-color vibe between him and Reed, he'd be dead meat in Forks for the rest of his life. Earley kicked off his caulk boots and reached for the basin and soap. Reed handed them over and went to the stove for the kettle.

"You're getting around pretty well on that thing," Earley

said, watching him walk. He wished Reed had put on different pants. Those gauzy things clung to his ass.

"I'm a runner," said Reed. "I've had every leg injury going. Shin splints, sprains, tendonitis, torn ligament. I don't know when to give up." He poured hot water into the basin, then dipped in a washcloth, wrung out the excess and laid it across Earley's forehead. Earley tensed at his touch.

"You don't have to—"

"I want to," said Reed. "It's the least I can do." He dabbed the steaming cloth along Earley's brow, wiping away sweat and sawdust as he moved it gently over his cheekbone, the side of his beard. A few drops of hot water dribbled down Earley's bare throat, soaking the neck of his undershirt.

"How'd you get this?" Reed asked, one finger stroking the bald strip of skin where the scar tissue parted the stubble.

"Hatchet," said Earley. "Splitting kindling when I was stoned, drunk and stupid."

Reed smiled. "Like last night?"

"Cut it out," Earley stood quickly, pushing his hand away. "I'm heading over to Zan's. I just stopped in to make sure your leg was okay."

"Bullshit," said Reed. "You came home because you want me too."

Earley's hand had flown out in a fist before he even made a decision about it. Reed crumpled against the dinette table, clutching his stomach. He made a guttural grunting noise, retching up air.

"You okay?" Earley asked, with his fist still cocked. Reed staggered forward and punched him hard under the jawbone.

"Now I am," Reed rasped, balling his fists like a prep school boxer.

Earley saw that Reed's knuckles had split and were bleeding. He tasted the metal and salt tang of blood on his own lower lip and grabbed at Reed savagely. He's half my size and his leg's broken; this isn't fair, he thought as they grappled, but they weren't fighting anymore: Earley was pressing his cut mouth to Reed's and Reed's mouth was gasping against his, and Earley was bending him over the cedar slab table, shoving the dishes away to bear down on his body, relentless.

TWENTY-TWO

Earley knocked off work early on Friday and drove into Forks by himself. He was looking for Clay Johannsen, the chopper pilot who contracted wood runs for Gillies' mill. He'd heard various rumors of where Clay was living these days—he moved almost weekly, from fishing boat cabin to trailer to biker chick's sofabed—but he figured that someone at Gillies' would know how to track the man down.

Reed was going to be pissed at him. That was a given. At breakfast, Reed had gone off on one of his rants about stopping the Royalton clearcut, insisting that Earley come back and get him before he drove down to the mill. Earley hadn't said yes, but he hadn't said no either; he had simply avoided the question and let Reed assume he'd agreed. And leaving

Reed up at the bus while he went into town was the tip of the iceberg: both of them knew Zan was coming tonight. Earley's guilt-ridden thrashings with Reed didn't stand a chance next to the real thing. He was dying to get Zan in bed, and he knew that Reed knew it. Whatever he did, Reed was going to be pissed.

Earley bounced his truck into the mud-rutted lot outside Gillies'. The mill was in full swing, workers swarming like hornets. Two crews were offloading their day's haul of logs; Earley was glad neither log truck was Harlan's. At the end of the lot, he spotted a purple-and-black motorcycle parked at an angle, its front wheel stretched out on a long, Easy Rider–style axle. Clay's Harley. Only a true timber madman would ride a hog in a place that got ten feet of rainfall a year, Earley thought as he parked alongside it. The spikes of his caulks pulled up divots with every step, caking his feet with a layer of clay. He heard the scream of bandsaws tearing into raw wood and the magnified clanking of cranes dropping logs into place. The air was thick with pine resin and the spicy grit of cedar sawdust; Earley could feel it right down to his lungs.

He swung open the office door, surprised to find nobody at the cash register. He rapped on the doorframe to Vern's inner office and looked inside. Nobody there either. Well, it was payday—someone had to show up pretty soon.

Earley spotted a topo map on Vern's desk and stepped closer to look at it. His eye swept from the glacial formations on top of Olympus to the coast, looking for the familiar double-S curve and twin forks of Suhammish Creek. There were red-numbered sections blocked off on both sides. Earley traced the west fork from clearcut Unit A-46 to the spot where he'd parked his bus, in the wedge of virgin forest that started at the creek and stretched to the summit of Suhammish Peak. That section was outlined in yellow. Two thousand acres, he thought. It must be the whole flank of the mountain.

"The fuck are you doing here?"

Earley turned. Vern was glaring at him from the door. "I ought to plug your thick skull. Tramping into a man's private office."

"Keep your shirt on, I'm not in your cashbox. Just checking this map."

"That's your future in black and white. Harlan Walkonis catch up with you yet?"

"Yeah, he drove up my driveway and let off some noise."

"More than noise," said Vern, spitting a gob of snoose into a Coke can. "Those bulldozers gonna be rolling the end of this month."

"You got a spare copy of this?" Earley picked up the map.

"Not for you," Vern said. "And I got no time for weighing out your pissant shake bolts today. I'm up to my eyeballs in serious lumber."

"I'm not here to sell," Earley told him. "I'm looking for Clay-borne."

"He's up in the air. Flying in some equipment for Gus Ritchie's outfit, up near Lake Ozette. You looking to order a flyout? 'Cause I've got his schedule right here on my desk." Vern riffled through piles of paper and squinted down at a clipboard. "How about the tenth at ten? Even you ought to be able to keep track of that."

Earley decided to sidestep the sarcasm. If Vern Gillies needed to feel a bit smarter by telling himself other people were stupider, that was his problem. "You're on," Earley said, quietly sliding the topo map under his jacket.

The aisles of the FoodMart were full of tired housewives with overstuffed carts. Earley turned each corner warily. He was sure that he'd run into Margie, still wearing her pink cafeteria smock, loading up on Doritos and Tab for another long weekend alone. He wondered if Margie knew that Harlan was trying to force him out of his clearing. Probably not. Even if Harlan's new chippie had already booted him back home, he wasn't the kind of guy who told things to his wife.

What would he say to Margie if he did run into her? Earley had always prided himself on doing the right thing by women— assuming that they didn't dump him, of course, which they usually did—but he knew he'd left Margie marooned in her loneliness, nobody home but the ghosts of her kids. He winced at the thought of her running into him here, buying dinner for both of his other lovers.

"Hey, Ritter!" The voice was a man's. Earley turned to see Scoter Gillies, flashing his snaggle-toothed grin as he slouched over, lugging a twelve-pack of Colt 45. "What the sam fuck are those things, mutant scallions?"

"Pretty much." Earley turned, shamefaced, and tossed three leeks into the top of his cart with the lentils and ginger root.

Scoter let out a low whistle. "You know how to cook with this shit?"

"I'm strictly Swanson's TV. Reed does most of the cooking."

"Your splitter? I heard where he tried to make firewood out of his anklebone."

"He's one hurting boy." Earley tried to match Scoter's tone. He felt as if he was impersonating some former self, like a tired comedian hauling out shopworn routines.

Scoter nodded. "Hard times, man. So you're cutting solo?"

"Done cutting, just stacking it up for the chopper. I've got shitloads of cedar up top of the ridge, half a mile from the road as the crow flies and twice that on foot."

"Who's flying you, Clay J?"

"I just signed him up at your dad's."

Scoter nodded. "Don't count on him making it. Old Clayborne's been looking a little red-rimmed in the nasal department these days."

"He always did have a touch of the sniffing sickness."

"Touch my ass, he's a medicine cabinet on legs," Scoter said. "I bet you could barter him some of that Maui if lame boy is interested. Think on it." He thumped Earley hard on the back and winked. It was just normal guy stuff, but it made Earley twitch. What would Scoter have said if he knew about him and Reed? Touch my ass, indeed.

Earley forced a smile and said, "Later." He swung his cart towards the front of the store, found a checkout that wasn't too busy and piled his things onto the rubber conveyor. The cashier finished bagging the order ahead of his and turned to face him. It was Amber Walkonis. She looked at Earley with a suspicious squint.

"You're that friend of my mom's," she said.

Earley added a blue pouch of Drum to his grocery pile. The last thing he wanted to do was get Margie in trouble. "You're Harlan's kid, right? I know your old man," he said, wondering if Amber was still shacking up with her boyfriend Miguel. Her eyelids were thick with mascara and liner, as if she was already trying to pass for the much older woman she'd look like too soon. She'd inherited Margie's big bust, but also her thickness; at sixteen, her flesh was already squeezed over her waistband. Her face was her father's, cheeks carved out of ham.

"What's this thing?" she said, lifting the ginger without showing any more interest in Earley. "It don't have a price marked."

"I can't believe you went shopping without me," said Reed, slamming grocery bags onto the counter. "We're out of all sorts of stuff. Ginger. Tamari."

"I got your tamari," said Earley. "And ginger, and leeks, and all sorts of fancy-ass crap no one else in Forks eats." He slapped down a pile of Reed's mail: three letters from environmental groups and six magazines sent Please Forward from Berkeley.

"You just didn't want to be seen with me."

"Bullshit," said Earley, too loudly. "I was afraid I'd miss Clay if I drove all the way up to get you. And while I was down there I stopped to pick up some dinner for Zan."

"Yeah, for *Zan*." Reed's voice sounded petulant.

Earley took a deep breath, reminding himself it was tacky to slug guys on crutches. "For all three of us, asshole."

"Don't call me an asshole, you asshole."

"All right," Earley said, "you're a prick."

It took Reed a moment to realize Earley was joking. Then he burst out laughing. "Hey, you know those humongous banana slugs we always find in the compost?"

"Yeah," Earley said. "What about them?" He took Vern's folded topo map from his pocket and stuck it in the storage rack next to his fly kit. He'd show it to Reed when he had enough patience, which wasn't right now.

Reed picked up one of his library books and opened it up to a page he'd bookmarked with a Zig-Zag. "'Slugs are hermaphrodites; each has both male and female sex organs and is capable of self-fertilization if no mate is found.'"

"They can fuck themselves?"

"Wait. 'A potential pair may follow one another and cavort

for a day; then copulate for another two or three days and nights, exchanging sperm reciprocally.'"

Earley cracked open a beer. "Remind me to be a slug in my next incarnation."

"Um, not so fast. 'The penis—an inch long—is so large and turgid that withdrawal is apparently difficult. The solution sometimes is to gnaw it off.'" Reed closed the book. "So much for your next incarnation."

"This is what you've been doing all day? Reading slug porn?"

"Believe me, I'd rather be working." Reed helped himself to a gulp of Earley's beer. "Did you stop off at Bogachiel?"

Earley shook his head, moving away from him. "Figured I'd have enough time for a waterfall shower before Zan shows up." He pushed a few cans of garbanzos and tuna fish onto the shelf.

"I could use one myself. I'm as rank as a goat." Reed glanced at his watch, which he'd hung from a nail near the stove. "We've got enough time to drive over to Bogachiel now. She never gets here before sunset."

"You can't get your cast wet," said Earley.

"You could make me one of those Hefty bag boots you made Zan," said Reed. "Duct tape all over the thighs. That was kinky." He slid his hand between Earley's legs.

Earley removed it. No way in hell was he going to get kinky with Reed in the men's room at Bogachiel. It was a Friday night stop-off for mill rats and logging crews getting spruced up for a night at the Cedar, and practically everyone else that he knew.

"I'm fine with the creek," he said, touching Reed's shoulder. "Think you could get down there?"

"I could climb to the top of Mount Kilimanjaro," said Reed. "I'm a hobbling fool."

Reed left his crutch inside the bus. "I'm walking much better," he said as he picked his slow way down the trail. "I'll be back on the job in no time."

"Uh-huh. Tell me if you need a hand," Earley said, stepping up and over a moss-covered blowdown that was sprouting a whole colonnade of new saplings.

Reed hesitated. "You think you could pick me up again?"

Earley squinted at him. Did he really need help, or was this just a ploy for more contact? Reed seemed to sense Earley's reluctance. His wide eyes looked plaintive, as if he'd already guessed what the answer would be and was worried he shouldn't have asked. Why make a federal case of it? thought Earley, just give him a hand. He stepped back over the nurse log and lifted Reed up in his arms. "Just call me Rhett Butler," he drawled.

"You *are* Rhett Butler." Reed kissed Earley's neck, in the scruff of his beard.

"No 'count two-timing Southern boy. That would be me."

"I am so goddamn happy," Reed said. "I just want you to know that."

"I do," Earley said, brusquely setting Reed down on the opposite side of the log. He didn't like talking about this kind of thing, never had; he felt equally awkward when women insisted on putting a name onto feelings that didn't belong in words. Things were what they were. There was no need to blurt.

It took them a long time to reach the gorge. They could hear the dull roar of the falls up ahead. A low slice of sun rayed out under the gunmetal cloud mass, striping the trail with the shadows of trees. They passed the steep gully where Reed's ruined mattress lay splayed across rocks, and turned onto the switchback trail, sending down showers of gravel. The last stretch was steep, and Reed leaned against Earley's arm. I like how this feels, Earley realized. I like being useful to someone.

The water was high, and the falls tumbled noisily, sending off sheer veils of mist. Both of them stripped, and when Earley looked up and saw Reed's slender body against a green backdrop of moss and maidenhair ferns, his breath caught in his throat. All this time he'd been holding back, telling himself it was Reed who'd been hitting on him, but deep in his gut Earley knew the desire ran both ways. And desire was the tip of the iceberg. The word for what Earley was feeling as he looked at Reed was much harder to face. He shoved it away. I'm in love with Zan, he reminded himself. You can't be in love with two people.

Reed turned towards him, naked. "You ready to bag me?" he asked.

Earley dug through his backpack, relieved to have something concrete to do. He set the two towels and soap on a rock, then took out the duct tape and trash bag and brought them to Reed.

"Step in," he said, flapping the bag open. Reed obeyed. Earley knelt down to gather the plastic around his foot, tying it off at the ankle with duct tape. He unrolled the tape in a slow spiral upwards till he saw Reed's dick, right at face level, rising to meet him. Reed slid his hand under his stiffening penis.

"Kiss it," he said.

Earley felt a revulsion well up in his throat. This was a boundary that they hadn't crossed, for all their feverish kissing and groping. The thought made him queasy.

"I can't," he said, standing up quickly.

"You want me too, Earley. Look at yourself." Reed took a step forward, sliding his hands around Earley's buttocks and arching his back so their dicks clashed like swords. Earley felt an electric shock race through his body. Was it rage or arousal?

"Suck mine," he said, hating the harsh note he heard in his voice, the pounding he felt in his veins. He grabbed Reed by the shoulders, pushing him downwards. Reed swung his lame leg to one side, grunting with effort, and lowered himself to the opposite knee. Then he took Earley's penis in both hands, as if he were praying, and leaned forward, taking him into his mouth.

Earley shut his eyes, breathing hard. I've crossed the line, he thought. Now I'm a faggot. Reed spluttered and spat him out, gagging. "Sorry," he mumbled, and tried again. Earley winced. He could feel Reed's teeth scraping his skin; he tried not to think of banana slugs mating. Reed seemed to be trying to figure out what he should do with his tongue. He shifted position and Earley recoiled.

This has got to be the most incompetent blow job I've ever had, Earley thought as Reed fumbled and chewed. Sure, Reed was new on this side of the table, but hadn't he ever *had* one? He ought to have some kind of notion of what would feel good; he'd been serviced by Zan. Earley thought of her lips gliding over his foreskin, and it sent a shudder of ecstasy through his whole body. Reed gagged again, choking.

"I'm sorry," he muttered.

"It's okay," Earley breathed as Reed took him back in, more smoothly this time. "That feels good." He realized he wasn't lying; it *did* feel good. A shiver ran through him. He felt himself gasp.

Lips are lips, Earley thought; tongues are tongues. Male or female, what did it matter? He closed his eyes tight and succumbed to the waves of sensation. When he opened them up, he was looking at Zan.

TWENTY-THREE

For an instant he thought he'd imagined her, summoning her into flesh by sheer force of desire. But no, there she was, on the edge of the cliff overlooking the gorge, staring at them in stunned disbelief.

"Zan," Earley blurted, pulling away as Reed twisted to look. She turned and stamped into the woods. "Wait," he cried, knowing the word was ridiculous, even if she could have heard his voice over the roar of the waterfall. He lunged at the cliff, scrambling up the sheer rockface, grabbing on to bare roots, finding toeholds in gravel. He could hear Reed below, struggling to pull himself up on his cast, but he didn't look back or hesitate. Nothing mattered but getting to Zan.

Earley came over the top of the cliff near his cabin site. He struggled through brush, dodging blackberry brambles and devil's club, fighting his way towards the path to the bus. He ran through the trees to the sound of glass breaking.

Zan had yanked his axe out of the chopping block and was slamming it through the bus's side windows. "Stop that," he shouted. She swung again. The window shattered and shards of glass crashed into the kitchen and fell in the mud at her feet.

Earley grabbed her right arm at the shoulder and wrist. "Drop it," he said. Zan resisted, twisting against his grasp. Earley forced the axe out of her hand and threw it as far as he could into the woods. "What the hell are you doing?"

"You bastards," she said.

"Can I let go of you now, or are you going to kill me?"

"Let go or I *will* kill you."

"Okay," Earley said, backing away with his hands up.

"Not funny." She glared at him.

"Neither is trashing my bus." Earley's chest heaved as he gulped for breath. He had streaks of mud on his belly and arms, with thin stripes of blood where the brambles had grabbed him. Zan stared at him for a long time, as if she was seeing him for the first time. He felt as if she could read every thought in his head, all the shame and confusion and heartache that churned through his guts like a whirlpool. Zan's eyes seemed unnaturally bright. Beneath all her fury, he sensed something else, something he couldn't identify. He had the peculiar sensation that she was about to break down.

"So how long have you two"— she started, and changed her mind. "Why is Reed's leg in a trash bag?"

Now that was one question he didn't expect. "Broke his ankle."

"When?"

Earley thought. "Tuesday, I guess."

Zan's eyebrows knit into a thundercloud. "Neither one of you thought about coming to tell me? I guess you were too busy fucking each other."

"It's not like that."

"What is it like?" she said. "Better than me?"

"No," Earley said. "Not at all."

"You know he's in love with you." It wasn't a question. Her eyes were dark, wounded. "If you weren't so blind you'd have noticed it ages ago. It's been in his eyes since the first night he met you. I knew I would lose him."

Earley looked down at the violin curves of her body, so different from Reed's skinny frame. "Did you know he was gay?"

"Reed isn't gay," Zan said bitterly. "It's you. He's in love with *you.*"

"I don't get it," said Earley.

"No, you wouldn't," she said. "You don't have a clue how much power you've got, just by being yourself. That's what makes you so . . ." Her voice scraped and broke. She looked up at him, biting her lip, and Earley realized she had just told him she loved him. His heart lurched with pleasure. Zan loved him, enough to smash windows when she thought he'd fallen for somebody else. She wasn't disgusted, or angry at him; she was feeling abandoned. "I never thought you'd take him up on it, Earley. Guess it serves me right, getting you both in the same bed."

"Why is this any different? 'Cause you're not the only one who gets both of us?"

"Fuck you," said Zan, lunging at him again. Earley caught both her wrists.

"You shouldn't do that to a naked man," he said, pressing his body against hers. "I might get ideas."

Zan lifted her knee to his groin, with just enough pressure to show him how much she could hurt him. "Don't pull that brute strength crap on me. I'm not helpless."

"Who said you were?" Zan was a lot of things, but helpless was not on the list. Even now she was changing her tune. Earley let out a groan. Her knee was still pressing against his balls, but now it was moving in slow, deliberate circles, massaging him, making him hard. He could feel her body heat right through her clothes, the jut of her nipples against his bare chest.

"Can Reed make you feel like that?" she whispered.

No, Earley thought, and neither can anyone else. Talk about helpless. He looked down at Zan, wondering what she would do to his balls if he kissed her. I love you too, he thought, feeling the unformed words scrape at the back of his throat. Say it, he thought. Just say it out loud. You can do it. He took a deep breath.

"Earley? Zan?" Reed called from the path, his voice tense and anxious.

Earley groaned, cursing under his breath. Zan slipped out of his grasp, turning towards Reed as he limped to the edge of the clearing.

"What's all that glass?" Reed asked. "What got broken?"

"Your ankle," said Zan. "A few windows. Few promises."

Reed stopped walking. He had Earley's backpack slung over one shoulder and their towels and clothes heaped up in his arms. Earley's irritation surged at the notion that Reed had picked up after him. Like a wife, he thought. Though Reed's hard-on wasn't especially wifely. He noticed Zan looking from his dick to Reed's. A defiant half-smile played over her lips. "All right, then, if that's how it is. Both at once. I've been wanting to try that." She walked to the clearing beside Earley's truck and kicked off her boots, testing the cushiony moss with her toes.

"Either of you want to join me?" Zan crossed her hands at the hem of her T-shirt and peeled it off slowly, her arms rising over her head so her breasts strained against her lace bra. She reached back to unhook it. Earley felt the roof of his mouth go dry. A minute ago she'd been threatening him with a knee in the crotch, and now she was acting like some kind of stripper. I can't figure her out, he thought. Maybe that's how she does it. Keeps changing the rules until you surrender and follow her blindly.

Reed dropped the clothes he was holding and went straight to Zan, kissing her with a sudden ferocity. Earley was struck again by how easily their bodies fit together, no bending or stooping to bring mouth to mouth. They looked made for each other, like Adam and Eve. Adam and Eve with a Hefty-bagged leg on the male of the species. Earley watched as Reed spread his palms over Zan's breasts, kneading the soft flesh like dough as he rammed his tongue into her mouth. He's not looking so gay at the moment, he thought. And I'm missing out. He took a step towards them.

Zan and Reed turned to him at the same moment, wrapping their arms around him in a three-way embrace. Earley felt hands running over his back and caressing his ass. Were they Zan's or Reed's? He lowered his face and felt both their mouths rising towards his. He closed his eyes, lost in a landscape of tongues, lips and fingers.

"Isn't this better?" breathed Zan, sliding her hand around Earley's cock. He looked down to see she had Reed's in her other hand.

"Handlebars," she said, pulling them closer.

That was the last thing that anyone said. Earley had no idea how long they made love to each other, rolling over and over in all that lush moss, trying every conceivable coupling of body parts, sticky with sweat-brine, insatiable. He lost track of all boundaries. Their bodies flowed into each other like tidewater. Earley's mind swam with images, wordless and fluid. He thought of the ocean, the wet, shifting places where surf and sand merge, of anemones, clustered in tidal pools, sucking and pulsing together as if they were part of the same organism. As if they were one.

Earley lay on his back in the damp moss with Zan and Reed nestled on top of him. Somebody's fingers were still tracing slow, lazy arcs on his belly. He didn't know whose and he didn't care. He looked up at the crowns of the trees, the granular shafts of light filtering down through the canopy. The sky had a strange golden clarity, as if the whole world had been varnished. The spiraling trill of a thrush filled his ears. I'm part of this world, he thought. I'm connected to all of this *life*.

He could hear sounds of an animal thrashing through brush, somewhere down the access road. Probably a deer. He remembered the Roosevelt elk on the Rainforest Trail, how the bull had made way for him, letting him into the herd. This is joy, Earley thought. This is what people mean when they talk about joy.

Zan let out a sigh of contentment, resting her cheek in the damp patch of fur on his breastbone, right over his heart. Reed lay next to her, wrapping his arms around both of their bodies.

"I'm staying," said Zan.

"Well, I hope so," said Earley.

"I don't mean this weekend. For good."

Reed raised his head. "What?"

Zan toyed with his ponytail, twining the hair around one of her fingers. "The tree-planting season is practically over. It's getting too warm. I can be Earley's splitter till you get your cast off."

"You're going to take over my job?" Reed's voice sounded sharp.

"You don't think I'm strong enough?"

"It isn't a question of strength," said Reed.

"What's it a question of? Balls, beard, testosterone?"

Reed turned his face towards Earley's. "What do you think about this?"

"Sssh," Earley said. While they were talking, the sounds on the road had grown louder and closer. Those aren't hooves, Earley realized; those are footfalls. He twisted his head to look past his truck.

"What the fuck?" Harlan Walkonis was standing by Earley's right fender, his face red with sweat and exertion. Zan froze at the sound of his voice. Harlan was gaping at them, and Earley realized what he must look like, splayed out on the ground with a nude man and woman lying on top of his body. He scrambled an arm towards Zan's T-shirt, but he couldn't reach it without exposing himself and the others. Harlan smirked, eyeing Reed's and Zan's buttocks, the black plastic wrapped around Reed's broken leg. "Kinky shit, Ritter. No wonder you live in the middle of nowhere."

Earley could see Reed's face color and Zan flinch from Harlan's view. He decided to brazen it out. "I do what I want, asshole. Why'd you come tiptoeing up here like some goddamn spy?"

"Very funny. It's gonna take more than some Volvo parked sideways to keep Royalton off your ass."

"Volvo?" Earley looked at Zan's face, which was inches from his.

"I got stuck in a ditch on the way up."

"What's this about Royalton?" Reed demanded, twisting his head around. Harlan looked startled, and Earley realized that he'd assumed the blond ponytail belonged to a woman.

"I'm serving you papers. You hippie fucks are evicted."

"You can't evict us," said Reed, rolling over to face him. "We have a legally signed stumpage contract with access rights."

Harlan eyed his crotch, glowering. "Your contract's on A-46. You're squatting on Royalton land and we'll bulldoze your bus if you don't drive it out of here."

"Let us get dressed and we'll talk, okay?" Reed covered himself with his forearm and struggled the rest of the way to his feet.

"I'm kind of liking the view," Harlan said, his eyes roaming hungrily over Zan's breasts. "I could do with a bit of that free love myself." He reached for his belt.

Earley stood up. He could feel his cock and balls swinging, exposed, as he loomed over Harlan, his voice low and dangerous. "Get the fuck out. If you ever set foot on my land again, I'll blow a hole right through your waterbed."

Harlan paused. "How'd you know I have a waterbed?"

Earley looked at him, caught. He hadn't meant to get into the whole Margie thing, even though it was fanning the flames of his hatred. He looked Harlan right in the eye. "Stay home for a change, you might know what goes on there."

"You son of a bitch." Harlan's hand reached for something on the back of his belt. Earley leapt on him instantly, twisting his wrist till it snapped. Harlan screamed in pain, dropping a handgun into the mud. A white-hot, blind rage tore through Earley's whole body. His hand drew back into a hard, swinging fist. He was his old man. He was little Earl, diving over his brother to save his hide, taking the blow like a punching bag. And he was himself, Earley Jude, here and now, with his full strength and fury unleashed, pounding Harlan's red face till his fists turned to meat.

"Stop it," yelled Reed, hanging on to his back. Earley shook him off as a bear shakes a hound and kept right on punching.

Harlan staggered and sank to his knees, reaching out for his gun. Before he could touch it, Zan grabbed a crowbar from the back of the truck and swung it down hard on the back of his head. Harlan fell like a tree.

Earley stepped back. All three of them stared down at Harlan's still body.

"Jesus," Reed whimpered. "Oh Christ."

"He was trying to shoot you," said Zan, her voice shaking. She took a step backwards. "He isn't dead. Tell me he isn't dead."

Earley knelt down next to Harlan. "Heart's beating. You just knocked him out." He laid his palm over the matted brown hair on Harlan's scalp. It came back up bloody. "I better get him to the hospital."

"No cops," Zan said wildly. "No cops, Reed!"

"Ssh," said Reed. "We've got to take care of him."

"What if they find me here?" Zan's voice rose in a panic. She backed up against Earley's truck, her eyes huge and flat, like a cornered animal. "I can't, Reed. If anyone finds me, you know what they'll do."

Earley didn't know what she was talking about. "How far down is your car?"

"What?" Zan stared at him blankly.

"Your Volvo. Harlan's truck is behind it. I'll drive him in that. Can I carry him down, or should I take my pickup?" Earley's voice sounded patient and calm, as if he was teaching Zan how to tie trout flies, not trying to figure out how to transport a man with a head wound to an emergency room thirty miles to the north. I'm on autopilot, he thought, stepping into his boots. Someone's phoning it in.

"It's far," Zan said, her voice thin and childlike. "I drove off the road."

Earley folded her into his arms. "I'll take care of you," he said. Zan buried her face in his chest. He could feel her whole body shaking with choked-off sobs.

"Earley," she whispered. And that was all.

TWENTY-FOUR

The hospital receptionist stared up at Earley. "You again?"

"This one deserved it."

She frowned. A couple of paramedics in sea green scrubs came with a gurney and rolled Harlan through double doors. One of the men wore a shower cap. Earley wondered why, and then wondered how he could be thinking about that when Zan might have killed Margie's husband. The ride into town had been hairy. Harlan had groaned once or twice, but most of the time he remained inert, his bulk shifting with every tight curve. Every time he slammed up against Earley's right shoulder, Earley found himself flinching, as if he'd been jumped by a corpse.

The receptionist passed him a clipboard. Her lips were as

thin as a bobby pin. "I can't check him in without his insurance and social security card. Are you family?"

"No way."

"Is there somebody else I can call?"

Earley hesitated, imagining Margie getting the news by phone. "I'll go get her," he said, heading for the glass doors.

"Wait. You can't leave him here. Sir!"

The doors parted for Earley, and he was outside.

The lights in the trailer were low. As Earley drove up, he saw the blue flickering of a TV in the living room. He could picture Margie slumped on the Naugahyde couch, forking up dinner and staring at *Happy Days* reruns for company. She deserves better, he thought as he walked up the flagstone path. Better than Harlan, and better than me.

He rang the front doorbell and stood on the welcome mat, shifting his feet. Behind the aluminum door, he could hear Margie padding across the shag rug. "Amber Ann? Is that you?" She opened the door and her face went from startled to angry in two seconds flat. "You've got some nerve coming round here when—"

He cut her off. "Margie. Harlan's in the hospital."

"What?" Margie stared at him. "What happened? Why are you—"

"There was a fight."

"Christ, Earley, what did you do?" It wasn't me, he started to say, but thought better of it. Margie grabbed a windbreaker and walked out the door. "Drive me," she said. "You can tell me the rest on the way."

A Coke machine rattled and buzzed. Earley sat in the hospital waiting room, memorizing the fake woodgrain swirls on the paneling, sucking a cup of cold coffee. The noise from the snowy TV set got under his skin, but he didn't turn it off; someone must want it, he figured, though he was the last person left in the room. He wondered how long it would be until Margie came out, if she even remembered that he was still here. *I can't leave her stranded,* he thought, even though he was dying to get back to his bus, back to Zan and Reed.

He took Harlan's keys from his pocket for the thirtieth time, twisting them in his fingers. His knuckles were swollen and one of his eyes throbbed. He wondered if Harlan was still alive, what would happen to them if he wasn't.

Margie came in, her purse clutched to her side. "Thanks for waiting," she said.

"Any news?"

"He's got a concussion. While they were stitching the back of his head, he opened his eyes and said, 'Fucking Japs.' Apparently that's a good sign." She took Earley's coffee cup, filled it from the water fountain and plopped in a couple of Alka Seltzers, drinking it down before they had a chance to fizz.

"I'm sorry," he said.

Margie shrugged. "He pulled a gun on you. What were you gonna do, let him plug you? He would've. It's okay for him to shack up with that blonde, but let *me* take one step to the left and forget it."

"Let's get out of this place." Earley rose. "If you're ready, I mean."

Margie nodded. "He's sleeping. They're keeping him here for a couple more days to check out his brain function. He had a skull fracture and seventeen stitches. Harlan's just lucky his head is so thick. Oh, and he broke his wrist."

"*I* broke his wrist," Earley said.

"I figured," said Margie. She took Earley's hand, soothing his split knuckles. "Nobody ever got into a fight over me before."

Earley winced inwardly. What would Margie say when she found out the truth, that Harlan had caught him buck naked with Reed? And Zan, who had been such a bitch to her back at the bar? I should tell her myself, he thought. Better she hears it from my lips than Harlan's.

"Margie . . ." he started, and couldn't find words. Margie looked at him, hopeful. Oh Lord, Earley thought. Was it evil of him to wish Harlan would have some amnesia or something? He couldn't bear to break Margie's heart any further. At least not tonight. Let it ride, he thought, holding the door open for her.

"Thanks," she said shyly.

Some gentleman, he thought. If you only knew.

.   .   .

Earley drove past the neon of Scoter's motel and headed through town, past the Cedar Bar Lounge and the Shamrock. The moon had sunk under the clouds and the sky arched above them like navy blue crepe, like his grandmother's going-to-church suit. Margie gazed out the window without saying much. After awhile she leaned her cheek onto his upper arm, closing her eyes. "I can feel you steering," she said.

Earley turned his head, resting his lips on the soft gray that parted her hair. He pulled up in front of her trailer. "I hope you can sleep," he said.

Margie paused. "Aren't you coming with me?"

"I can't. Not tonight."

Margie looked at him. "What about Harlan's truck?" she said, struggling to keep her voice even. She wants something from me, thought Earley. I best head it off.

"I'll bring it back to you tomorrow."

"What if I need it tonight?" she said. Earley reached into his pocket to roll up a smoke. Margie's eyes flicked across his face, noting his silence. She folded her arms. "You don't want me to see where you live."

I don't want you to see who I live with, he thought, trying to picture how Zan would react if he showed up with Margie. "That's not it at all," he said, hoping he sounded convincing. "You've had a rough night. It's a half-hour drive and the roads are the pits."

"Are you kidding? This truck is a tank."

"Margie—"

"What if the hospital calls me at four in the morning? My car's in the shop."

"It is?" he said, swallowing hard.

Margie glared at him. "Drive me to your place," she said. "This is bullshit."

There was no way around it. Earley backed up. "If you're sure."

Harlan's double-cab crew truck lumbered uphill, high-beams raking the trunks of the trees. Earley braked at the crossroads. "Remember this fork," he told Margie. "If you turn the wrong way, you'll be heading for Suhammish clearcut. Nothing up there but a few chunks of cedar and miles of bad road."

Margie grabbed at the dash as the truck rattled over some washboard. "I didn't realize you were this far off the highway."

"It ain't the suburbs," he said, shifting down to first gear. The ditch on the side of the road was a deep gash of mud. He couldn't remember how far Zan had gotten before she'd abandoned her Volvo. On every tight curve, he expected to find himself facing her taillights. Pray she's already asleep, he begged, even though he was dead certain that Zan and Reed would be waiting up, anxious for news about Harlan's condition. He twisted the steering wheel, frowning.

His headlights swung over the dirt road and caught something metal. Earley stepped on the brake and found himself facing the grille of his pickup truck, right where he'd left it. There was a raw gouge of earth and a poacher's spade left on the roadside; no Volvo. He felt all the air leave his lungs, as if someone had kicked him. "Where is she?" he stammered.

Margie turned her head. "She?" The syllable arched like the back of a cat.

Earley tried feebly to cover his tracks. "Reed's girlfriend. Zan. You remember."

"*Oh* yeah," Margie said. "I remember her well." She was looking at Earley like someone deciphering code. It must show in my face, he thought. Fuck, I can't hide this. She's gone. He pushed open the door.

"Thanks for the lift," he said, fighting the panic that welled in his gut. "You got all the turns straight?"

"Aren't you going to ask me inside?"

He shook his head quickly. "It's not a good time."

Margie looked down at her lap. "It won't ever be a good time, will it, Earley?"

Not now, he groaned to himself. Why did women always roll out these impossible questions at just the wrong moment? He was tempted to say she was right, just to shut her up, but he laid a big hand on her forearm instead.

"Margie, I gotta get up there. I'll call you tomorrow, okay?"

"Sure," she said, nodding, her mouth a straight line. "You don't have a phone."

Reed stood up the second he saw Earley enter. "How is he?"

"Where's Zan?" Earley swiveled his head, as if she might be hiding somewhere in the bus. Reed had already taped Hefty bags over the cracked kitchen windows; Earley noticed the hems of his trousers were caked with mud.

Earley leaned over Reed. He could feel the rage rising again, that sickening heat at the back of his scalp. "You dug her out, didn't you? You helped her leave."

"I had to." Reed's eyes didn't flinch. "It wasn't the first time."

Earley swallowed hard. "What?"

"Sit down. There's some stuff you don't know."

Earley folded his arms and stood waiting. His throat felt constricted, as if he was choking on something. His swollen eye throbbed.

"First tell me. Is Harlan still . . . ?"

"Just a concussion."

"Thank God." Reed cracked open a beer. He drank most of it down before he said anything else. "Zan was too panicked to wait anymore. She was sure there'd be cops."

Earley remembered her screaming, "No cops," and an unbidden memory needled his brain: how tense Zan had looked in Seattle when Reed made that joke about getting arrested.

"Is she wanted for something?"

Reed nodded. "There was this guy at the restaurant where

she worked in Berkeley. I think he was kind of retarded. He worked as a dishwasher."

Earley sat down and reached for Reed's beer. His mind was racing so fast he could barely make sense of the words Reed was saying. Somehow he already knew where the whole thing was leading.

"Frankie started hanging around after work. When Zan left the restaurant, he'd walk on the opposite side of the street and just stare at her. Never did anything, just gave her the creeps. Then one night he followed her into the—"

"How did she kill him?"

Reed stared at Earley. "She *told* you?"

He shook his head. How did I know? he thought. "Knife, gun? What?"

"Knife. In the stomach. He bled to death while she was calling for help. She was too freaked out to wait for the cops." Reed looked Earley right in the eye. "I bought her the bus ticket north. Gave her eight hundred bucks to get started and swore that I'd never tell anyone."

"Fuck." Earley stared at his hands.

"It was self-defense," Reed said. "The guy tried to rape her."

Earley nodded. He could still see the look on Zan's face as she went after Harlan, the fear in her eyes when he reached for that belt. Maybe that's how I knew it, he thought. There was something he'd recognized, all the way back, some deep flash of terror and pain that had passed through him like an electrical charge the first time they'd made love. He had wanted to save Zan from something, without knowing what it was. Reed was still talking, he realized.

". . . so she panicked and left him. I begged her to turn herself in and plead self-defense, but she's always been out of her mind about cops. I used to wonder if she'd been in the Weather Underground or something. Her name when I met her was Linda."

Earley stared at him. This part he hadn't expected. "Her name isn't Zan?"

"Linda Ortega."

"She's Mexican?"

"Half. Grew up outside San Diego. Or that's what she told me."

"Not Guam?" Earley could feel his voice shaking.

"I never heard that one before," said Reed. "She makes it sound real every time. Sometimes I wonder if she knows the difference."

"Damn." Earley stared at a crack in the table, blinking back tears. He felt dizzy, uprooted. Why did it shock him so much to find out Zan had used a false name, even more than it shocked him to learn she had stabbed a man?

I don't know the first thing about her, he thought. Not one goddamn thing. He remembered the first time he'd met her, the sharp, teasing way she had reeled off her name. Zan Koutros, Greek on both sides. Alexandra, but who has the time. Turned sixteen in Baja. Was anything she'd ever told him the truth? If he'd fallen in love with a whole pack of lies, were his feelings lies too?

No, he thought. They were as real as it gets.

"You asked me one time why I let her leave me," said Reed. "Now you know."

Earley looked at his face, at those ghostly blue eyes. Wrong, he thought. I don't know anything.

"What should we do with Harlan's gun?" Reed asked. "Keep it as evidence?"

Zan still thinks she killed him, Earley realized. I've got to tell her that Harlan pulled through, or she'll panic and bolt. If she hasn't already. He stood up so fast that his head slammed against the low curve of the ceiling.

Reed grimaced. "Are you all right?"

"No," Earley said, and ran out of the bus.

Earley made several wrong turns on the logging roads up to the planters' camp. He remembered Zan giving directions, sandwiched between him and Reed, but most of the landmarks she'd mentioned were lost in the darkness. Every mistake that he made added fuel to his panic. He was driving so fast his truck bounced like a jackrabbit. Finally his headlights swung over the wickiup high on the ridge.

He jumped out of the truck and peeled back the flap of the

kitchen yurt, staring in at the firelit circle of planters who turned his way. He saw at a glance that Zan wasn't among them. The canvas dome was as hot as a sauna, the air thick and garlicky. Young Nick was ladling some kind of tea at the woodstove.

"Namaste," he said. "Want some yerba?"

Earley shook his head. "I'm looking for Zan."

"She's not here," said Just Nick, enthroned on a blanket-topped hay bale across from the woodstove. "She split a few hours ago. Took all her stuff."

Earley's heart seemed to freeze in his chest. "Where did she go?"

Just Nick met his eye with a satisfied glint. Earley noticed his hand was on Cassie's thigh. "If Zan wanted you to know, she would have told you."

"She left something for you," Cassie droned. "It's in our tent."

Earley whirled around, frantic. He ducked through the door and lit out for Zan's tent, his boots pounding into the packed mud and straw. She couldn't be gone. She just couldn't. He pulled back the green and gray tent flap and struck his Bic lighter, frantically sweeping his head for a note, a sign, anything.

Zan's cot was a bare slab of canvas. The hay-strewn floor on her side of the tent was muddy and trampled, the stump table stripped. And then Earley saw it, hung from a hook on the tent frame: her red dress. He gathered it into his arms and buried his face in it, breathing her in. A lingering fragrance of almonds still clung to the fabric, diaphanous, empty.

TWENTY-FIVE

The top of Olympus glowed crimson at dawn. The sky was stippled with thin smears of cloud, and the firs barely moved. Good flying weather, thought Earley, mechanically pulling suspenders up onto his shoulders and zipping the fly of his high-water pants. At least something's gone right.

For the past three days he had worked himself into a stupor, criss-crossing the clearcut with ropes on his back and binding the cedar they'd cut into bundles. They stood around on the slope at odd angles, like demented haystacks left on a tipped field.

Reed wanted to help. He'd gotten used to his cast and was walking at close to his usual speed, but the thought of negotiating that steep, mud-gashed bowl on a crutch was absurd. "You'd just slow me down," Earley told him.

The truth was that he was relieved to have the excuse of Reed's broken ankle; he wanted to be by himself. Earley knew that Reed knew it, and knew that it hurt him, and he didn't care. Not enough to act differently, anyway. All he could think of was Zan. He kept picturing her huddled up in a Greyhound station, eyes haunted, heading for God knows where. He tried to imagine her sticking a knife into somebody's guts. Was she packing a weapon, or had it been something she'd grabbed from the restaurant kitchen because she was frightened?

Who was she, this woman he loved, whose absence he felt as a physical pang, like a diver who'd surfaced too fast and come up with the bends? Earley wondered what name she'd use next, if she'd ever stop running. He hoped against hope that she'd write to his G.P.O. box sooner or later, giving him bread crumbs to follow. He couldn't accept that he might never see her again.

If only she'd waited to find out that Harlan pulled through. Reed had told Earley how terrified Zan had been that night, certain that even if Harlan survived, he'd press charges and drag her in front of the cops. As if Harlan Walkonis would ever admit he'd been clocked by a woman. And though Reed swore that Zan had promised to wait for news up at the treeplanters' camp, Earley couldn't forgive him for letting her go. I would have gone with her, he thought. In a heartbeat. I would never have left her alone.

He came home after dark, ate Reed's gourmet dinners in silence and dropped off to sleep like a stone down a well. Reed seemed to intuit that he shouldn't join him in bed, and moved through the bus with a martyred sulk that drove Earley crazy.

Last night, when Earley stood up after dinner to head to his room, Reed had slammed down the coffeepot. "Look, I don't care what we do or don't do. We don't have to have sex. But don't freeze me out like this. I can't take any more."

"It's not about you," Earley said.

"Oh bullshit, you won't even look at me. How is that not about me?" Reed was angry. "You know something, Earley? Zan's left me flat *twice*. If it hadn't been Harlan, it would have been something else. Zan runs away from things. That's who she is."

Earley didn't say anything. Reed reached for his hand. "I miss her as much as you do," he said. "So why can't we comfort each other?"

"I can't," Earley said. "It was different when Zan was a part of it too."

"What, you'll sleep with me if there's a woman between us and not if there's not? I don't get it."

"It's just how it is. I'm not saying it makes any sense."

"You're damn straight."

"That's right," Earley said, dropping Reed's hand. "That's the problem. I'm damn straight."

"Oh yeah? Who the fuck was that kissing me, your evil twin?" Reed glared at him, seething. "You made the first move. You're as two-tone as I am."

"I'm not," Earley snapped. "And the harder you push me, the more I'll back off. So leave me alone."

Reed looked at the floor. His jaw muscles were twitching. "It always turns out that way, doesn't it? The one who wants more is the one who gets left in the dirt."

Earley took a deep breath. "I'm sorry, lil' dude. I can't be what you want."

Reed's blue eyes bored into his. "You are so fucking dense. Don't you get it? You *are* what I want. I'm in love with you."

"Why?" Earley blurted.

"Just wacky, I guess. Do you honestly want me to answer that?"

"I don't know what I want anymore," Earley had said. He could feel the tears gathering under his lashes.

"I do," said Reed. "So I guess I'm the lucky one." He rose up on his toes to give Earley a kiss, sliding both arms around his broad back. Earley didn't resist.

The bus door swung open. "There's coffee," Reed called. Earley turned. How long have I been standing out here, staring up at this mountain? he wondered. Long enough for Reed to fire up a woodstove and brew a fresh pot of coffee. Long.

"Thanks," he said, ducking his head as he climbed up the steps. The inside of the bus smelled like bacon. Reed flipped over an omelette, then shook up a skillet of home fries. Earley noticed a pile of squeezed orange rinds heaped in the compost pail.

"This is one hell of a breakfast you're making."

"Well, hell, it's my first flyout ever."

So that was why he was so cheerful. Earley stood still for a moment. He hadn't intended to bring Reed along. He poured himself coffee and slopped in some sugar and cream. "How's your leg? Are you sure you're up to—"

Reed turned before he even finished his sentence. "I wouldn't miss it," he said in a voice that refused to accept any arguments. He wrapped his arms around Earley's back, sliding a hand underneath his suspenders. "What time do we meet them?"

Earley lit one cigarette off the butt of another one as they drove up to the clearcut. Reed glanced at him. "Never saw you do that before," he said. "Nervous?"

"Nah. Our part is cake. All we do is help Scoter stack bolts in his truck. That, and hope Clay's not too strung out to fly." Earley pictured Clay at the Cedar, hunched over his double tequila, and wondered what hair of what dog he'd been hitting this morning. Not that it made any difference. Clay was a whiz in the air, no matter what crap he pumped into his body. It was like handing Keith Richards a Stratocaster. Put a joystick in front of him, Clay would get sober.

Earley blew smoke out the window and stubbed out his cigarette. "Try to be cool with these guys," he said.

"What do you mean?" Reed bristled. "No sucking your cock in the clearcut?"

"Don't be sarcastic," said Earley. "God only knows what kind of rumors Harlan's been spreading. If Scoter suspects any part of it's true, we'll be dead meat in Forks. There's guys around here who would lynch us."

Reed raised his eyebrows. "Bisexual loggers. That's one of those *really* short lists." The word *bisexual* hit Earley's ear like a slap. Reed grinned at him, singing some song that went, "I'm a lumberjack and I'm okay . . ."

"Shut the fuck up," Earley growled. He rounded the bend and pulled into the clearcut, angling into the same set of ruts he had parked in for months.

It was nearly an hour before they heard a rumble of diesel and chains coming up the old access road. "That truck sounds Cro-Magnon," said Reed.

"Probably is," Earley said. "Scoter's dad is a tightfisted bastard. You'll see when he weighs us out. Probably charge us for wear on his tire chains." He got to his feet as an eighteen-wheel flatbed rolled into the clearing. Reed did the same, pushing down on his crutch. Scoter cut off his engine and hopped from the cab.

"You call that a road?" he said.

"I've driven on worse," Earley said.

"Fuckin' hillbilly. I bet you've *lived* on worse." Scoter pushed back his cap and stared up at the Suhammish clearcut.

"Hey, did you hear about Harlan? They're sending him home tonight."

"So there's no brain damage?" Reed asked.

"How could they tell?" Scoter cackled as if he had just laid an egg.

Earley wondered if "home" meant to Margie, or to his new squeeze, but he figured he'd better not ask. "D'you happen to see our friend Clayborne this morning?"

"Fuckin' A. Think I'd waste my life driving up to this boondock if Clay didn't show? So who did your leg—Doctor Al?" Scoter's question caught Reed off guard.

"I didn't catch his name."

"Mustache?" Reed nodded. "The best! The man's a prescribing fool. Did you score any 'Ludes?"

Reed shook his head. "Darvon, Tylenol III."

"Codeine, I *love* codeine! I gotta break me a leg or two." Scoter looked wistful. "Either of you got a smoke I could bum?"

Earley noticed the ravens long before he heard Clay's chopper. There were three of them, high in the crown of a spar tree, shifting restively and trading guttural croaks as if to say, what the hell is *that?* The whir of the rotors came next, from behind the ridge. As the chopper suddenly lifted up into view, the three ravens rose into the air with an indignant clatter of wings.

"Thar she blows!" called Scoter, waving both arms. Earley stepped forward, shielding his eyes from the sun. Clay's cockpit window was open, and Earley could see him hunched over his joystick, the glare of the windshield reflected in his mirrored shades. He circled the clearcut a couple of times, angling low, taking stock of the bundles that Earley had flagged for him. Then he steered down towards the two trucks and hovered right over their heads, parked in midair like a thundercloud. Earley motioned to Reed to stand clear as Clay leaned out the side door and dropped down a thick rope with a hook on the end.

"Get on." Clay's amplified voice boomed out over the ratcheting din of the rotor blades. "Gonna start up at the top."

Earley wished he was doing the opposite, picking up the closer-in bundles first and saving the long flights for later, when he'd be exhausted, but this was Clay's party. Anyway, there was no way to discuss it, with Clay up above in that deafening chopper. "Stand by to unload," he shouted at Scoter and Reed. "I'll come down when I can."

He stepped onto the hook, grabbed the rope in both hands and pulled, signaling that he was ready. Clay touched his controls and, without any warning, Earley felt himself lifted straight up in the sky. A surge of adrenaline rushed through his veins and a wild whoop escaped him, as if he were riding a bronco, or white-water rafting. The land seemed to rise up and meet him as he swung above it. He could see his own shadow, foreshortened into a dark blot, moving over the ground.

Earley yodeled and bounced as the chopper flew over the

gully and up the sheer rockface. The mudslides, the stumps, the bright slashes of wildflowers swam in a blur far below like a hallucination. They got to the top of the ridge and Clay eased him down gently, a foot at a time, until Earley was on the ground.

Clay's amplified voice boomed out again. "Hook it," he called. Earley went to the first bundle and secured the hook, working as fast as he could. He could feel the impatient throb of the helicopter hovering overhead, shadowing him like a raptor.

He stood clear and waved up a hand signal, shading his eyes as the cedar he'd busted his back for rose up in the sky. Clay ferried it down towards the flatbed truck, so far below that it looked like a piece from a model train set. He could just make out Scoter's and Reed's silhouettes. If not for Reed's limp, there'd be no way to tell who was who from this distance.

Earley made his way to the next bundle, watching anxiously as the chopper slowed over the truckbed and lowered its load. He should've flown back with the first one and showed Reed how to offload the hook. Leaving Scoter in charge was a hell of a question mark.

Unloading the first bundle seemed to take three times as long as it should. Earley waited and watched, feeling helpless. After several long minutes, he heard Clay's voice booming something that sounded like, "Clear out." The two tiny figures stepped off the truckbed, one quickly, one laboring clumsily sideways.

The quicker one raised its hand high and the chopper rose, heading back uphill towards Earley.

The next several trips went the same way. Earley kept thinking, *this* time they'll get it, but every unload took as long as the first. After three or four passes, Clay lowered the rope down towards Earley and spoke through his bullhorn.

"Fuckin' Laurel and Hardy act. Ride down and show 'em what's what."

Earley stepped onto the hook and they flew back down. Clay let Earley off a few yards from the truck, then veered over the treeline and disappeared.

Reed looked up. "Where is he going?"

"Just taking a break. Little loop de loop." Earley strode to the truck.

"About time," Scoter grumbled. "He's lame, and I'm time and a half. I'm s'posed to be resting my ass in the cab reading *Penthouse*, not slogging your shit for you."

"Life's tough all over," said Earley. "Let's see what we got." He swung himself up on the truckbed and took a deep breath. The bundles were jumbled on top of each other, and one had tipped over, spilling a logjam of cedar bolts onto the truckbed.

"We screwed up the first one," said Reed, looking sheepish.

Earley nodded. "We're gonna have to restack this whole mess or the rest of the load'll collapse. Won't take but ten minutes."

"I'll be in the cab," Scoter said. "It's your fuckin' wood."

Earley shrugged and began stacking shake bolts. Reed sat

on the edge of the truckbed and swung up his broken leg. It took him a long time to get to his feet. "I'm not tailor-made for this move," he said, gritting his teeth.

"Too bad you can't work the top." Earley tossed the heavy bolts into a stack as if they were firewood. "Hooking's the gravy job. Nothing to climb on or fit into place."

"Plus you get to fly on a rope," said Reed. "Ever see *La Dolce Vita*?"

"What?"

"Movie," said Reed. "Never mind." He moved to Earley's side, and the two of them stood tossing wood like a well-oiled machine. Neither one of them spoke. There was no sound but their breathing, the dry chunk of wood on wood. Earley remembered how well he and Reed had worked together right from the first, how relieved he had been when his new partner turned out to understand silence.

They restacked the bundles in what seemed like no time. "Don't unhook the next till it's toed in right here." Earley pointed. "As long as it's still on the rope, you can swing it around pretty easily."

"Cool." Reed was flushed and his skin had a sheen of sweat. He looked happy.

Earley pushed back the brim of his cap and squinted up towards the sky. "Listen," he said, and they froze in place, straining to hear. The faint noise of distant rotor blades came up from somewhere behind the ridge.

Earley shook his head, awed. "Fucker's on his way back. It's like he could hear we were finished, he's that wired in. Spooky."

"Let me go up," said Reed.

"What?"

"You said yourself I'd be better at that than unloading. And I want to fly."

"Your leg's in a cast."

"So what? It plays." Earley looked at him blankly. Reed shrugged. "Heard that from a three-fingered bluesman. Best picker I've heard." He wobbled three fingers.

The sound of the chopper was closer now. Earley twisted his head as it cleared the ridge. He looked back at Reed. "I really don't think you can—"

"I can do anything." Reed's eyes flashed, defiant. "Are you going to stop me?"

"It doesn't make sense."

"Hey, man, I'm free, white and twenty-one. I'm going up."

The shadow of Clay's helicopter fell over them both. Earley looked up and saw it move into place, hovering right overhead and then edging a couple of yards to one side. Clay leaned forward, his sunglasses glinting, and dropped down the hook.

"Some other time," Earley shouted to Reed, and stepped towards the hook rope. Reed looked up at the chopper's gray belly above, then leaned forward quickly and kissed Earley right on the mouth.

Earley recoiled. "Are you nuts?" he hissed as he swiveled his head, convinced against logic that Clay could see through the floor of his chopper and Scoter could see through the back of his truck. Reed's lips curled into a triumphant smile. He stepped onto the hook, tugged hard on the rope and was lifted up into the air.

Earley scrambled backwards. Even over the engine and rotor noise, he could hear Reed's voice echo his own first exuberant whoop.

"YESSSSS!" Reed roared, arching his back to look up at the sky. "I'm flying!" His hair blew loose as the chopper began its ascent, angling over the uneven rows of vast stumps, the deep gash of the gully. He let out a yodel of unbridled joy.

Earley lifted his hand to ward off the sun's glare, and Reed lifted his hand in return. He thinks I'm waving to him, Earley realized with a sickening jolt. The air seemed to freeze in his lungs as Reed grinned and returned the wave, losing his balance. His right leg swung forward in its heavy cast and his body jerked after it, teetering over the edge of the hook. He twisted to grab at the rope, and his fingers missed, grabbing at air.

Earley stood rooted as Reed hung suspended in space for the briefest of moments, then plunged through the air like a stone.

TWENTY-SIX

Earley charged up the mountain as fast as he could, dodging stumps and dead limbs. He got to the gully and plowed straight through the creek, scrambling up the far bank on his hands and knees, grabbing at roots and stones. It seemed like forever until he reached Reed.

Reed's body lay twisted at an impossible angle, his neck to one side and his body splayed out like a marionette. Earley sank to his knees, his chest heaving.

"Buddy," he said. "Lil' dude." He lifted Reed's wrist, felt nothing, and pressed his ear down on Reed's ribcage. His own heart was pounding so hard that he couldn't be sure what he heard or didn't hear. Please, he begged silently, sliding his palm over Reed's chest, but he knew already, had known from the moment he saw Reed tumble off into the sky. But he's warm, he thought wildly. How can his skin still be warm? He lifted Reed into his arms and sat cradling him as the sound of the helicopter drew close overhead.

Clay lowered his craft onto a minuscule patch of semi-flat land between two massive stumps, so close to Earley that he felt the wind off its rotor blades pulling at him like a whirlpool. The sun glinted off Clay's mirrored glasses and dogtags.

"Get him in here," he barked through his bullhorn, "We gotta get him to the medics." Earley just stared at him.

Clay's panic rose. "*Move*, you fuck! Move him out."

Earley shook his head. His mouth tried to form the words "too late," but he couldn't find his voice. Clay cut his engine. The rotor blades ground to a slow halt, bathing the clearcut in silence. The sun seemed to beat down on Earley's head, baking in pulses. I'm going insane, he thought. I'm going to crack.

Clay pounded his dashboard with both fists. "Fuck," he said. "I'm gonna lose my damn license. You sure he's—?"

"I'm sure." Earley's voice sounded distant, like someone else speaking a long way away. "What do we do? Take him to the ER, the cops?"

"Oh Christ," said Clay. "*Fuck.*"

Earley rose to his feet, holding Reed in his arms. He walked to the chopper and stared through the window at Clay. "If you mention your license again," he said, "I'll tear out your throat."

·   ·   ·

The state police were incredulous. "Why would you take up a guy with a broken leg?"

Clay's scalp was shaved bald, with a couple raw scratches where he'd botched the job. Earley noticed that his index finger was missing a joint. He wore a wide strip of leather around his left wrist and a skull ring of heavy chrome, worn upside down so its teeth seemed to gnaw at his knuckle.

"I thought it was Ritter," he said, shooting Earley a poisonous glance. "I'm forty feet in the air—how the fuck am I s'posed to know who's yanking my hook rope?"

"A hook rope's for wood, not for people." The sergeant was crewcut and stocky, with a thick neck that rolled over his collar. The tag on his uniform pocket read "Buck."

"My fault," Earley said, staring down at his mud-caked boots. "I should've stopped him."

"Why didn't you?" the sergeant asked.

Earley paused, remembering Reed's ecstatic shouts as he rose in the air. The memory rolled backwards: Reed's kiss, and the last thing that Earley had said to him, the last words he'd heard in his life: "Are you nuts?" Earley swallowed and bit his lip. Don't fall apart, he prayed. Not here. Not now.

"Do you know his—Reed's—family?"

Earley shook his head, numb. "I know he's from Marblehead, Mass."

"Parents still live there?"

"Far as I know. They're divorced, though, so maybe not both." Earley thought of the postcards of sailboats and lobsters he'd picked up from their G.P.O. box, along with Reed's forwarded stacks of *The Nation*, the package his mother had sent with a down vest and wool socks from the L.L. Bean catalog. Reed had been angry about it, and Earley had wondered why; he wished someone would send *him* free work clothes.

"Alton," said Sergeant Buck, gazing at his report. "You got a first name on his father? I'm not going to call Information and tell the wrong guy that his son tumbled out of a plane."

"Helicopter," said Clay. Sergeant Buck didn't bother to answer. He stood and went into the back office, coming back out with Reed's wallet.

"Let's see what he had on him." Earley squirmed as Sergeant Buck took out Reed's Visa card, California driver's license, his Berkeley student ID. He peered at the photos, then handed them off to a deputy. "I need a home number and next of kin. Student ID should pan out. If it doesn't, try Visa. They can always track a guy down."

The deputy nodded and went to the phone. Sergeant Buck sat back down in his desk chair and sighed. "You know, maybe if you boys had to do the job I have to do today—call up some stranger and tell him his son broke his neck—you'd think twice about breaking every damn rule that you come across."

Earley looked down at his boots again. "I'll call him myself if you want. It's hard to imagine how I could feel worse."

"It's my job," said the sergeant, his voice clipped. "I do my job."

Clay shifted his weight in his hard wooden chair. "Are you done with me yet?" he asked, scratching his arm. Sergeant Buck looked at him as if he were a cockroach.

"Oh, we're just beginning," he said.

Earley stumbled back out to his truck. The interrogation had taken three hours. Reed's father was going to fly into Sea-Tac tomorrow to pick up the body; he'd asked Earley to gather Reed's things, and then changed his mind. "I'll get them myself," he had said in a tense, flattened voice. "I want to see where Reed was living."

Earley's whole body ached, as if he, and not Reed, had been dropped from the sky. All during the drive to the hospital morgue, at the state trooper station, he'd fought back his tears. Now he felt as if something inside him had been cauterized, sealed off forever, and he would be numb for the rest of his life. Every movement he made felt surreal and suspended. He couldn't make sense of the actions he usually did without thinking: inserting a key into the ignition and shifting into reverse felt like things he had done once in some other lifetime, which he only dimly remembered. Earley put his hand onto the throttle. I've got to tell Zan, he thought. But how can I find her?

And that's when the tears started. Earley's sobs heaved up from the core of his being like lava, choking him, scraping his throat, uncontrollable. He was crying for Reed and for Zan, for himself, for the thought that he'd never hold either of them in his arms again, that he, Earley Ritter, card-carrying loner, had gotten more love than he'd known what to do with, had swum in it, swirled in it, given his heart to not one but two people, and now he had lost it forever. Gone, he thought, empty. Emptier now, because Earley had learned, for a few shining months, how it felt to be full.

Earley had arranged to meet Bowen Alton at the funeral home where Reed's body was being embalmed. He couldn't have missed him. Reed's father was lean as a greyhound, with an aquiline nose and tan hair, turning silver and sparse at the temples. He was wearing a navy blue blazer, a club tie and chinos, as if he were attending some alumni event and not picking up his son's corpse. Earley had dressed in his newest and cleanest clothes, and he still felt like something you'd find in a laundromat lint trap. He took a step forward and held out his hand.

"I'm Earley," he said. "I'm Reed's friend."

Whatever Bowen might have expected, it hadn't been him. He had glanced Earley's way as he stepped from his truck, and dismissed him as some local workman who happened to be in the same place. Now he peered at him, taking in Earley's bulk, his dead tooth, untrimmed beard and long hair, and Earley could feel the dismay that clicked into his eyes. Bowen shook Earley's hand in a tight, viselike grip, withdrawing his own hand so quickly that Earley nearly expected him to wipe it off with a handkerchief. "I don't need to tell you how shocked we were," he said.

You and me both, Earley thought, but all he could say was, "I'm so sorry."

Bowen nodded, as if that empty, ritual phrase bore some actual comfort. He paused for a moment, about to say something, but changed his mind. He took a set of keys with a Hertz rental tag from his pocket. "I'll follow you up to the house," he said.

Earley glanced at the parking lot and spotted a silver Oldsmobile Cutlass parked by the curb. "I don't think so," he said. "The road's pretty rugged."

"It's rented," said Bowen. "I'm not concerned about wear and tear."

"I'm not talking wear and tear, I'm talking arrival. I'm twelve miles up an ungraded dirt road with a ton of spring washout. Unless you've got four-wheel drive, you're gonna wind up sticking out of some drainage ditch, miss your flight home and all. I'll drive you up there and back to your car."

Bowen glanced over at Earley's mud-crusted pickup, with its rust-riddled wheel wells and tarp-covered toolbed. "All right," he said, pursing his lips.

Earley opened the passenger door for him, carefully lifting the bungees and twine so it stayed on its hinge. He thought about telling Reed's father that Reed had invented the system, but decided against it. Let Bowen choose what, if anything, they ought to talk about. Earley slammed his own door shut and started the engine.

Weather, it seemed, was all Bowen was willing to broach. He noticed the "Logging Capital of the World" sign on the out-skirts of town that boasted an average rainfall of 126 inches a year. "Must be why it's so verdant," he said, launching into an oddly bright speech about touring through Ireland and Wales, and then falling suddenly silent. Earley glanced at him, trying to prove he was listening, and saw that Bowen's eyes had gone helpless, consumed by grief. Leave him alone, Earley thought. Don't say anything useless. He gazed out the window.

Route 101 unspooled ahead of them, one hairpin curve at a time. The roadsides were lush with wildflowers: foxgloves, yarrow, yellow cat's ear, even some late rhododendrons, and the trunks of the fir forest rose up like pillars, filtering sunlight in muted diagonal shafts. The day was so lovely that it seemed impossible they could be headed on such a dark errand. It hasn't sunk in yet, thought Earley. I still don't believe it. His sleep had been haunted by dreams of Reed falling, not from Clay's chopper, but over the edge of the waterfall gully, where they had thrown his burnt mattress.

And there was one more thing that haunted him, waking and sleeping. He kept hearing Sergeant Buck's gravelly voice asking, "Did Reed seem depressed? Was there any reason he might have been tempted to take his own life?" Earley had stared at him, struck to the root. The fall was an accident, surely; the weight of the cast had thrown Reed off balance. That's what they'd agreed on. And Reed had been far from depressed. Earley pictured him pouring Tabasco all over his omelette, unable to stifle the lopsided grin he'd had on his face ever since they had woken up side by side in Earley's big bed. The memory seared through his brain like a knife.

"No, nothing like that," he had told Sergeant Buck, but the question had sent a barb into his darkest imaginings. He replayed the moments before Reed's fall over and over obsessively, reliving each detail as if he were picking a scab. He died waving to me, Earley thought. Was he trying to kiss me good-bye?

No, he told himself, not even close. Reed's kiss had been more like a challenge: I dare you to let Scoter see us. And I didn't dare, Earley thought. I turned away, and he slipped through my fingers.

"Watch it," said Bowen, and Earley realized his pickup had drifted out onto the oncoming traffic lane.

"Sorry," he said again. That seemed to be his refrain with this guy. The word was pathetic, but what else could he offer him? Sorrow was all he had left. Earley reached for his Drum pouch and stuck a rolled cigarette into his mouth, catching a look from Reed's father as he lit it up. "It's tobacco," he said.

"May I have one?"

"Yeah, sure, of course." Earley nearly tripped over himself

with relief. He handed his suede pouch to Bowen, who drew out a lopsided home-roll and twisted it tighter. Earley fumbled to coax a flame from his sputtering lighter and Bowen leaned towards it. Earley noticed that he had the same long, improbably straight eyelashes as Reed, though his eyes weren't as blue.

Bowen inhaled deeply and turned towards the window, sending smoke streaming out through both nostrils. "I quit twenty years ago," he said, and looked back at Earley. "He was my only son."

Earley couldn't even choke out an "I'm sorry." He nodded and bit his lip.

Bowen didn't speak again until they were most of the way up the access road. Earley noticed him clutching the armrest as they jostled over bare roots and gullies. "Long way off the road," he offered, and ten minutes later, "We're almost there." Bowen didn't respond. Earley couldn't decide whether he should be upset or grateful that Reed's father was not going to pump him for details or, worse, explanations. He tried to imagine Reed sitting next to this man at a Thanksgiving dinner, or talking to him about music, and came up blank. But hell, at least Bowen was *there*. If Earley had died in the woods, there'd be no silver Oldsmobiles rented.

They bumped over a rock and the truck's engine sputtered and died. "Oh shit," Earley said. He looked down at the gas gauge and saw that the needle had sunk below Empty. Story of my goddamn life, he thought, punching the wheel. "Got a couple of saw cans in back," he told Bowen, and went out to peel back the tarp. The first can he hefted was empty. So was the second. Fuck, he thought. I've got to drain my damn Husqy. In front of the Crown Prince of Marblehead.

Earley twisted off his chainsaw's gas cap and funneled fuel into a can, then took it around to the side of the truck and poured all of it in. He screwed both the gas caps back on, pulled the tarp into place and got back in the cab. "Ought to get us back to Forks, at least," he said.

"Ought to?" said Bowen.

"I've got some more gas at the bus," Earley mumbled. Bowen turned his head towards him and Earley thought, You heard me right, buddy. Bus. Not some eighteen-room mansion with gold toilet seats for your privileged ass. Some of us work for a living. He sped up the last stretch of road and pulled into his clearing. Without even turning his head, he could feel Bowen stiffening, galled by the plastic bags over the five broken windows, the tin cans and beer bottles, the mottled pink longjohns that sagged from the clothesline, the splitting maul chunked in the chopping block. Shake-rat deluxe, thought Earley, defiant. Your son called it home.

Bowen swallowed and reached for the door. "Careful," said Earley. "That hinge is real dicey. Reed made it." He reached across Bowen and eased the door open. They got out and walked to the bus.

Earley had gone into Reed's room that morning. He'd dug through Reed's duffel and moved the remains of his stash to an old creosote bucket out back by the woodpile. There wasn't much left, but he figured Reed wouldn't have wanted his father to find it. It wasn't a pure act of conscience, though; there would be times ahead, Earley knew, when he'd need to get wasted.

The rest of Reed's room was untouched, as he'd left it. Earley pulled back the curtain and stepped aside. Bowen took in the milk crate end table with its oil lamp and pile of books, the discarded work gloves beside the unmade single bed. "I don't know what my son thought he was playing at here," he said bitterly. "What a damned waste."

Your son put my dick in his mouth, Earley thought. I could pop your snot-nosed, superior bubble with one word of truth. "I'll be in the back," he said, turning. "His stuff is all here." Except for his drugs. And his caulk boots. And his mandolin.

Earley hadn't meant to keep that from Bowen, at first; it was just that the instrument happened to be in his room. Reed had played him to sleep one night, a week and a lifetime ago. You can't have it, he thought at the stranger in Reed's room. You can't have the part of him you never knew. He looked at the teardrop-shaped instrument with its twin strings, remembering the gypsyish tune Reed had played him. A surge of pure longing rose through Earley's body. God help me, he thought. I'm going to lose it. He sat on the edge of his bed with his head in his hands. He could hear Bowen packing things, moving around. Make this be over, he begged to the universe. Just make it stop.

Neither man spoke on the long drive back down to the funeral parlor. As Earley turned into the parking lot, he saw a hearse parked behind Bowen's rental. Reed's in there, thought Earley. My lil' dude, my buddy. He glanced over at Bowen and noticed the way he was cradling Reed's duffel, as though he were holding a child on his lap. We both miss him, thought Earley. He's lost to us both.

Bowen turned towards him. "Thank you," he said in a choked voice. He lifted the hinge and climbed out of the truck, turning back to press something into Earley's hand. "For the gas," he said. It was a folded bill. A fifty.

TWENTY-SEVEN

Earley drove over to Chester Marczupiak's Texaco and filled his tank. He'd have enough extra cash left to get ploughed at the Cedar, but he couldn't face seeing anyone there. The rumors had swept through town like a wildfire. If anyone looked at him funny, he might have to hurt them, and he couldn't muster the energy. His whole body felt like a bruise.

He went into the station and paid Chester with Bowen's fifty, stuffing the change in his jeans pocket as he walked back to his truck. He heard something ping on the pavement and roll past: a dime. It had fallen right through the same hole in his pocket. Earley stared for a moment, unable to choose between letting it stay there and hunkering down on his haunches to get it. This isn't a major decision, he thought, but it was beyond him. His brain felt like rain clouds.

Margie was driving past in her rusty orange Pinto. As soon as she saw Earley standing there, she braked and pulled into the lot. Earley swallowed hard, wondering what Harlan had told her. She left her car door swinging open as she hurried towards him, her eyes full of sympathy.

"Scoter told me about Reed. I'm so sorry."

There was that word again. It was pitiful, really. Could this be the best that people could offer each other? A word that meant nothing, healed nothing, changed nothing, not one god-damn thing.

Margie put her arms around Earley's waist. He looked over her shoulder, anxiously scanning for oncoming traffic. "We better be careful. If someone tells Harlan . . ."

"You already told him," said Margie, "and I could care less what anyone thinks." She hugged Earley tight, pressing her soft body against his. He could feel her heart beating, the warmth of her arms. It was like being wrapped in a blanket.

He closed his eyes, letting her hold him. "Margie," he whispered.

"You poor man." She pressed her cheek into his chest.

"I loved him," he blurted.

"I know you did, Earley." She stroked his bare arm.

"No, you don't know. I loved him." Earley realized it was the first time he'd said it aloud. Never to Reed, he thought. Coward. And now it's too late.

Margie stepped back and stared at him. "Jesus. Oh, Jesus. *You?*"

What in hell made me tell her? thought Earley, despairing. He glanced back at the station, as if Chester had heard every word through his plate-glass window. Was what he had said even true, had he really loved Reed in the way he loved women? Was that even possible? Nothing made sense any more.

Margie's eyes brimmed with a feeling that he didn't recognize, not disgust but something more fragile. "I didn't realize."

"Neither did I," Earley said.

Margie took half a step backward, tilting her neck to look up at his face, as if she couldn't see from so close. "So that's what was up all this time, why you haven't been . . ." She shook her head, staring, unable to take it in.

Earley didn't know what he should say or do. He couldn't meet Margie's eye. This is what it'll be like from now on, he thought. I've got nowhere to hide.

"Harlan said you were both screwing what's her name."

That too, thought Earley. He pictured himself with his arms wrapped around Zan and Reed, the three of them rolling around in the moss, the unbounded bliss they had found in each other. How could anyone else understand? He didn't understand it himself; he just knew it was gone, gone forever.

"I've got to go home now," he mumbled.

Margie nodded, her face strained. "I'm here if you need me."

"I know you are. Thanks, Margie." Earley bent down and kissed her on top of the head. She squeezed her eyes shut and clung to his body as if she were drowning.

"You're welcome," she whispered. They stood for a long time

like that, holding on to each other. Then Earley let go and got back in his truck.

Earley could feel the millworkers' eyes on him when he went to Gillies' to cash out. He'd been a magnet for gossip all week. Every place he went, somebody was staring, or smirking, or both. He's the one, he imagined them thinking, the one who was fucking three people at once, the one who cracked Harlan Walkonis' skull when he caught them, the one whose partner fell out of the sky.

When Vern Gillies gouged him as usual, skimming a huge cut for Scoter and Clay off his paycheck, Earley was almost relieved to be treated like everyone else. It didn't feel right to be taking Reed's cut of the money, but he didn't know what else to do with it. Vern worked a wad of tobacco between his stained teeth as he watched Earley stuff the cash into his pocket. "You driven that bus off the Royalton clearcut yet?"

"Hell no," Earley said. "And I don't plan to, either. I live where I live."

"They'll be booting you out in a week and a half."

"Let 'em try," Earley said. "I got nothing to lose."

Vern shrugged and spit into a bottle as Earley walked back out the door. I'll fight this, he thought. I'm going to build my damn cabin in spite of them all. That's what Reed would have done.

· · · ·

It had taken him over a week to go back to the clearcut. The state police had closed the case, classifying Reed's fall as an accident. Clay's license was suspended for six to eight weeks; he was told he would lose it for good if he ever let anyone ride on his hook rope again.

Earley had finished the rest of the flyout on foot, traversing the steep terrain time and again to hook bundles, and then to unload them back into the truck. He welcomed the numbness that came with exhaustion. The ache in his bones didn't bother him nearly as much as driving alone to his bus at the end of the day. Everything there was a treacherous road map that led either to Reed or to Zan. He was haunted by thoughts of her, out there somewhere alone in the world, beyond his reach.

He went to the post office every morning. One day, he imagined, a postcard might be there in Zan's jagged handwriting, telling him how he could find her. Earley pictured himself climbing into the driver's seat of the school bus and rumbling down off his mountainside, headed for . . . where? She had talked about Canada once; was she hiding out somewhere on Vancouver Island? How long would she wait before she risked contact? Reed could have told me, he thought, and a hot pang of grief seared the back of his throat as he realized Zan didn't know Reed was dead. If she does send a postcard, she'll write to us both. And her name won't be Zan.

He went to his bedroom and buried his face in the futon, yanking the covers up over his head. The sheets stunk of sweat, but he couldn't face washing them. He hadn't done laundry in weeks, hadn't showered since Reed was alive, and the animal stink of his own skin repulsed him. His thoughts eddied and spun like a whirlpool, pulling him down. It was painful to think of Zan running away, but thinking of Reed was unbearable. *If I'd grabbed for the hook just a few seconds sooner, if I hadn't turned when he kissed me . . .* The echoes were endless.

And it didn't make any difference what Sergeant Buck had concluded—Earley still had those dreams every night, about Reed's body falling, and worse than that, one night, a dream in which he'd pushed Reed off a cliff.

He awoke drenched in sweat, gulping air like a hooked bass. He stumbled outside, stark naked and barefoot, his heart racing. Where had he hidden that pot of Reed's? The bourbon he'd bought with his blood money?

Earley walked into the woods. He didn't know where he was going and he didn't care, as long as it got him away from his nightmare. The sky overhead was starless, a cloud-wrapped wool gray, and he had no idea if it was still evening, past midnight, the dark before dawn. His feet crunched on branches and sharp stones, thorns tore at his skin, but the pain didn't matter, none of it mattered, nothing was real except loss. He stumbled on blindly, led by some force that subsumed his own will, like an animal making its way down a trail not because he had made a decision but simply because this was where the trail led.

Earley stood at the edge of the gorge. Either his eyes had accustomed themselves to the gray or he had some sixth sense that let him know just where the ledge was, the rim of the much greater darkness below. He could picture the jagged tumble of boulders beneath him, where Reed's mattress lay. He could hear the dull tumble of waterfall off to his left, could feel the seduction of sky at his feet.

I'm Reed, he thought. I'm dangling alone at the end of a rope, and one step in the air puts an end to all pain. Could I do it?

He thought of himself bruised and broken below, of his neck snapped like Reed's. There'd be no one to find him or carry him home; he'd make some wild creature a meal. What hole would he tear in the world if he left it? Would anyone notice if he disappeared, leaving nothing behind but a '58 GMC pickup and a blue-painted bus in the woods? What was holding his feet to the ledge?

It must be fear, Earley figured, though he didn't feel anything that he recognized as being frightened, no heart-pounding, eye-bulging panic. What did he have to fear? That he wouldn't die right away, or that he would? That his gramma had really been right about hellfire and brimstone?

It came down to one simple thing: a step forward or back. An impulse, like everything else, that you followed or choked.

Maybe I'll land on that mattress, he thought. If I'm meant to survive, I will.

Earley closed his eyes, swaying, and felt himself pitch into space. He felt every pore wake as he plunged, felt a shout of sheer terror boil out of his lungs, felt the air rushing past him, the sensation of time itself frozen, suspended above him like Clay's helicopter, its rotor blades shredding the air into glittering shards. But I didn't mean to, he thought. Not like this. He felt his arms and chest flatten, his knees thudding onto the ground, one landing on bare rock, the other on something wet, springy, improbably soft.

He had fallen halfway on Reed's mattress. Shit, he thought, wincing. I *missed*.

His right leg was throbbing. Blood gushed from his kneecap. He shifted his weight and rolled gingerly onto the mattress, feeling his heart knock against his ribs. Everything hurts, he thought. Guess I'm not dead.

Earley had no idea how long he lay there. The mattress cover was soggy with mildew and rain, but it still held a sharp, acrid smell of charred lamp oil. He pressed his cheek into it, closed his eyes, letting the memories flood him. I had that, he thought. I had that much love in my life. I can have it again.

He pushed himself up on his hands and good knee. Sore, but his body was working; in Reed's words, it played. He rocked back on his haunches and stood, slowly unfurling himself to his full height. The sky was beginning to lighten. Above, he could make out a faint tinge of pearl, not quite pink, like the lip of a shell.

Earley picked his way over the boulders that lined the steep gorge. The gash on his right leg was pulsing with pain and the palms of his hands throbbed. Alive, he thought. Blood moving through my veins. Welcome.

He followed the gorge towards the sound of the waterfall, clambering over the rocks to the spot where the creekbed had shifted its course many lifetimes ago, leaving its higher fork dry and the lower one moist and impossibly fertile. Even the rocks here were bursting with life, silver-green lichen yielding to mosses, then bracken and fern. Skunk cabbage unfurled in the mud between bunchberry dogwoods, and fallen logs nursed colonnades of new seedlings. The roar of the water was constant.

The falls tumbled over a moss-green cliff, silvered with dew-drops that shone in the first rays of low-slanting sunlight. A sheer veil of mist undulated around the white water. Earley stepped into the spray, letting its soothing coolness caress his bruised skin. Then he took a deep breath and stepped under the waterfall's icy cascade.

The water streamed over his head, onto his eyelids and over his knotted, sore shoulders. The cold made his heart pump.

He thought about Zan, far away from him now, all by herself in the treacherous world; about Márgie, back home on her waterbed, wondering if she would ever be loved again; and he thought about Reed, laid to rest in the ground, who would stay in his heart for the rest of his life.

The sun caught the mist, iridescent. Good-bye, my buddy, Earley thought as he lifted his arms to the cascading water. We're finally taking that shower together. He tipped back his head and just stood there, alive on the earth.